EXPANDED UNIVERSE

VOLUME ONE

ROBERT A. HEINLEIN

CAEZIK
SF & FANTASY
ARC MANOR
ROCKVILLE, MARYLAND

*

SHAHID MAHMUD
PUBLISHER

www.CaezikSF.com

ISBN: 978-1-64710-056-8

First CAEZIK Hardcover Edition. 1st Printing, July 2022.
1 2 3 4 5 6 7 8 9 10

An imprint of Arc Manor LLC

www.CaezikSF.com

To William Targ

—— CONTENTS ————————————————

FOREWORD

Warning! Truth in advertising requires me to tell you that this volume contains *The Worlds of Robert A. Heinlein*, published 1966. But this new volume is about three times as long. It contains fiction stories that have never before appeared in book form, nonfiction articles not available elsewhere, a 30-year updating on my 1950 prognostications (as well as the 15-year updating that appeared in *The Worlds of R.A.H.*), with the usual weasel-worded excuses as to why I guessed wrong—and (ruffles & flourishes) not one but *two* scenarios for the year 2000, one for people who like happy endings and another for people who can take bad news without a quiver—as long as it happens to somebody else.

On these I will do a really free-swinging job as the probability (by a formula I just now derived) that either I or this soi-disant civilization will be extinct by 2000 A.D. approaches 99.92+%. This makes it unlikely that I will again have to explain my mistakes.

But do not assume that *I* will be the one extinct. My great-great-great-grandfather Lawrence Heinlein died prematurely at the age of ninety-seven, through having carelessly left his cabin one winter morning without his gun—and found a buck deer on the ice of his pond. Lack of his gun did not stop my triple-great-grandfather; this skinful of meat must *not* be allowed to escape. He went out on the ice and bull-dogged the buck, quite successfully.

But in throwing the deer my ancestor slipped on the ice, went down, and a point of the buck's rack stabbed between his ribs and pierced his heart.

9

No doubt it taught him a lesson—it certainly taught *me* one. So far I've beaten the odds three times: continued to live when the official prognosis called for something less active. So I intend to be careful—not chopped down in my prime the way my ancestor was. I shan't bulldog any buck deer, or cross against the lights, or reach bare-handed into dark places favored by black widow spiders, or—most especially!—leave my quarters without being adequately armed.

Perhaps the warmest pleasure in life is the knowledge that one has no enemies. The easiest way to achieve this is by outliving them. No action is necessary; time wounds all heels.

In this peaceful crusade I have been surprisingly successful; most of those rascals are dead ... and three of the survivors are in very poor health. The curve seems to indicate that by late 1984 I won't have an enemy anywhere in the world.

Of course someone else may appoint himself my enemy (all my enemies are self-appointed) but I would not expect such an unlikely event to affect the curve much. There appears to be some unnamed ESP force at work here; the record shows that it is not healthy to hate me.

I don't have anything to do with this. The character can be more than a thousand miles away, with me doing my utter best to follow Sergeant Dogberry's advice; nevertheless it happens: He starts losing weight, suffering from insomnia and from nightmares, headaches, stomach trouble, and, after a bit, he starts hearing voices.

The terminal stages vary greatly. Anyhow, they are unpleasant and I should not be writing about such things as I am supposed to be writing a blurb that will persuade you to buy this book despite the fact that nearly a third of it is copy you may have seen before.

Aside from this foreword the items in this book are arranged in the order in which written, each with a comment as to how and why it was written (money, usually, but also—Well, money)—then a bridging comment telling what I was writing or doing between that item and the next.

The span is forty years. But these are not my memoirs of those four decades. The writing business is not such as to evoke amusing memoirs (yes, I do mean you and you and you and especially *you*). A writer spends his professional time in solitary confinement, refusing

10

to accept telephone calls and declining to see visitors, surrounded by a dreary forest of reference books and somewhat-organized papers. The high point of his day is the breathless excitement of waiting for the postman. (The low point is usually immediately thereafter.)

How can one write entertaining memoirs about such an occupation? Answer: By writing about what this scrivener did when *not* writing, or by resorting to fiction, or both. Usually both.

I could write entertaining memoirs about things I did when not writing. I shan't do so because a) I hope those incidents have been forgotten, or b) I hope that any not forgotten are covered by the statute of limitations.

Meanwhile I hope you enjoy this. The fiction is plainly marked fiction; the nonfiction is as truthful as I can make it—and here and there, tucked into space that would otherwise be blank are anecdotes and trivia ranging from edifying to outrageous.

Each copy is guaranteed—or double your money back—to be printed on genuine paper of enough pages to hold the covers apart.

—R.A.H., 1980

FOREWORD

The beginning of 1939 found me flat broke following a disastrous political campaign (I ran a strong second best, but in politics there are no prizes for place or show). I was highly skilled in ordnance, gunnery, and fire control for Naval vessels, a skill for which there was no demand ashore—and I had a piece of paper from the Secretary of the Navy telling me that I was a waste of space—"totally and permanently disabled" was the phraseology. I "owned" a heavily-mortgaged house.

About then Thrilling Wonder Stories *ran a house ad reading (more or less):*

GIANT PRIZE CONTEST—Amateur Writers!!!!!!
First Prize $50 Fifty Dollars $50

In 1939 one could fill three station wagons with fifty dollars worth of groceries. Today I can pick up fifty dollars in groceries unassisted—perhaps I've grown stronger. So I wrote the story "Life-Line." It took me four days—I am a slow typist. But I did not send it to Thrilling Wonder; *I sent it to* Astounding, *figuring they would not be so swamped with amateur short stories.*

Astounding *bought it … for $70, or $20 more than that "Grand Prize"—and there was never a chance that I would ever again look for honest work.*

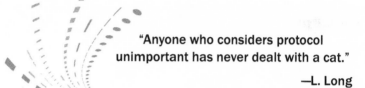

"Anyone who considers protocol
unimportant has never dealt with a cat."

—L. Long

The chairman rapped loudly for order. Gradually the catcalls and boos died away as several self-appointed sergeants-at-arms persuaded a few hot-headed individuals to sit down. The speaker on the rostrum by the chairman seemed unaware of the disturbance. His bland, faintly insolent face was impassive. The chairman turned to the speaker and addressed him in a voice in which anger and annoyance were barely restrained.

"Dr. Pinero"—the "Doctor" was faintly stressed—"I must apologize to you for the unseemly outburst during your remarks. I am surprised that my colleagues should so far forget the dignity proper to men of science as to interrupt a speaker, no matter"—he paused and set his mouth—"no matter how great the provocation." Pinero smiled in his face, a smile that was in some way an open insult. The chairman visibly controlled his temper and continued: "I am anxious that the program be concluded decently and in order. I want you to finish your remarks. Nevertheless, I must ask you to refrain from affronting our intelligence with ideas that any educated man knows to be fallacious. Please confine yourself to your discovery—if you have made one."

Pinero spread his fat, white hands, palms down. "How can I possibly put a new idea into your heads, if I do not first remove your delusions?"

The audience stirred and muttered. Someone shouted from the rear of the hall: "Throw the charlatan out! We've had enough."

The chairman pounded his gavel.

"Gentlemen! Please!"

Then to Pinero, "Must I remind you that you are not a member of this body, and that we did not invite you?"

Pinero's eyebrows lifted. "So? I seem to remember an invitation on the letterhead of the Academy."

The chairman chewed his lower lip before replying. "True, I wrote that invitation myself. But it was at the request of one of the trustees—a fine, public-spirited gentleman, but not a scientist, not a member of the Academy."

Pinero smiled his irritating smile. "So? I should have guessed. Old Bidwell, not so, of Amalgamated Life Insurance? And he wanted his trained seals to expose me as a fraud, yes? For if I can tell a man the day of his own death, no one will buy his pretty policies. But how can you expose me, if you will not listen to me first? Even supposing you had the wit to understand me? Bah! He has sent jackals to tear down a lion." He deliberately turned his back on them.

The muttering of the crowd swelled and took on a vicious tone. The chairman cried vainly for order. There arose a figure in the front row.

"Mr. Chairman!"

The chairman grasped the opening and shouted: "Gentlemen! Dr. Van Rhein-Smitt has the floor." The commotion died away.

The doctor cleared his throat, smoothed the forelock of his beautiful white hair, and thrust one hand into a side pocket of his smartly tailored trousers. He assumed his women's-club manner.

"Mr. Chairman, fellow members of the Academy of Science, let us have tolerance. Even a murderer has the right to say his say before the State exacts its tribute. Shall we do less? Even though one may be intellectually certain of the verdict? I grant Dr. Pinero every consideration that should be given by this august body to any unaffiliated colleague, even though"—he bowed slightly in Pinero's direction—"we may not be familiar with the university which bestowed his degree. If what he has to say is false, it cannot harm us. If what he has to say is true, we should know it." His mellow, cultivated voice rolled on, soothing and calming. "If the eminent doctor's manner appears a trifle inurbane for our tastes, we must bear in mind that the doctor may be from a place,

16

or a stratum, not so meticulous in these matters. Now our good friend and benefactor has asked us to hear this person and carefully assess the merit of his claims. Let us do so with dignity and decorum."

He sat down to a rumble of applause, comfortably aware that he had enhanced his reputation as an intellectual leader. Tomorrow the papers would again mention the good sense and persuasive personality of "America's Handsomest University President." Who knows; maybe now old Bidwell would come through with that swimming-pool donation.

When the applause had ceased, the chairman turned to where the center of the disturbance sat, hands folded over his little round belly, face serene.

"Will you continue, Dr. Pinero?"

"Why should I?"

The chairman shrugged his shoulders. "You came for that purpose."

Pinero arose. "So true. So very true. But was I wise to come? Is there anyone here who has an open mind, who can stare a bare fact in the face without blushing? I think not. Even that so-beautiful gentleman who asked you to hear me out has already judged me and condemned me. He seeks order, not truth. Suppose truth defies order, will he accept it? Will you? I think not. Still, if I do not speak, you will win your point by default. The little man in the street will think that you little men have exposed me, Pinero, as a hoaxer, a pretender.

"I will repeat my discovery. In simple language, I have invented a technique to tell how long a man will live. I can give you advance billing of the Angel of Death. I can tell you when the Black Camel will kneel at your door. In five minutes' time, with my apparatus, I can tell any of you how many grains of sand are still left in your hourglass." He paused and folded his arms across his chest. For a moment no one spoke. The audience grew restless.

Finally the chairman intervened. "You aren't finished, Dr. Pinero?"

"What more is there to say?"

"You haven't told us how your discovery works."

Pinero's eyebrows shot up. "You suggest that I should turn over the fruits of my work for children to play with? This is dangerous knowledge, my friend. I keep it for the man who understands it, myself." He tapped his chest.

17

"How are we to know that you have anything back of your wild claims?"

"So simple. You send a committee to watch me demonstrate. If it works, fine. You admit it and tell the world so. If it does not work, I am discredited, and will apologize. Even I, Pinero, will apologize."

A slender, stoop-shouldered man stood up in the back of the hall. The chair recognized him and he spoke.

"Mr. Chairman, how can the eminent doctor seriously propose such a course? Does he expect us to wait around for twenty or thirty years for someone to die and prove his claims?"

Pinero ignored the chair and answered directly.

"*Pfui!* Such nonsense! Are you so ignorant of statistics that you do not know that in any large group there is at least one who will die in the immediate future? I make you a proposition. Let me test each one of you in this room, and I will name the man who will die within the fortnight, yes, and the day and hour of his death." He glanced fiercely around the room. "Do you accept?"

Another figure got to his feet, a portly man who spoke in measured syllables. "I, for one, cannot countenance such an experiment. As a medical man, I have noted with sorrow the plain marks of serious heart trouble in many of our older colleagues. If Dr. Pinero knows those symptoms, as he may, and were he to select as his victim one of their number, the man so selected would be likely to die on schedule, whether the distinguished speaker's mechanical egg timer works or not."

Another speaker backed him up at once. "Dr. Shepard is right. Why should we waste time on voodoo tricks? It is my belief that this person who calls himself *Dr.* Pinero wants to use this body to give his statements authority. If we participate in this farce, we play into his hands. I don't know what his racket is, but you can bet that he has figured out some way to use us for advertising his schemes. I move, Mr. Chairman, that we proceed with our regular business."

The motion carried by acclamation, but Pinero did not sit down. Amidst cries of "Order! Order!" he shook his untidy head at them, and had his say.

"Barbarians! Imbeciles! Stupid dolts! Your kind have blocked the recognition of every great discovery since time began. Such ignorant canaille are enough to start Galileo spinning in his grave. That fat fool down there twiddling his elk's tooth calls himself a medical man. Witch doctor would be a better term! That little bald-headed runt over there—You! You style yourself a philosopher, and prate about life and time in your neat categories. What do you know of either one? How can you ever learn when you won't examine the truth when you have a chance? Bah!" He spat upon the stage. "You call this an Academy of Science. I call it an undertakers' convention, interested only in embalming the ideas of your red-blooded predecessors."

He paused for breath and was grasped on each side by two members of the platform committee and rushed out the wings. Several reporters arose hastily from the press table and followed him. The chairman declared the meeting adjourned.

The newspapermen caught up with Pinero as he was going out by the stage door. He walked with a light, springy step, and whistled a little tune. There was no trace of the belligerence he had shown a moment before. They crowded about him. "How about an interview, doc?" "What d'yuh think of modern education?" "You certainly told 'em. What are your views on life after death?" "Take off your hat, doc, and look at the birdie."

He grinned at them all. "One at a time, boys, and not so fast. I used to be a newspaperman myself. How about coming up to my place?"

A few minutes later they were trying to find places to sit down in Pinero's messy bed-living room, and lighting his cigars. Pinero looked around and beamed. "What'll it be, boys? Scotch or Bourbon?" When that was taken care of he got down to business. "Now, boys, what do you want to know?"

"Lay it on the line, doc. Have you got something, or haven't you?"

"Most assuredly I have something, my young friend."

"Then tell us how it works. That guff you handed the profs won't get you anywhere now."

"Please, my dear fellow. It is my invention. I expect to make money with it. Would you have me give it away to the first person who asks for it?"

"See here, doc, you've got to give us something if you expect to get a break in the morning papers. What do you use? A crystal ball?"

"No, not quite. Would you like to see my apparatus?"

"Sure. Now we're getting somewhere."

He ushered them into an adjoining room, and waved his hand. "There it is, boys." The mass of equipment that met their eyes vaguely resembled a medico's office X-ray gear. Beyond the obvious fact that it used electrical power, and that some of the dials were calibrated in familiar terms, a casual inspection gave no clue to its actual use.

"What's the principle, doc?"

Pinero pursed his lips and considered. "No doubt you are all familiar with the truism that life is electrical in nature. Well, that truism isn't worth a damn, but it will help to give you an idea of the principle. You have also been told that time is a fourth dimension. Maybe you believe it, perhaps not. It has been said so many times that it has ceased to have any meaning. It is simply a cliché that windbags use to impress fools. But I want you to try to visualize it now, and try to feel it emotionally."

He stepped up to one of the reporters. "Suppose we take you as an example. Your name is Rogers, is it not? Very well, Rogers, you are a space-time event having duration four ways. You are not quite six feet tall, you are about twenty inches wide and perhaps ten inches thick. In time, there stretches behind you more of this space-time event, reaching to, perhaps, 1905, of which we see a cross section here at right angles to the time axis, and as thick as the present. At the far end is a baby, smelling of sour milk and drooling its breakfast on its bib. At the other end lies, perhaps, an old man some place in the 1980s. Imagine this space-time event, which we call Rogers, as a long pink worm, continuous through the years. It stretches past us here in 1939, and the cross section we see appears as a single, discrete body. But that is illusion. There is physical continuity to this pink worm, enduring, through the years. As a matter of fact, there is physical continuity in this concept to the entire race, for these pink worms branch off from other pink worms. In this fashion the race is like a vine whose branches intertwine and send out shoots. Only by taking a cross section of the vine would we fall into the error of believing that the shootlets were discrete individuals."

He paused and looked around at their faces. One of them, a dour, hard-bitten chap, put in a word.

"That's all very pretty, Pinero, if true, but where does that get you?"

Pinero favored him with an unresentful smile. "Patience, my friend. I asked you to think of life as electrical. Now think of our long, pink worm as a conductor of electricity. You have heard, perhaps, of the fact that electrical engineers can, by certain measurements, predict the exact location of a break in a transatlantic cable without ever leaving the shore. I do the same with our pink worms. By applying my instruments to the cross section here in this room I can tell where the break occurs; that is to say, where death takes place. Or, if you like, I can reverse the connections and tell you the date of your birth. But that is uninteresting; you already know it."

The dour individual sneered. "I've caught you, doc. If what you say about the race being like a vine of pink worms is true, you can't tell birthdays, because the connection with the race is continuous at birth. Your electrical conductor reaches on back through the mother into a man's remotest ancestors."

Pinero beamed. "True, and clever, my friend. But you have pushed the analogy too far. It is not done in the precise manner in which one measures the length of an electrical conductor. In some ways it is more like measuring the length of a long corridor by bouncing an echo off the far end. At birth there is a sort of twist in the corridor, and, by proper calibration, I can detect the echo from that twist."

"Let's see you prove it!"

"Certainly, my dear friend. Will you be a subject?"

One of the others spoke up. "He's called your bluff, Luke. Put up or shut up."

"I'm game. What do I do?"

"First write the date of your birth on a sheet of paper, and hand it to one of your colleagues."

Luke complied. "Now what?"

"Remove your outer clothing and step upon these scales. Now tell me, were you ever very much thinner, or very much fatter, than you are now? No? What did you weigh at birth? Ten pounds? A fine bouncing baby boy. They don't come so big anymore."

"What is all this flubdubbery?"

21

"I am trying to approximate the average cross section of our long pink conductor, my dear Luke. Now will you seat yourself here? Then place this electrode in your mouth. No, it will not hurt you; the voltage is quite low, less than one microvolt, but I must have a good connection." The doctor left him and went behind his apparatus, where he lowered a hood over his head before touching his controls. Some of the exposed dials came to life and a low humming came from the machine. It stopped and the doctor popped out of his little hideaway.

"I get sometime in February, 1902. Who has the piece of paper with the date?"

It was produced and unfolded. The custodian read, "February 22, 1902."

The stillness that followed was broken by a voice from the edge of the little group. "Doc, can I have another drink?"

The tension relaxed, and several spoke at once: "Try it on me, doc," "Me first, doc; I'm an orphan and really want to know." "How about it, doc? Give us all a little loose play."

He smilingly complied, ducking in and out of the hood like a gopher from its hole. When they all had twin slips of paper to prove the doctor's skill, Luke broke a long silence.

"How about showing how you predict death, Pinero?"

No one answered. Several of them nudged Luke forward. "Go ahead, smart guy. You asked for it." He allowed himself to be seated in the chair. Pinero changed some of the switches, then entered the hood. When the humming ceased he came out, rubbing his hands briskly together.

"Well, that's all there is to see, boys. Got enough for a story?"

"Hey, what about the prediction? When does Luke get his 'thirty?"

Luke faced him. "Yes, how about it?"

Pinero looked pained. "Gentlemen, I am surprised at you. I give that information for a fee. Besides, it is a professional confidence. I never tell anyone but the client who consults me."

"I don't mind. Go ahead and tell them."

"I am very sorry. I really must refuse. I only agreed to show you how; not to give the results."

Luke ground the butt of his cigarette into the floor. "It's a hoax, boys. He probably looked up the age of every reporter in town just to be ready to pull this. It won't wash, Pinero."

Pinero gazed at him sadly. "Are you married, my friend?"

"No."

"Do you have anyone dependent on you? Any close relatives?"

"No. Why? Do you want to adopt me?"

Pinero shook his head. "I am very sorry for you, my dear Luke. You will die before tomorrow."

DEATH PUNCHES TIME CLOCK

... within twenty minutes of Pinero's strange prediction, Timons was struck by a falling sign while walking down Broadway toward the offices of the *Daily Herald* where he was employed.

Dr. Pinero declined to comment but confirmed the story that he had predicted Timons' death by means of his so-called chronovitameter. Chief of Police Roy ...

Does the FUTURE worry you?????
Don't waste money on
fortune tellers—
Consult
Dr. Hugo Pinero, Bio-Consultant
He will help you plan for the
future by infallible
SCIENTIFIC METHODS
No "Spirit" Messages
$10,000 Bond posted in
forfeit to back
our predictions
Circular on request
SANDS of TIME, Inc.
Majestic Bldg., Suite 700
(adv.)

Legal Notice

To whom it may concern, greetings; I, John
Cabot Winthrop III, of the firm of Winthrop, Winthrop, Ditmars and Winthrop, Attorneys-at-law, do
affirm that Hugo Pinero of this city did hand to me
ten thousand dollars in lawful money of the United
States, and did instruct me to place it in escrow with
a chartered bank of my selection with escrow instructions as follows:

The entire bond shall be forfeit, and shall forth-
with be paid to the first client of Hugo Pinero and/or
Sands of Time, Inc., who shall exceed his life tenure
as predicted by Hugo Pinero by one per centum, or
the estate of the first client who shall fail of such predicted tenure in a like amount, whichever occurs first
in point of time.

Subscribed and sworn,
John Cabot Winthrop III.

Subscribed and sworn to before me
this 2nd day of April, 1939.
Albert M. Swanson
Notary Public in and for this
county and State. My commission expires
June 17, 1939.

"Good evening, Mr. and Mrs. Radio Audience, let's go to press!
Flash! Hugo Pinero, the Miracle Man from Nowhere, has made his
thousandth death prediction without anyone claiming the reward he
offered to the first person who catches him failing to call the turn.
With thirteen of his clients already dead, it is mathematically certain
that he has a private line to the main office of the Old Man with the
Scythe. That is one piece of news I don't want to know about before
it happens. Your coast-to-coast correspondent will *not* be a client of
Prophet Pinero—"

The judge's watery baritone cut through the stale air of the court-room. "Please, Mr. Weems, let us return to our subject. This court granted your prayer for a temporary restraining order, and now you ask that it be made permanent. In rebuttal, Dr. Pinero claims that you have presented no cause and asks that the injunction be lifted, and that I order your client to cease from attempts to interfere with what Pinero describes as a simple, lawful business. As you are not address-ing a jury, please omit the rhetoric and tell me in plain language why I should not grant his prayer."

Mr. Weems jerked his chin nervously, making his flabby gray dewlap drag across his high stiff collar, and resumed:

"May it please the honorable court, I represent the public—"

"Just a moment. I thought you were appearing for Amalgamated Life Insurance."

"I am, your honor, in a formal sense. In a wider sense I represent several other of the major assurance, fiduciary and financial institu-tions, their stockholders and policy holders, who constitute a major-ity of the citizenry. In addition we feel that we protect the interests of the entire population, unorganized, inarticulate and otherwise unprotected."

"I thought that I represented the public," observed the judge dryly. "I am afraid I must regard you as appearing for your client of record. But continue. What is your thesis?"

The elderly barrister attempted to swallow his Adam's apple, then began again: "Your honor, we contend that there are two separate reasons why this injunction should be made permanent, and, further, that each reason is sufficient alone.

"In the first place, this person is engaged in the practice of sooth-saying, an occupation proscribed both in common law and in statute. He is a common fortuneteller, a vagabond charlatan who preys on the gullibility of the public. He is cleverer than the ordinary gypsy palm reader, astrologer, or table tipper, and to the same extent more dan-gerous. He makes false claims of modern scientific methods to give a spurious dignity to the thaumaturgy. We have here in court leading representatives of the Academy of Science to give expert witness as to the absurdity of his claims.

"In the second place, even if this person's claims were true—granting for the sake of argument such an absurdity—" Mr. Weems permitted himself a thin-lipped smile—"we contend that his activities are contrary to the public interest in general, and unlawfully injurious to the interests of my client in particular. We are prepared to produce numerous exhibits with the legal custodians to prove that this person did publish, or cause to have published, utterances urging the public to dispense with the priceless boon of life insurance to the great detriment of their welfare and to the financial damage of my client."

Pinero arose in his place. "Your honor, may I say a few words?"

"What is it?"

"I believe I can simplify the situation if permitted to make a brief analysis."

"Your honor," put in Weems, "this is most irregular."

"Patience, Mr. Weems. Your interests will be protected. It seems to me that we need more light and less noise in this matter. If Dr. Pinero can shorten the proceedings by speaking at this time, I am inclined to let him. Proceed, Dr. Pinero."

"Thank you, your honor. Taking the last of Mr. Weems' points first. I am prepared to stipulate that I published the utterances he speaks of—"

"One moment, doctor. You have chosen to act as your own attorney. Are you sure you are competent to protect your own interests?"

"I am prepared to chance it, your honor. Our friends here can easily prove what I stipulate."

"Very well. You may proceed."

"I will stipulate that many persons have canceled life-insurance policies as a result thereof, but I challenge them to show that anyone so doing has suffered any loss or damage therefrom. It is true that the Amalgamated has lost business through my activities, but that is the natural result of my discovery, which has made their policies as obsolete as the bow and arrow. If an injunction is granted on that ground, I shall set up a coal-oil-lamp factory, and then ask for an injunction against the Edison and General Electric companies to forbid them to manufacture incandescent bulbs.

"I will stipulate that I am engaged in the business of making predictions of death, but I deny that I am practicing magic, black, white or rainbow-colored. If to make predictions by methods of scientific accuracy is illegal, then the actuaries of the Amalgamated have been guilty for years, in that they predict the exact percentage that will die each year in any given large group. I predict death retail; the Amalgamated predicts it wholesale. If their actions are legal, how can mine be illegal?

"I admit that it makes a difference whether I can do what I claim, or not; and I will stipulate that the so-called expert witnesses from the Academy of Science will testify that I cannot. But they know nothing of my method and cannot give truly expert testimony on it—"

"Just a moment, doctor. Mr. Weems, is it true that your expert witnesses are not conversant with Dr. Pinero's theory and methods?"

Mr. Weems looked worried. He drummed on the table top, then answered. "Will the court grant me a few moments' indulgence?"

"Certainly."

Mr. Weems held a hurried whispered consultation with his cohorts, then faced the bench. "We have a procedure to suggest, your honor. If Dr. Pinero will take the stand and explain the theory and practice of his alleged method, then these distinguished scientists will be able to advise the court as to the validity of his claims."

The judge looked inquiringly at Pinero, who responded: "I will not willingly agree to that. Whether my process is true or false, it would be dangerous to let it fall into the hands of fools and quacks"—he waved his hand at the group of professors seated in the front row, paused and smiled maliciously—"as these gentlemen know quite well. Furthermore, it is not necessary to know the process in order to prove that it will work. Is it necessary to understand the complex miracle of biological reproduction in order to observe that a hen lays eggs? Is it necessary for me to re-educate this entire body of self-appointed custodians of wisdom—cure them of their ingrown superstitions—in order to prove that my predictions are correct?

"There are but two ways of forming an opinion in science. One is the scientific method; the other, the scholastic. One can judge from experiment, or one can blindly accept authority. To the scientific mind, experimental proof is all-important, and theory is merely a convenience in description, to be junked when it no longer fits. To the academic mind, authority is everything, and facts are junked when they do not fit theory laid down by authority.

"It is this point of view—academic minds clinging like oysters to disproved theories—that has blocked every advance of knowledge in history. I am prepared to prove my method by experiment, and, like Galileo in another court, I insist, 'It still moves!'

"Once before I offered such proof to this same body of self-styled experts, and they rejected it. I renew my offer; let me measure the life length of the members of the Academy of Science. Let them appoint a committee to judge the results. I will seal my findings in two sets of envelopes; on the outside of each envelope in one set will appear the name of a member; on the inside, the date of his death. In the other envelopes I will place names; on the outside I will place dates. Let the committee place the envelopes in a vault, then meet from time to time to open the appropriate envelopes. In such a large body of men some deaths may be expected, if Amalgamated actuaries can be trusted, every week or two. In such a fashion they will accumulate data very rapidly to prove that Pinero is a liar, or no."

He stopped, and thrust out his chest until it almost caught up with his little round belly. He glared at the sweating savants. "Well?"

The judge raised his eyebrows, and caught Mr. Weems' eye. "Do you accept?"

"Your honor, I think the proposal highly improper—"

The judge cut him short. "I warn you that I shall rule against you if you do not accept, or propose an equally reasonable method of arriving at the truth."

Weems opened his mouth, changed his mind, looked up and down the faces of the learned witnesses, and faced the bench. "We accept, your honor."

"Very well. Arrange the details between you. The temporary injunction is lifted, and Dr. Pinero must not be molested in the pursuit of his business. Decision on the petition for permanent injunction is reserved without prejudice pending the accumulation of evidence. Before we leave this matter I wish to comment on the theory implied by you, Mr. Weems, when you claimed damage to your client. There has grown up in the minds of certain groups in this country the notion that because a man or corporation has made a profit out of the public for a number of years, the government and the courts are charged with the duty of guaranteeing such profit in the future, even in the face of changing circumstances and contrary to public interest. This strange doctrine is not supported by statute nor common law. Neither individuals nor corporations have any right to come into court and ask that the clock of history be stopped, or turned back."

Bidwell grunted in annoyance. "Weems, if you can't think up anything better than that, Amalgamated is going to need a new chief attorney. It's been ten weeks since you lost the injunction, and that little wart is coining money hand over fist. Meantime, every insurance firm in the country's going broke. Hoskins, what's our loss ratio?"

"It's hard to say, Mr. Bidwell. It gets worse every day. We've paid off thirteen big policies this week; all of them taken out since Pinero started operations."

A spare little man spoke up. "I say, Bidwell, we aren't accepting any new applicants for United, until we have time to check and be sure that they have not consulted Pinero. Can't we afford to wait until the scientists show him up?"

Bidwell snorted. "You blasted optimist! They won't show him up. Aldrich, can't you face a fact? The fat little pest has something; how, I don't know. This is a fight to the finish. If we wait, we're licked." He threw his cigar into a cuspidor, and bit savagely into a fresh one. "Clear out of here, all of you! I'll handle this my way. You, too, Aldrich. United may wait, but Amalgamated won't."

Weems cleared his throat apprehensively. "Mr. Bidwell, I trust you will consult me before embarking on any major change in policy?"

Bidwell grunted. They filed out. When they were all gone and the door closed, Bidwell snapped the switch of the interoffice announcer. "O.K.; send him in."

The outer door opened. A slight, dapper figure stood for a moment at the threshold. His small, dark eyes glanced quickly about the room before he entered, then he moved up to Bidwell with a quick, soft tread. He spoke to Bidwell in a flat, emotionless voice. His face remained impassive except for the live, animal eyes. "You wanted to talk to me?"

"Yes."

"What's the proposition?"

"Sit down, and we'll talk."

Pinero met the young couple at the door of his inner office.

"Come in, my dears, come in. Sit down. Make yourselves at home. Now tell me, what do you want of Pinero? Surely such young people are not anxious about the final roll call?"

The boy's pleasant young face showed slight confusion. "Well, you see, Dr. Pinero, I'm Ed Hartley and this is my wife, Betty. We're going to have ... that is, Betty is expecting a baby and, well—"

Pinero smiled benignly. "I understand. You want to know how long you will live in order to make the best possible provision for the youngster. Quite wise. Do you both want readings, or just yourself?"

The girl answered, "Both of us, we think."

Pinero beamed at her. "Quite so. I agree. Your reading presents certain technical difficulties at this time, but I can give you some information now. Now come into my laboratory, my dears, and we'll commence."

He rang for their case histories, then showed them into his workshop. "Mrs. Hartley first, please. If you will go behind that screen and remove your shoes and your outer clothing, please."

He turned away and made some minor adjustments of his apparatus. Ed nodded to his wife, who slipped behind the screen and reappeared almost at once, dressed in a slip. Pinero glanced up.

"This way, my dear. First we must weigh you. There. Now take your place on the stand. This electrode in your mouth. No, Ed, you mustn't touch her while she is in the circuit. It won't take a minute. Remain quiet."

He dove under the machine's hood and the dials sprang into life. Very shortly he came out, with a perturbed look on his face. "Ed, did you touch her?"

"No, doctor." Pinero ducked back again and remained a little longer. When he came out this time, he told the girl to get down and dress. He turned to her husband.

"Ed, make yourself ready."

"What's Betty's reading, doctor?"

"There is a little difficulty. I want to test you first."

When he came out from taking the youth's reading, his face was more troubled than ever. Ed inquired as to his trouble. Pinero shrugged his shoulders and brought a smile to his lips.

"Nothing to concern you, my boy. A little mechanical misadjustment, I think. But I shan't be able to give you two your readings today. I shall need to overhaul my machine. Can you come back tomorrow?"

"Why, I think so. Say, I'm sorry about your machine. I hope it isn't serious."

"It isn't, I'm sure. Will you come back into my office and visit for a bit?"

"Thank you, doctor. You are very kind."

"But, Ed, I've got to meet Ellen."

Pinero turned the full force of his personality on her. "Won't you grant me a few moments, my dear young lady? I am old, and like the sparkle of young folks' company. I get very little of it. Please." He nudged them gently into his office and seated them. Then he ordered lemonade and cookies sent in, offered them cigarettes and lit a cigar.

Forty minutes later Ed listened entranced, while Betty was quite evidently acutely nervous and anxious to leave, as the doctor spun out a story concerning his adventures as a young man in Tierra del Fuego. When the doctor stopped to relight his cigar, she stood up.

"Doctor, we really must leave. Couldn't we hear the rest tomorrow?"

"Tomorrow? There will not be time tomorrow."

"But you haven't time today, either. Your secretary has rung five times."

"Couldn't you spare me just a few more minutes?"

"I really can't today, doctor. I have an appointment. There is someone waiting for me."

"There is no way to induce you?"

"I'm afraid not. Come, Ed."

After they had gone, the doctor stepped to the window and stared out over the city. Presently he picked out two tiny figures as they left the office building. He watched them hurry to the corner, wait for the lights to change, then start across the street. When they were part way across, there came the scream of a siren. The two little figures hesi-

31

tated, started back, stopped and turned. Then a car was upon them. As the car slammed to a stop, they showed up from beneath it, no longer two figures, but simply a limp, unorganized heap of clothing.

Presently the doctor turned away from the window. Then he picked up his phone and spoke to his secretary.

"Cancel my appointments for the rest of the day. ... No. ... No one. ... I don't care; cancel them."

Then he sat down in his chair. His cigar went out. Long after dark he held it, still unlighted.

Pinero sat down at his dining table and contemplated the gourmet's luncheon spread before him. He had ordered this meal with particular care, and had come home a little early in order to enjoy it fully.

Somewhat later he let a few drops of Fiori D'Alpini roll down his throat. The heavy, fragrant syrup warmed his mouth and reminded him of the little mountain flowers for which it was named. He sighed. It had been a good meal, an exquisite meal, and had justified the exotic liqueur.

His musing was interrupted by a disturbance at the front door. The voice of his elderly maidservant was raised in remonstrance. A heavy male voice interrupted her. The commotion moved down the hall and the dining-room door was pushed open.

"*Madonna mia! Non si puo' entrare!* The master is eating!"

"Never mind, Angela. I have time to see these gentlemen. You may go."

Pinero faced the surly-faced spokesman of the intruders. "You have business with me; yes?"

"You bet we have. Decent people have had enough of your damned nonsense."

"And so?"

The caller did not answer at once. A smaller, dapper individual moved out from behind him and faced Pinero.

"We might as well begin." The chairman of the committee placed a key in the lock box and opened it. "Wenzell, will you help me pick out today's envelopes?" He was interrupted by a touch on his arm.

"Dr. Baird, you are wanted on the telephone."

"Very well. Bring the instrument here."

When it was fetched he placed the receiver to his ear. "Hello. ... Yes; speaking. ... What? ... No, we have heard nothing. ... Destroyed the machine, you say. ... Dead! How? ... No! No statement. None at all. ... Call me later."

He slammed the instrument down and pushed it from him.

"What's up?"

"Who's dead now?"

Baird held up one hand. "Quiet, gentlemen, please! Pinero was murdered a few moments ago at his home."

"Murdered!"

"That isn't all. About the same time vandals broke into his office and smashed his apparatus."

No one spoke at first. The committee members glanced around at each other. No one seemed anxious to be the first to comment.

Finally one spoke up! "Get it out."

"Get what out?"

"Pinero's envelope. It's in there, too. I've seen it."

Baird located it, and slowly tore it open. He unfolded the single sheet of paper and scanned it.

"Well? Out with it!"

"One thirteen P.M. ... today."

They took this in silence.

Their dynamic calm was broken by a member across the table from Baird reaching for the lock box. Baird interposed a hand.

"What do you want?"

"My prediction. It's in there—we're all in there."

"Yes, yes."

"We're all in there."

"Let's have them."

Baird placed both hands over the box. He held the eye of the man opposite him, but did not speak. He licked his lips. The corner of his mouth twitched. His hands shook. Still he did not speak. The man opposite relaxed back into his chair.

"You're right, of course," he said.

"Bring me that wastebasket." Baird's voice was low and strained, but steady.

He accepted it and dumped the litter on the rug. He placed the tin basket on the table before him. He tore half a dozen envelopes across, set a match to them, and dropped them in the basket. Then he started tearing a double handful at a time, and fed the fire steadily. The smoke made him cough, and tears ran out of his smarting eyes. Someone got up and opened a window. When Baird was through, he pushed the basket away from him, looked down and spoke.

"I'm afraid I've ruined this table top."

FOREWORD

For any wordsmith the most valuable word in the English language is that short, ugly, Anglo-Saxon monosyllable: **No!!!** *It is one of the peculiarities in the attitude of the public toward the writing profession that a person who would never expect a free ride from a taxi driver, or free groceries from a market, or free gilkwoks from a gilkwok dealer, will without the slightest embarrassment ask a professional writer for free gifts of his stock in trade.*

This chutzpah is endemic in science fiction fans, acute in organized SF fans, and at its virulent worst in organized fans-who-publish-fan-magazines.

The following story came into existence shortly after I sold my first story—and resulted from my having not yet learned to say No!

SUCCESSFUL OPERATION

"**H**ow dare you make such a suggestion!"

The State Physician doggedly stuck by his position. "I would not make it, sire, if your life were not at stake. There is no other surgeon in the Fatherland who can transplant a pituitary gland but Doctor Lans."

"You will operate!"

The medico shook his head. "You would die, Leader. My skill is not adequate."

The Leader stormed about the apartment. He seemed about to give way to one of the girlish bursts of anger that even the inner state clique feared so much. Surprisingly he capitulated.

"Bring him here!" he ordered.

Doctor Lans faced the Leader with inherent dignity, a dignity and presence that three years of "protective custody" had been unable to shake. The pallor and gauntness of the concentration camp lay upon him, but his race was used to oppression. "I see," he said. "Yes, I see ... I can perform that operation. What are your terms?"

"Terms?" The Leader was aghast. "Terms, you filthy swine? You are being given a chance to redeem in part the sins of your race!"

The surgeon raised his brows. "Do you not think that I *know* that you would not have sent for me had there been any other course available to you? Obviously, my services have become valuable."

"You'll do as you are told! You and your kind are lucky to be alive."

"Nevertheless I shall not operate without my fee."

"I said you are lucky to be alive—"The tone was an open threat.

Lans spread his hands, did not answer.

"Well—I am informed that you have a family …"

The surgeon moistened his lips. His Emma—they would hurt his Emma … and his little Rose. But he must be brave, as Emma would have him be. He was playing for high stakes—for all of them. "They cannot be worse off dead," he answered firmly, "than they are now."

It was many hours before the Leader was convinced that Lans could not be budged. He should have known—the surgeon had learned fortitude at his mother's breast.

"What is your fee?"

"A passport for myself and my family."

"Good riddance!"

"My personal fortune restored to me—"

"Very well."

"—to be paid in gold before I operate!"

The Leader started to object automatically, then checked himself. Let the presumptuous fool think so! It could be corrected after the operation.

"And the operation to take place in a hospital on foreign soil."

"Preposterous!"

"I must insist."

"You do not trust me?"

Lans stared straight back into his eyes without replying. The Leader struck him, hard, across the mouth. The surgeon made no effort to avoid the blow, but took it, with no change of expression. …

"You are willing to go through with it, Samuel?"The younger man looked at Doctor Lans without fear as he answered,

"Certainly, Doctor."

"I can not guarantee that you will recover. The Leader's pituitary gland is diseased; your younger body may or may not be able to stand up under it—that is the chance you take."

"I know it—but I am out of the concentration camp!"

"Yes. Yes, that is true. And if you do recover, you are free. And I will attend you myself, until you are well enough to travel."

Samuel smiled. "It will be a positive joy to be sick in a country where there are no concentration camps!"

"Very well, then. Let us commence."

They returned to the silent, nervous group at the other end of the room. Grimly, the money was counted out, every penny that the famous surgeon had laid claim to before the Leader had decided that men of his religion had no need for money. Lans placed half of the gold in a money belt and strapped it around his waist. His wife concealed the other half somewhere about her ample person.

It was an hour and twenty minutes later that Lans put down the last instrument, nodded to the surgeons assisting him, and commenced to strip off operating gloves. He took one last look at his two patients before he left the room. They were anonymous under the sterile gowns and dressings. Had he not known, he could not have told dictator from oppressed. Come to think about it, with the exchange of those two tiny glands there was something of the dictator in his victim, and something of the victim in the dictator.

Doctor Lans returned to the hospital later in the day, after seeing his wife and daughter settled in a first class hotel. It was an extravagance, in view of his uncertain prospects as a refugee, but they had enjoyed no luxuries for years back *there*—he did not think of it as his home country—and it was justified this once.

He enquired at the office of the hospital for his second patient. The clerk looked puzzled. "But he is not here."

"Not here?"

"Why, no. He was moved at the same time as His Excellency—back to your country."

Lans did not argue. The trick was obvious; it was too late to do anything for poor Samuel. He thanked his God that he had had the foresight to place himself and his family beyond the reach of such brutal injustice before operating. He thanked the clerk and left.

The Leader recovered consciousness at last. His brain was confused—then he recalled the events before he had gone to sleep. The operation!—it must be over! And he was alive! He had never admitted to anyone how terribly frightened he had been at the prospect. But he had lived—he had lived!

He groped around for the bell cord, and, failing to find it, gradually forced his eyes to focus on the room. What outrageous nonsense was this? This was no sort of a room for the Leader to convalesce in. He took in the dirty white-washed ceiling, and the bare wooden floor with distaste. And the bed! It was no more than a cot!

He shouted. Someone came in, a man wearing the uniform of a trooper in his favorite corps. He started to give him the tongue-lashing of his life, before having him arrested. But he was cut short.

"Cut out that racket, you unholy pig!"

At first he was too astounded to answer, then he shrieked, "Stand at attention when you address your Leader! Salute!"

The man looked dumbfounded, then guffawed. "Like this, maybe?" He stepped to the side of the cot, struck a pose with his right arm raised in salute. He carried a rubber truncheon in it. "Hail to the Leader!" he shouted, and brought his arm down smartly. The truncheon crashed into the Leader's cheekbone.

Another trooper came in to see what the noise was while the first was still laughing at his witticism. "What's up, Jon? Say, you'd better not handle that monkey too rough—he's still carried on the hospital list." He glanced casually at the Leader's bloody face.

"Him? Didn't you know?" He pulled him to one side and whispered.

The second's eyes widened; he grinned. "So? They don't want him to get well, eh? Well, I could use some exercise this morning—"

"Let's get Fats," the other suggested. "He always has such amusing ideas."

"Good idea." He stepped to the door, and bellowed, "Hey, Fats!"

They didn't really start in on him until Fats was there to help.

FOREWORD

LIFE-LINE, MISFIT, LET THERE BE LIGHT, ELSEWHEN, PIED PIPER, IF THIS GOES ON—, REQUIEM, THE ROADS MUST ROLL, COVENTRY, BLOWUPS HAPPEN—for eleven months, mid March 1939 through mid February 1940, I wrote every day ... and that ended my bondage; BLOWUPS HAPPEN paid off the last of that pesky mortgage—eight years ahead of time.

BLOWUPS HAPPEN was the first of my stories to be published in hard covers, in Groff Conklin's first anthology, The Best of Science Fiction, *1946. In the meantime there had been World War II, Hiroshima, The Smyth Report—so I went over my 1940 manuscript most carefully, correcting some figures I had merely guessed at in early 1940.*

This week I have compared the two versions, 1940 and 1946, word by word—there isn't a dime's worth of difference between them ... and I now see, as a result of the enormous increase in the art in 33 years, more errors in the '46 version than I spotted in the '40 version when I checked it in '46.

I do not intend ever again to try to update a story to make it fit new art. Such updating can't save a poor story and isn't necessary for a good story. All of H. G. Wells' SF stories are hopelessly dated ... and they remain the best, *the most gripping science fiction stories to be found anywhere. My* Beyond This Horizon *(1941) states that* H. sapiens *has forty-eight chromosomes, a "fact" that "everybody knew" in 1941. Now "everybody knows" that the "correct" number is forty-six. I shan't change it.*

The version of "Blowups Happen" here following is exactly, word for word, the way it was first written in February 1940.

41

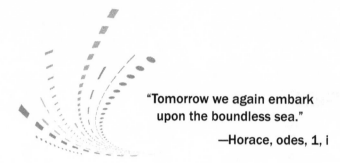

"Tomorrow we again embark
upon the boundless sea."

—Horace, odes, 1, i

"**P**ut down that wrench!"

The man addressed turned slowly around and faced the speaker. His expression was hidden by a grotesque helmet, part of a heavy, leaden armor which shielded his entire body, but the tone of voice in which he answered showed nervous exasperation.

"What the hell's eating on you, Doc?" He made no move to replace the tool in question.

They faced each other like two helmeted, arrayed fencers, watching for an opening. The first speaker's voice came from behind his mask a shade higher in key and more peremptory in tone. "You heard me, Harper. Put down that wrench at once, and come away from that 'trigger.' Erickson!"

A third armored figure came around the shield which separated the uranium bomb proper from the control room in which the first two stood. "Whatcha want, Doc?"

"Harper is relieved from watch. You take over as engineer-of-the-watch. Send for the standby engineer."

"Very well." His voice and manner were phlegmatic as he accepted the situation without comment. The atomic engineer whom he had just relieved glanced from one to the other, then carefully replaced the wrench in its rack.

"Just as you say, Dr. Silard—but send for your relief, too. I shall demand an immediate hearing!" Harper swept indignantly out, his lead-sheathed boots clumping on the floor plates.

Dr. Silard waited unhappily for the ensuing twenty minutes until his own relief arrived. Perhaps he had been hasty. Maybe he was wrong in thinking that Harper had at last broken under the strain of tending the most dangerous machine in the world—an atomic power plant. But if he had made a mistake, it had to be on the safe side— slips *must not happen* in this business; not when a slip might result in the atomic detonation of two and a half tons of uranium.

He tried to visualize what that would mean, and failed. He had been told that uranium was potentially forty million times as explosive as TNT. The figure was meaningless that way. He thought of it, instead, as a hundred million tons of high explosive, two hundred million aircraft bombs as big as the biggest ever used. It still did not mean anything. He had once seen such a bomb dropped, when he had been serving as a temperament analyst for army aircraft pilots. The bomb had left a hole big enough to hide an apartment house. He could not imagine the explosion of a thousand such bombs, much less a hundred million of them.

Perhaps these atomic engineers could. Perhaps, with their greater mathematical ability and closer comprehension of what actually went on inside the nuclear fission chamber—the "bomb"—they had some vivid glimpse of the mind-shattering horror locked up beyond that shield. If so, no wonder they tended to blow up—

He sighed. Erickson looked up from the linear resonant accelerator on which he had been making some adjustment. "What's the trouble, Doc?"

"Nothing. I'm sorry I had to relieve Harper."

Silard could feel the shrewd glance of the big Scandinavian. "Not getting the jitters yourself, are you, Doc? Sometimes you squirrel sleuths blow up, too—"

"Me? I don't think so. I'm scared of that thing in there—I'd be crazy if I weren't."

"So am I," Erickson told him soberly, and went back to his work.

The accelerator's snout disappeared in the shield between them and the bomb, where it fed a steady stream of terrifically speeded up subatomic bullets to the beryllium target located within the bomb itself. The tortured beryllium yielded up neutrons, which shot out in all directions through the uranium mass. Some of these neutrons struck uranium atoms squarely on their nuclei and split them in two. The fragments were new elements, barium, xenon, rubidium—depending on the proportions in which each atom split. The new elements were usually unstable isotopes and broke down into a dozen more elements by radioactive disintegration in a progressive chain reaction.

But these chain reactions were comparatively unimportant; it was the original splitting of the uranium nucleus, with the release of the awe-inspiring energy that bound it together—an incredible two hundred million electron-volts—that was important—and perilous.

For, while uranium isotope 235 may be split by bombarding it with neutrons from an outside source, the splitting itself gives up more neutrons which, in turn, may land in other uranium nuclei and split them. If conditions are favorable to a progressively increasing reaction of this sort, it may get out of hand, build up in an unmeasurable fraction of a microsecond into a complete atomic explosion—an explosion which would dwarf the eruption of Krakatoa to popgun size; an explosion so far beyond all human experience as to be as completely incomprehensible as the idea of personal death. It could be feared, but not understood.

But a self-perpetuating sequence of nuclear splitting *just under the level of complete explosion* was necessary to the operation of the power plant. To split the first uranium nucleus by bombarding it with neutrons from the beryllium target took more power than the death of the atom gave up. In order that the output of power from the system should exceed the power input in useful proportion it was imperative that each atom split by a neutron from the beryllium target should cause the splitting of many more.

It was equally imperative that this chain of reactions should always tend to dampen, to die out. It must not build up, or the entire mass would explode within a time interval too short to be measured by any means whatsoever.

Nor would there be anyone left to measure it.

The atomic engineer on duty at the bomb could control this reaction by means of the "trigger," a term the engineers used to include the linear resonant accelerator, the beryllium target, and the adjacent controls, instrument board, and power sources. That is to say, he could vary the bombardment on the beryllium target to increase or decrease the power output of the plant, and he could tell from his instruments that the internal reaction was dampened—or, rather, that it had been dampened the split second before. He could not possibly know what was actually happening *now* within the bomb—subatomic speeds are too great and the time intervals too small. He was like the bird that flew backward; he could see where he had been, but he never knew where he was going.

Nevertheless, it was his responsibility, and his alone, not only to maintain the bomb at a high input-output efficiency, but to see that the reaction never passed the critical point and progressed into mass explosion.

But that was impossible. He could not be sure; he could never be sure.

He could bring to the job all of the skill and learning of the finest technical education, and use it to reduce the hazard to the lowest mathematical probability, but the blind laws of chance which appear to rule in subatomic action might turn up a royal flush against him and defeat his most skillful play.

And each atomic engineer knew it, knew that he gambled not only with his own life, but with the lives of countless others, perhaps with the lives of every human being on the planet. Nobody knew quite what such an explosion would do. The most conservative estimate assumed that, in addition to destroying the plant and its personnel completely, it would tear a chunk out of the populous and heavily traveled Los Angeles-Oklahoma Road City a hundred miles to the north.

That was the official, optimistic viewpoint on which the plant had been authorized, and based on mathematics which predicted that a mass of uranium would itself be disrupted on a molar scale, and thereby rendered comparatively harmless, before progressive and accelerated atomic explosion could infect the entire mass.

The atomic engineers, by and large, did not place faith in the official theory. They judged theoretical mathematical prediction for what it was worth—precisely nothing, until confirmed by experiment.

But even from the official viewpoint, each atomic engineer while on watch carried not only his own life in his hands, but the lives of many others—how many, it was better not to think about. No pilot, no general, no surgeon ever carried such a daily, inescapable, ever-present weight of responsibility for the lives of other people as these men carried every time they went on watch, every time they touched a vernier screw or read a dial.

They were selected not alone for their intelligence and technical training, but quite as much for their characters and sense of social responsibility. Sensitive men were needed—men who could fully appreciate the importance of the charge intrusted to them; no other sort would do. But the burden of responsibility was too great to be borne indefinitely by a sensitive man.

It was, of necessity, a psychologically unstable condition. Insanity was an occupational disease.

Dr. Cummings appeared, still buckling the straps of the armor worn to guard against stray radiation. "What's up?" he asked Silard.

"I had to relieve Harper."

"So I guessed. I met him coming up. He was sore as hell—just glared at me."

"I know. He wants an immediate hearing. That's why I had to send for you."

Cummings grunted, then nodded toward the engineer, anonymous in all-inclosing armor. "Who'd I draw?"

"Erickson."

"Good enough. Squareheads can't go crazy—eh, Gus?"

Erickson looked up momentarily and answered, "That's your problem," and returned to his work.

Cummings turned back to Silard and commented: "Psychiatrists don't seem very popular around here. O.K.—I relieve you, sir."

"Very well, sir."

Silard threaded his way through the zigzag in the tanks of water which surrounded the disintegration room. Once outside this outer shield, he divested himself of the cumbersome armor, disposed of it in the locker room provided, and hurried to a lift. He left the lift at the tube station, underground, and looked around for an unoccupied capsule. Finding one, he strapped himself in, sealed the gasketed door, and settled the back of his head into the rest against the expected surge of acceleration.

Five minutes later he knocked at the door of the office of the general superintendent, twenty miles away.

The power plant proper was located in a bowl of desert hills on the Arizona plateau. Everything not necessary to the immediate operation of the plant—administrative offices, television station and so forth—lay beyond the hills. The buildings housing these auxiliary functions were of the most durable construction technical ingenuity could devise. It was hoped that, if *Der Tag* ever came, occupants would stand approximately the chance of survival of a man going over Niagara Falls in a barrel.

Silard knocked again. He was greeted by a male secretary. Steinke. Silard recalled reading his case history. Formerly one of the most brilliant of the young engineers, he had suffered a blanking out of the ability to handle mathematical operations. A plain case of *fugue*, but there had been nothing that the poor devil could do about it—he had been anxious enough with his conscious mind to stay on duty. He had been rehabilitated as an office worker.

Steinke ushered him into the superintendent's private office. Harper was there before him, and returned his greeting with icy politeness. The superintendent was cordial, but Silard thought he looked tired, as if the twenty-four-hour-a-day strain was too much for him.

"Come in, Doctor, come in. Sit down. Now tell me about this. I'm a little surprised. I thought Harper was one of my steadiest men."

"I don't say he isn't, sir."

"Well?"

"He may be perfectly all right, but your instructions to me are not to take any chances."

"Quite right." The superintendent gave the engineer, silent and tense in his chair, a troubled glance, then returned his attention to Silard. "Suppose you tell me about it."

Silard took a deep breath. "While on watch as psychological observer at the control station I noticed that the engineer of the watch seemed preoccupied and less responsive to stimuli than usual. During my off-watch observation of this case, over a period of the past several days, I have suspected an increasing lack of attention. For example, while playing contract bridge, he now occasionally asks for a review of the bidding, which is contrary to his former behavior pattern.

"Other similar data are available. To cut it short, at 3:11 today, while on watch, I saw Harper, with no apparent reasonable purpose in mind, pick up a wrench used only for operating the valves of the water shield and approach the trigger. I relieved him of duty and sent him out of the control room."

"Chief!" Harper calmed himself somewhat and continued: "If this witch doctor knew a wrench from an oscillator, he'd know what I was doing. The wrench was on the wrong rack. I noticed it, and picked it up to return it to its proper place. On the way, I stopped to check the readings!"

The superintendent turned inquiringly to Dr. Silard.

"That may be true. Granting that it is true," answered the psychiatrist doggedly, "my diagnosis still stands. Your behavior pattern has altered; your present actions are unpredictable, and I can't approve you for responsible work without a complete checkup."

General Superintendent King drummed on the desk top and sighed. Then he spoke slowly to Harper: "Cal, you're a good boy, and, believe me, I know how you feel. But there is no way to avoid it— you've got to go up for the psychometricals, and accept whatever disposition the board makes of you." He paused, but Harper maintained an expressionless silence. "Tell you what, son—why don't you take a few days leave? Then, when you come back, you can go up before the board, or transfer to another department away from the bomb, whichever you prefer." He looked to Silard for approval, and received a nod.

But Harper was not mollified. "No, chief," he protested. "It won't do. Can't you see what's wrong? It's this constant supervision. Somebody always watching the back of your neck, *expecting* you to go crazy. A man can't even shave in private. We're jumpy about the most innocent acts, for fear some head doctor, half batty himself, will see it and decide it's a sign we're slipping. Good grief, what do you expect?" His outburst having run its course, he subsided into a flippant cynicism that did not quite jell. "O.K.—never mind the straitjacket; I'll go quietly. You're a good Joe in spite of it, chief," he added, "and I'm glad to have worked under you. Good-bye."

King kept the pain in his eyes out of his voice.

"Wait a minute, Cal—you're not through here. Let's forget about the vacation. I'm transferring you to the radiation laboratory. You belong in research, anyhow; I'd never have spared you from it to stand watches if I hadn't been short on Number One men.

"As for the constant psychological observation, I hate it as much as you do. I don't suppose you know that they watch me about twice as hard as they watch you duty engineers." Harper showed his surprise, but Silard nodded in sober confirmation. "But we have to have this supervision. Do you remember Manning? No, he was before your time. We didn't have psychological observers then. Manning was able and brilliant. Furthermore, he was always cheerful; nothing seemed to bother him.

"I was glad to have him on the bomb, for he was always alert, and never seemed nervous about working with it—in fact, he grew more buoyant and cheerful the longer he stood control watches. I should have known that was a very bad sign, but I didn't, and there was no observer to tell me so.

"His technician had to slug him one night. He found him dismounting the safety interlocks on the trigger. Poor old Manning never pulled out of it—he's been violently insane ever since. After Manning cracked up we worked out the present system of two qualified engineers and an observer for every watch. It seemed the only thing to do."

"I suppose so, chief," Harper mused, his face no longer sullen, but still unhappy. "It's a hell of a situation just the same."

"That's putting it mildly." King rose and put out his hand. "Cal, unless you're dead set on leaving us, I'll expect to see you at the radiation laboratory tomorrow. Another thing—I don't often recommend this, but it might do you good to get drunk tonight."

King had signed to Silard to remain after the young man left. Once the door was closed he turned back to the psychiatrist. "There goes another one—and one of the best. Doctor, what am I going to do?"

Silard pulled at his cheek. "I don't know," he admitted. "The hell of it is, Harper's absolutely right. It does increase the strain on them to know that they are being watched—and yet they have to be watched. Your psychiatric staff isn't doing too well, either. It makes us nervous to be around the bomb—the more so because we don't understand it. And it's a strain on us to be hated and despised as we are. Scientific detachment is difficult under such conditions; I'm getting jumpy myself."

King ceased pacing the floor and faced the doctor. "But there must be *some* solution—" he insisted.

Silard shook his head. "It's beyond me, Superintendent. I see no solution from the standpoint of psychology."

"No? Hm-m-m. Doctor, who is the top man in your field?"

"Eh?"

"Who is the recognized Number One man in handling this sort of thing?"

"Why, that's hard to say. Naturally, there isn't any one leading psychiatrist in the world; we specialize too much. I know what you mean, though. You don't want the best industrial-temperament psychometrician; you want the best all-around man for psychoses nonlesional and situational. That would be Lentz."

"Go on."

"Well—he covers the whole field of environmental adjustment. He's the man who correlated the theory of optimum tonicity with the relaxation technique that Korzybski had developed empirically. He actually worked under Korzybski himself, when he was a young student—it's the only thing he's vain about."

"He did? Then he must be pretty old; Korzybski died in—What year did he die?"

"I started to say that you must know his work in symbology—theory of abstraction and calculus of statement, all that sort of thing—because of its applications to engineering and mathematical physics."

"*That* Lentz—yes, of course. But I had never thought of him as a psychiatrist."

"No, you wouldn't, in your field. Nevertheless, we are inclined to credit him with having done as much to check and reduce the pandemic neuroses of the Crazy Years as any other man, and more than any man left alive."

"Where is he?"

"Why, Chicago, I suppose. At the Institute."

"Get him here."

"Eh?"

"Get him down here. Get on that visiphone and locate him. Then have Steinke call the port of Chicago, and hire a stratocar to stand by for him. I want to see him as soon as possible—before the day is out." King sat up in his chair with the air of a man who is once more master of himself and the situation. His spirit knew that warming replenishment that comes only with reaching a decision. The harassed expression was gone.

Silard looked dumbfounded. "But, Superintendent," he expostulated, "You can't ring for Dr. Lentz as if he were a junior clerk. He's ... he's *Lentz*."

"Certainly—that's why I want him. But I'm not a neurotic clubwoman looking for sympathy, either. He'll come. If necessary, turn on the heat from Washington. Have the White House call him. But get him here at once. Move!" King strode out of the office.

When Erickson came off watch he inquired around and found that Harper had left for town. Accordingly, he dispensed with dinner at the base, shifted into "drinkin' clothes," and allowed himself to be dispatched via tube to Paradise.

Paradise, Arizona, was a hard little boom town, which owed its existence to the power plant. It was dedicated exclusively to the serious business of detaching the personnel of the plant from their inordinate salaries. In this worthy project they received much cooperation from the plant personnel themselves, each of whom was receiving from twice to ten times as much money each pay day as he had ever received in any other job, and none of whom was certain of living long enough to justify saving for old age. Besides, the company carried a sinking fund in Manhattan for their dependents; why be stingy?

It was said, with some truth, that any entertainment or luxury obtainable in New York City could be purchased in Paradise. The local chamber of commerce had appropriated the slogan of Reno, Nevada, "Biggest Little City in the World." The Reno boosters retaliated by claiming that, while any town that close to the atomic power plant undeniably brought thoughts of death and the hereafter, Hell's Gates would be a more appropriate name than Paradise.

Erickson started making the rounds. There were twenty-seven places licensed to sell liquor in the six blocks of the main street of Paradise. He expected to find Harper in one of them, and, knowing the man's habits and tastes, he expected to find him in the first two or three he tried.

He was not mistaken. He found Harper sitting alone at a table in the rear of DeLancey's Sans Souci Bar. DeLancey's was a favorite of both of them. There was an old-fashioned comfort about its chrome-plated bar and red leather furniture that appealed to them more than did the spectacular fittings of the up-to-the-minute places. DeLancey was conservative; he stuck to indirect lighting and soft music; his hostesses were required to be fully clothed, even in the evening.

The fifth of Scotch in front of Harper was about two thirds full. Erickson shoved three fingers in front of Harper's face and demanded, "Count!"

Three," announced Harper. "Sit down, Gus."

"That's correct," Erickson agreed, sliding his big frame into a low-slung chair. "You'll do—for now. What was the outcome?"

"Have a drink. Not," he went on, "that this Scotch is any good. I think Lance has taken to watering it. I surrendered, horse and foot."

"Lance wouldn't do that—stick to that theory and you'll sink in the sidewalk up to your knees. How come you capitulated? I thought you planned to beat 'em about the head and shoulders, at least."

"I did," mourned Harper, "but, cripes, Gus, the chief is right. If a brain mechanic says you're punchy, he has got to back him up and take you off the bomb. The chief can't afford to take a chance."

"Yeah, the chief's all right, but I can't learn to love our dear psychiatrists. Tell you what—let's find us one, and see if he can feel pain. I'll hold him while you slug 'im."

"Oh, forget it, Gus. Have a drink."

"A pious thought—but not Scotch. I'm going to have a martini; we ought to eat pretty soon."

"I'll have one, too."

"Do you good." Erickson lifted his blond head and bellowed, "Israfel!"

A large, black person appeared at his elbow. "Mistuh Erickson! Yes, suh!"

"Izzy, fetch two martinis. Make mine with Italian." He turned back to Harper. "What are you going to do now, Cal?"

"Radiation laboratory."

"Well, that's not so bad. I'd like to have a go at the matter of rocket fuels myself. I've got some ideas."

Harper looked mildly amused. "You mean atomic fuel for interplanetary flight? The problem's pretty well exhausted. No, son, the stratosphere is the ceiling until we think up something better than rockets. Of course, you *could* mount the bomb in a ship, and figure out some jury rig to convert its radiant output into push, but where does that get you? One bomb, one ship—and twenty years of mining in Little America has only produced enough pitchblende to make one bomb. That's disregarding the question of getting the company to lend you their one bomb for anything that doesn't pay dividends."

Erickson looked balky. "I don't concede that you've covered all the alternatives. What have we got? The early rocket boys went right ahead trying to build better rockets, serene in the belief that, by the time they could build rockets good enough to fly to the Moon, a fuel would be perfected that would do the trick. And they did build ships that were good enough—you could take any ship that makes the antipodes run, and refit it for the Moon—*if* you had a fuel that was sufficiently concentrated to maintain the necessary push for the whole run. But they haven't got it.

54

"And why not? Because we let 'em down, that's why. Because they're still depending on molecular energy, on chemical reactions, with atomic power sitting right here in our laps. It's not their fault— old D. D. Harriman had Rockets Consolidated underwrite the whole first issue of Antarctic Pitchblende, and took a big slice of it himself, in the expectation that we would produce something usable in the way of a concentrated rocket fuel. Did we do it? Like hell! The company went hog-wild for immediate commercial exploitation, and there's no fuel yet."

"But you haven't stated it properly," Harper objected. "There are just two forms of atomic power available—radioactivity and atomic disintegration. The first is too slow; the energy is there, but you can't wait years for it to come out—not in a rocketship. The second we can only manage in a large mass of uranium. There you are—stymied."

Erickson's Scandinavian stubbornness was just gathering for another try at the argument when the waiter arrived with the drinks. He set them down with a triumphant flourish. "There you are, suh!"

"Want to roll for them, Izzy?" Harper inquired.

"Don' mind if I do."

The Negro produced a leather dice cup, and Harper rolled. He selected his combinations with care and managed to get four aces and a jack in three rolls. Israfel took the cup. He rolled in the grand manner with a backward twist to his wrist. His score finished at five kings, and he courteously accepted the price of six drinks. Harper stirred the engraved cubes with his forefinger.

"*Izzy*," he asked, "are these the same dice I rolled with?"

"Why, Mistuh Harper!" The Negro's expression was pained.

"Skip it," Harper conceded. "I should know better than to gamble with you. I haven't won a roll from you in six weeks. What did you start to say, Gus?"

"I was just going to say that there ought to be a better way to get energy out of—"

But they were joined again, this time by something very seductive in an evening gown that appeared to have been sprayed on her lush figure. She was young, perhaps nineteen or twenty. "You boys lonely?" she asked as she flowed into a chair.

"Nice of you to ask, but we're not," Erickson denied with patient politeness. He jerked a thumb at a solitary figure seated across, the room. "Go talk to Hannigan; he's not busy."

She followed his gesture with her eyes, and answered with faint scorn: "Him? He's no use. He's been like that for three weeks—hasn't spoken to a soul. If you ask me, I'd say that he was cracking up."

"That so?" he observed noncommittally. "Here"—he fished out a five-dollar bill and handed it to her—"buy yourself a drink. Maybe we'll look you up later."

"Thanks, boys." The money disappeared under her clothing, and she stood up. "Just ask for Edith."

"Hannigan does look bad," Harper considered, noting the brooding stare and apathetic attitude, "and he has been awfully standoffish lately, for him. Do you suppose we're obliged to report him?"

"Don't let it worry you," advised Erickson. There's a spotter on the job now. Look." Harper followed his companion's eyes and recognized Dr. Mott of the psychological staff. He was leaning against the far end of the bar, and nursing a tall glass, which gave him protective coloration. But his stance was such that his field of vision included not only Hannigan, but Erickson and Harper as well.

"Yeah, and he's studying us as well," Harper added. "Damn it to hell, why does it make my back hair rise just to lay eyes on one of them?"

The question was rhetorical; Erickson ignored it. "Let's get out of here," he suggested, "and have dinner somewhere else."

"O.K."

DeLancey himself waited on them as they left. "Going so soon, gentlemen?" he asked, in a voice that implied that their departure would leave him no reason to stay open. "Beautiful lobster thermidor tonight. If you do not like it, you need not pay." He smiled brightly.

"Not sea food, Lance," Harper told him, "not tonight. Tell me— why do you stick around here when you know that the bomb is bound to get you in the long run? Aren't you afraid of it?"

The tavernkeeper's eyebrows shot up. "Afraid of the bomb? But it is my friend!"

"Makes you money, eh?"

"Oh, I do not mean that." He leaned toward them confidentially. "Five years ago I come here to make some money quickly for my family before my cancer of the stomach, it kills me. At the clinic, with the wonderful new radiants you gentlemen make with the aid of the bomb, I am cured—I live again. No, I am not afraid of the bomb, it is my good friend."

"Suppose it blows up?"

"When the good Lord needs me, He will take me." He crossed himself quickly.

As they turned away, Erickson commented in a low voice to Harper, "There's your answer, Cal—if all us engineers had his faith, the bomb wouldn't get us down."

Harper was unconvinced. "I don't know," he mused. "I don't think it's faith; I think it's lack of imagination—and knowledge."

Notwithstanding King's confidence, Lentz did not show up until the next day. The superintendent was subconsciously a little surprised at his visitor's appearance. He had pictured a master psychologist as wearing flowing hair, an imperial, and having piercing black eyes. But this man was not very tall, was heavy in his framework, and fat—almost gross. He might have been a butcher. Little, piggy, faded-blue eyes peered merrily out from beneath shaggy blond brows. There was no hair anywhere else on the enormous skull, and the apelike jaw was smooth and pink. He was dressed in mussed pajamas of unbleached linen. A long cigarette holder jutted permanently from one corner of a wide mouth, widened still more by a smile with suggested unmalicious amusement at the worst that life, or men, could do. He had gusto.

King found him remarkably easy to talk to.

At Lentz's suggestion the superintendent went first into the history of the atomic power plant, how the fission of the uranium atom by Dr. Otto Hahn in December, 1938, had opened up the way to atomic power. The door was opened just a crack; the process to be self-perpetuating and commercially usable required an enormously greater mass of uranium than there was available in the entire civilized world at that time.

But the discovery, fifteen years later, of enormous deposits of pitchblende in the old rock underlying Little America removed that obstacle. The deposits were similar to those previously worked at Great Bear Lake in the arctic north of Canada, but so much more extensive that the eventual possibility of accumulating enough uranium to build an atomic power plant became evident.

The demand for commercially usable, cheap power had never been satiated. Even the Douglas-Martin sunpower screens, used to drive the roaring road cities of the period and for a myriad other industrial purposes, were not sufficient to fill the ever-growing demand. They had saved the country from impending famine of oil and coal, but their maximum output of approximately one horsepower per square yard of sun-illuminated surface put a definite limit to the power from that source available in any given geographical area.

Atomic power was needed—was demanded.

But theoretical atomic physics predicted that a uranium mass sufficiently large to assist in its own disintegration might assist too well—blow up instantaneously, with such force that it would probably wreck every man-made structure on the globe and conceivably destroy the entire human race as well. They dared not build the bomb, even though the uranium was available.

"It was Destry's mechanics of infinitesimals that showed a way out of the dilemma," King went on. "His equations appeared to predict that an atomic explosion, once started, would disrupt the molar mass inclosing it so rapidly that neutron loss through the outer surface of the fragments would dampen the progression of the atomic explosion to zero before complete explosion could be reached.

"For the mass we use in the bomb, his equations predict a possible force of explosion one seventh of one percent of the force of complete explosion. That alone, of course, would be incomprehensibly destructive—about the equivalent of a hundred and forty thousand tons of TNT—enough to wreck this end of the State. Personally, I've never been sure that is all that would happen."

"Then why did you accept this job?" inquired Lentz.

King fiddled with items on his desk before replying. "I couldn't turn it down, Doctor—I *couldn't*. If I had refused, they would have gotten someone else—and it was an opportunity that comes to a physicist once in history."

Lentz nodded. "And probably they would have gotten someone not as competent. I understand, Dr. King—you were compelled by the 'truth-tropism' of the scientist. He must go where the data is to be found, even if it kills him. But about this fellow Destry, I've never liked his mathematics; he postulates too much."

King looked up in quick surprise, then recalled that this was the man who had refined and given rigor to the calculus of statement. "That's just the hitch," he agreed. "His work is brilliant, but I've never been sure that his predictions were worth the paper they were written on. Nor, apparently," he added bitterly, "do my junior engineers."

He told the psychiatrist of the difficulties they had had with personnel, of how the most carefully selected men would, sooner or later, crack under the strain. "At first I thought it might be some degenerating effect from the hard radiation that leaks out of the bomb, so we improved the screening and the personal armor. But it didn't help. One young fellow who had joined us after the new screening was installed became violent at dinner one night, and insisted that a pork chop was about to explode. I hate to think of what might have happened if he had been on duty at the bomb when he blew up."

The inauguration of the system of constant psychological observation had greatly reduced the probability of acute danger resulting from a watch engineer cracking up, but King was forced to admit that the system was not a success; there had actually been a marked increase in psychoneuroses, dating from that time.

"And that's the picture, Dr. Lentz. It gets worse all the time. It's getting me now. The strain is telling on me; I can't sleep, and I don't think my judgment is as good as it used to be—I have trouble making up my mind, of coming to a decision. Do you think you can do anything for us?"

But Lentz had no immediate relief for his anxiety. "Not so fast, superintendent," he countered. "You have given me the background, but I have no real data as yet. I must look around for a while, smell out the situation for myself, talk to your engineers, perhaps have a few drinks with them, and get acquainted. That is possible, is it not? Then in a few days, maybe, we'll know where we stand."

King had no alternative but to agree.

"And it is well that your young men do not know what I am here for. Suppose I am your old friend, a visiting physicist, eh?"

"Why, yes—of course. I can see to it that the idea gets around. But say—" King was reminded again of something that had bothered him from the time Silard had first suggested Lentz's name—"may I ask a personal question?"

The merry eyes were undisturbed.

"Go ahead."

"I can't help but be surprised that one man should attain eminence in two such widely differing fields as psychology and mathematics. And right now I'm perfectly convinced of your ability to pass yourself off as a physicist. I don't understand it."

The smile was more amused, without being in the least patronizing, nor offensive. "Same subject, symbology. You are a specialist; it would not necessarily come to your attention."

"I still don't follow you."

"No? Man lives in a world of ideas. Any phenomenon is so complex that he cannot possibly grasp the whole of it. He abstracts certain characteristics of a given phenomenon as an idea, then represents that idea as a symbol, be it a word or a mathematical sign. Human reaction is almost entirely reaction to symbols, and only negligibly to phenomena. As a matter of fact," he continued, removing the cigarette holder from his mouth and settling into his subject, "it can be demonstrated that the human mind can think only in terms of symbols.

"When we think, we let symbols operate on other symbols in certain, set fashions—rules of logic, or rules of mathematics. If the symbols have been abstracted so that they are structurally similar to the phenomena they stand for, and if the symbol operations are similar in structure and order to the operations of phenomena in the real world, we think sanely. If our logic-mathematics, or our word-symbols, have been poorly chosen, we do not think sanely.

"In mathematical physics you are concerned with making your symbology fit physical phenomena. In psychiatry I am concerned with precisely the same thing, except that I am more immediately concerned with the man who does the thinking than with the phenomena he is thinking about. But the same subject, always the same subject."

"We're not getting anyplace, ... Gus." Harper put down his slide rule and frowned.

"Seems like it, Cal," Erickson grudgingly admitted. "Damn it, though—there ought to be some reasonable way of tackling the problem. What do we need? Some form of concentrated, controllable power for rocket fuel. What have we got? Power galore in the bomb. There must be some way to bottle that power, and serve it out when we need it—and the answer is someplace in one of the radioactive series. I *know* it." He stared glumly around the laboratory as if expecting to find the answer written somewhere on the lead-sheathed walls.

"Don't be so down in the mouth about it. You've got me convinced there is an answer; let's figure out how to find it. In the first place the three natural radioactive series are out, aren't they?"

"Yes—at least we had agreed that all that ground had been fully covered before."

"O.K.; we have to assume that previous investigators have done what their notes show they have done—otherwise we might as well not believe anything, and start checking on everybody from Archimedes to date. Maybe that is indicated, but Methuselah himself couldn't carry out such an assignment. What have we got left?"

"Artificial radioactives."

"All right. Let's set up a list of them, both those that have been made up to now, and those that might possibly be made in the future. Call that our group—or rather, field, if you want to be pedantic about definitions. There are a limited number of operations that can be performed on each member of the group, and on the members taken in combination. Set it up."

Erickson did so, using the curious curlicues of the calculus of statement. Harper nodded. "All right—expand it."

Erickson looked up after a few moments, and asked, "Cal, have you any idea how many terms there are in the expansion?"

"No—hundreds, maybe thousands, I suppose."

"You're conservative. It reaches four figures without considering possible new radioactives. We couldn't finish such a research in a century." He chucked his pencil down and looked morose.

Cal Harper looked at him curiously, but with sympathy. "Gus," he said gently, "the bomb isn't getting you, too, is it?"

"I don't think so. Why?"

"I never saw you so willing to give up anything before. Naturally you and I will never finish any such job, but at the very worst we will have eliminated a lot of wrong answers for somebody else. Look at Edison—sixty years of experimenting, twenty hours a day, yet he never found out the one thing he was most interested in knowing. I guess if he could take it, we can."

Erickson pulled out of his funk to some extent. "I suppose so," he agreed. "Anyhow, maybe we could work out some techniques for carrying on a lot of experiments simultaneously."

Harper slapped him on the shoulder. "That's the ol' fight. Besides—we may not need to finish the research, or anything like it, to find a satisfactory fuel. The way I see it, there are probably a dozen, maybe a hundred, right answers. We may run across one of them any day. Anyhow, since you're willing to give me a hand with it in your off-watch time, I'm game to peck away at it till hell freezes."

Lentz puttered around the plant and the administration center for several days, until he was known to everyone by sight. He made himself pleasant and asked questions. He was soon regarded as a harmless nuisance, to be tolerated because he was a friend of the superintendent. He even poked his nose into the commercial power end of the plant, and had the mercury-steam-turbogenerator sequence explained to him in detail. This alone would have been sufficient to disarm any suspicion that he might be a psychiatrist, for the staff psychiatrists paid no attention to the hard-bitten technicians of the power-conversion unit. There was no need to; mental instability on their part could not affect the bomb, nor were they subject to the man-killing strain of social responsibility. Theirs was simply a job personally dangerous, a type of strain strong men have been inured to since the jungle.

In due course he got around to the unit of the radiation laboratory set aside for Calvin Harper's use. He rang the bell and waited. Harper answered the door, his antiradiation helmet shoved back from his face like a grotesque sunbonnet. "What is it?" he asked. "Oh—it's you, Dr. Lentz. Did you want to see me?"

"Why, yes and no," the older man answered. "I was just looking around the experimental station, and wondered what you do in here. Will I be in the way?"

"Not at all. Come in. Gus!"

Erickson got up from where he had been fussing over the power leads to their trigger—a modified cyclotron rather than a resonant accelerator. "Hello."

"Gus, this is Dr. Lentz—Gus Erickson."

"We've met," said Erickson, pulling off his gauntlet to shake hands. He had had a couple of drinks with Lentz in town and considered him a "nice old duck." "You're just between shows, but stick around and we'll start another run—not that there is much to see."

While Erickson continued with the setup, Harper conducted Lentz around the laboratory, explaining the line of research they were conducting, as happy as a father showing off twins. The psychiatrist listened with one ear and made appropriate comments while he studied the young scientist for signs of the instability he had noted to be recorded against him.

"You see," Harper explained, oblivious to the interest in himself, "we are testing radioactive materials to see if we can produce disintegration of the sort that takes place in the bomb, but in a minute, almost microscopic, mass. If we are successful, we can use the power of the bomb to make a safe, convenient, atomic fuel for rockets." He went on to explain their schedule of experimentation.

"I see," Lentz observed politely. "What metal are you examining now?"

Harper told him. "But it's not a case of examining one element—we've finished Isotope II with negative results. Our schedule calls next for running the same test on Isotope V. Like this." He hauled out a lead capsule, and showed the label to Lentz, who saw that it was, indeed, marked with the symbol of the fifth isotope. He hurried away to the shield around the target of the cyclotron, left open by Erickson.

Lentz saw that he had opened the capsule, and was performing some operation on it in a gingerly manner, having first lowered his helmet. Then he closed and clamped the target shield.

"O.K., Gus?" he called out. "Ready to roll?"

"Yeah, I guess so," Erickson assured him, coming around them. They crowded behind a thick metal shield that cut them off from direct sight of the setup.

"Will I need to put on armor?" inquired Lentz.

"No," Erickson reassured him, "we wear it because we are around the stuff day in and day out. You just stay behind the shield and you'll be all right. It's lead—backed up by eight inches of case-hardened armor plate."

Erickson glanced at Harper, who nodded, and fixed his eyes on a panel of instruments mounted behind the shield. Lentz saw Erickson press a push button at the top of the board, then heard a series of relays click on the far side of the shield. There was a short moment of silence.

The floor slapped his feet like some incredible bastinado. The concussion that beat on his ears was so intense that it paralyzed the auditory nerve almost before it could be recorded as sound. The air-conducted concussion wave flailed every inch of his body with a single, stinging, numbing blow. As he picked himself up, he found he was trembling uncontrollably and realized, for the first time, that he was getting old.

Harper was seated on the floor and had commenced to bleed from the nose. Erickson had gotten up; his cheek was cut. He touched a hand to the wound, then stood there, regarding the blood on his fingers with a puzzled expression on his face.

"Are you hurt?" Lentz inquired inanely. "What happened?"

Harper cut in. "Gus, we've done it! We've done it! Isotope V's turned the trick!"

Erickson looked still more bemused. "Five?" he said stupidly. "But that wasn't Five; that was Isotope II. I put it in myself."

"*You* put it in? *I* put it in! It was Five, I tell you!"

They stood staring at each other, still confused by the explosion, and each a little annoyed at the bone-headed stupidity the other displayed in the face of the obvious. Lentz diffidently interceded.

"Wait a minute, boys," he suggested. "Maybe there's a reason—Gus, you placed a quantity of the second isotope in the receiver?"

"Why, yes, certainly. I wasn't satisfied with the last run, and I wanted to check it."

Lentz nodded. "It's my fault, gentlemen," he admitted ruefully. "I came in and disturbed your routine, and both of you charged the receiver. I know Harper did, for I saw him do it—with Isotope V. I'm sorry."

Understanding broke over Harper's face, and he slapped the older man on the shoulder. "Don't be sorry," he laughed; "you can come around to our lab and help us make mistakes any time you feel in the mood. Can't he, Gus? This is the answer, Dr. Lentz; this is it!"

"But," the psychiatrist pointed out, "you don't know which isotope blew up."

"Nor care," Harper supplemented. "Maybe it was both, taken together. But we *will* know—this business is cracked now; we'll soon have it open." He gazed happily around at the wreckage.

In spite of Superintendent King's anxiety, Lentz refused to be hurried in passing judgment on the situation. Consequently, when he did present himself at King's office, and announced that he was ready to report, King was pleasantly surprised as well as relieved. "Well, I'm delighted," he said. "Sit down, Doctor, sit down. Have a cigar. What do we do about it?"

But Lentz stuck to his perennial cigarette and refused to be hurried. "I must have some information first. How important," he demanded, "is the power from your plant?"

King understood the implication at once. "If you are thinking about shutting down the bomb for more than a limited period, it can't be done."

"Why not? If the figures supplied me are correct, your output is less than thirteen percent of the total power used in the country."

"Yes, that is true, but you haven't considered the items that go into making up the total. A lot of it is domestic power, which householders get from sunscreens located on their own roofs. Another big slice is power for the moving roadways—that's sunpower again. The portion we provide here is the main power source for most of the heavy industries—steel, plastics, lithics, all kinds of manufacturing and processing. You might as well cut the heart out of a man—"

"But the food industry isn't basically dependent on you?" Lentz persisted.

"No. Food isn't basically a power industry—although we do supply a certain percentage of the power used in processing. I see your point, and will go on and concede that transportation—that is to say, distribution of food—could get along without us. But, good heavens, Doctor, you can't stop atomic power without causing the biggest panic this country has ever seen. It's the keystone of our whole industrial system."

"The country has lived through panics before, and we got past the oil shortage safely."

"Yes—because atomic power came along to take the place of oil. You don't realize what this would mean, Doctor. It would be worse than a war; in a system like ours, one thing depends on another. If you cut off the heavy industries all at once, everything else stops, too."

"Nevertheless, you had better dump the bomb." The uranium in the bomb was molten, its temperature being greater than twenty-four hundred degrees centigrade. The bomb could be dumped into a group of small containers, when it was desired to shut it down. The mass in any one container was too small to maintain progressive atomic disintegration.

King glanced involuntarily at the glass-inclosed relay mounted on his office wall, by which he, as well as the engineer on duty, could dump the bomb, if need be. "But I couldn't do that—or rather, if I did, the plant wouldn't stay shut down. The Directors would simply replace me with someone who *would* operate the bomb."

"You're right, of course." Lentz silently considered the situation for some time, then said, "Superintendent, will you order a car to fly me back to Chicago?"

"You're going, Doctor?"

"Yes." He took the cigarette holder from his face, and, for once, the smile of Olympian detachment was gone completely. His entire manner was sober, even tragic. "Short of shutting down the bomb, there is no solution to your problem—none whatsoever!

"I owe you a full explanation." Lentz continued, at length. "You are confronted here with recurring instances of situational psychoneurosis. Roughly, the symptoms manifest themselves as anxiety neurosis or some form of hysteria. The partial amnesia of your secretary, Steinke, is a good example of the latter. He might be cured with shock technique, but it would hardly be a kindness, as he has achieved a stable adjustment which puts him beyond the reach of the strain he could not stand.

"That other young fellow, Harper, whose blowup was the immediate cause of your sending for me, is an anxiety case. When the cause of the anxiety was eliminated from his matrix, he at once regained full sanity. But keep a close watch on his friend, Erickson—

"However, it is the cause, and prevention, of situational psychoneurosis we are concerned with here, rather than the forms in which it is manifested. In plain language, psychoneurosis situational simply refers to the common fact that, if you put a man in a situation that worries him more than he can stand, in time he blows up, one way or another.

"That is precisely the situation here. You take sensitive, intelligent young men, impress them with the fact that a single slip on their part, or even some fortuitous circumstance beyond their control, will result in the death of God knows how many other people, and then expect them to remain sane. It's ridiculous—impossible!"

"But, good heavens, Doctor, there must be some answer! There must!" He got up and paced around the room. Lentz noted, with pity, that King himself was riding the ragged edge of the very condition they were discussing.

"No," he said slowly. "No. Let me explain. You don't dare intrust the bomb to less sensitive, less socially conscious men. You might as well turn the controls over to a mindless idiot. And to psychoneurosis situational there are but two cures. The first obtains when the psychosis results from a misevaluation of environment. That cure calls for semantic readjustment. One assists the patient to evaluate correctly his environment. The worry disappears because there never was a real reason for worry in the situation itself, but simply in the wrong meaning the patient's mind had assigned to it.

67

"The second case is when the patient has correctly evaluated the situation, and rightly finds in it cause for extreme worry. His worry is perfectly sane and proper, but he cannot stand up under it indefinitely; it drives him crazy. The only possible cure is to change the situation. I have stayed here long enough to assure myself that such is the condition here. Your engineers have correctly evaluated the public danger of this bomb, and it will, with dreadful certainty, drive all of you crazy!

"The only possible solution is to dump the bomb—and leave it dumped."

King had continued his nervous pacing of the floor, as if the walls of the room itself were the cage of his dilemma. Now he stopped and appealed once more to the psychiatrist. "Isn't there *anything* I can do?"

"Nothing to cure. To alleviate—well, possibly."

"How?"

"Situational psychosis results from adrenaline exhaustion. When a man is placed under a nervous strain, his adrenal glands increase their secretion to help compensate for the strain. If the strain is too great and lasts too long, the adrenals aren't equal to the task, and he cracks. That is what you have here. Adrenaline therapy might stave off a mental breakdown, but it most assuredly would hasten a physical breakdown. But that would be safer from a viewpoint of public welfare—even though it assumes that physicists are expendable!

"Another thing occurs to me: If you selected any new watch engineers from the membership of churches that practice the confessional, it would increase the length of their usefulness."

King was plainly surprised. "I don't follow you."

"The patient unloads most of his worry on his confessor, who is not himself actually confronted by the situation, and can stand it. That is simply an ameliorative, however. I am convinced that, in this situation, eventual insanity is inevitable. But there is a lot of good sense in the confessional," he added. "It fills a basic human need. I think that is why the early psychoanalysts were so surprisingly successful, for all their limited knowledge." He fell silent for a while, then added, "If you will be so kind as to order a stratocab for me—"

"You've nothing more to suggest?"

"No. You had better turn your psychological staff loose on means of alleviation; they're able men, all of them."

King pressed a switch and spoke briefly to Steinke. Turning back to Lentz, he said, "You'll wait here until your car is ready?"

Lentz judged correctly that King desired it and agreed. Presently the tube delivery on King's desk went *ping!* The Superintendent removed a small white pasteboard, a calling card. He studied it with surprise and passed it over to Lentz. "I can't imagine why he should be calling on me," he observed, and added, "Would you like to meet him?"

Lentz read:

THOMAS P. HARRINGTON

CAPTAIN (MATHEMATICS)

UNITED STATES NAVY

DIRECTOR

U.S. NAVAL OBSERVATORY

"But I do know him," he said. "I'd be very pleased to see him."

Harrington was a man with something on his mind. He seemed relieved when Steinke had finished ushering him in, and had returned to the outer office. He commenced to speak at once, turning to Lentz, who was nearer to him than King. "You're King? … Why, Dr. Lentz! What are you doing here?"

"Visiting," answered Lentz, accurately but incompletely, as he shook hands. "This is Superintendent King over here. Superintendent King—Captain Harrington."

"How do you do, Captain—it's a pleasure to have you here."

"It's an honor to be here, sir."

"Sit down?"

"Thanks." He accepted a chair and laid a briefcase on a corner of King's desk. "Superintendent, you are entitled to an explanation as to why I have broken in on you like this—"

"Glad to have you." In fact, the routine of formal politeness was an anodyne to King's frayed nerves.

"That's kind of you, but—That secretary chap, the one that brought me in here, would it be too much to ask you to tell him to forget my name? I know it seems strange—"

"Not at all." King was mystified, but willing to grant any reasonable request of a distinguished colleague in science. He summoned Steinke to the interoffice visiphone and gave him his orders.

Lentz stood up and indicated that he was about to leave. He caught Harrington's eye. "I think you want a private palaver, Captain."

King looked from Harrington to Lentz and back to Harrington. The astronomer showed momentary indecision, then protested: "I have no objection at all myself; it's up to Dr. King. As a matter of fact," he added, "it might be a very good thing if you did sit in on it."

"I don't know what it is, Captain," observed King, "that you want to see me about, but Dr. Lentz is already here in a confidential capacity."

"Good! Then that's settled. I'll get right down to business. Dr. King, you know Destry's mechanics of infinitesimals?"

"Naturally." Lentz cocked a brow at King, who chose to ignore it.

"Yes, of course. Do you remember theorem six and the transformation between equations thirteen and fourteen?"

"I think so, but I'd want to see them." King got up and went over to a bookcase. Harrington stayed him with a hand.

"Don't bother. I have them here." He hauled out a key, unlocked his briefcase, and drew out a large, much-thumbed, loose-leaf notebook. "Here. You, too, Dr. Lentz. Are you familiar with this development?"

Lentz nodded. "I've had occasion to look into them."

"Good—I think it's agreed that the step between thirteen and fourteen is the key to the whole matter. Now, the change from thirteen to fourteen looks perfectly valid—and would be, in some fields. But suppose we expand it to show every possible phase of the matter, every link in the chain of reasoning."

He turned a page and showed them the same two equations broken down into nine intermediate equations. He placed a finger under an associated group of mathematical symbols. "Do you see that? Do you see what that implies?" He peered anxiously at their faces.

King studied it, his lips moving. "Yes ... I believe I do see. Odd ... I never looked at it just that way before—yet I've studied those equations until I've dreamed about them." He turned to Lentz. "Do you agree, Doctor?"

Lentz nodded slowly. "I believe so. ... Yes, I think I may say so."

Harrington should have been pleased; he wasn't. "I had hoped you could tell me I was wrong," he said, almost petulantly, "but I'm afraid there is no further doubt about it. Dr. Destry included an assumption valid in molar physics, but for which we have absolutely no assurance in atomic physics. I suppose you realize what this means to you, Dr. King?"

King's voice was a dry whisper. "Yes," he said, "yes—It means that if that bomb out there ever blows up, we must assume that it will go up all at once, rather than the way Destry predicted—and God help the human race!"

Captain Harrington cleared his throat to break the silence that followed. "Superintendent," he said, "I would not have ventured to call had it been simply a matter of disagreement as to interpretation of theoretical predictions—"

"You have something more to go on?"

"Yes and no. Probably you gentlemen think of the Naval Observatory as being exclusively preoccupied with ephemerides and tide tables. In a way you would be right—but we still have some time to devote to research as long as it doesn't cut into the appropriation. My special interest has always been lunar theory.

"I don't mean lunar ballistics," he continued. "I mean the much more interesting problem of its origin and history, the problem the younger Darwin struggled with, as well as my illustrious predecessor, Captain T. J. J. See. I think that it is obvious that any theory of lunar origin and history must take into account the surface features of the Moon—especially the mountains, the craters, that mark its face so prominently."

He paused momentarily, and Superintendent King put in: "Just a minute, Captain—I may be stupid, or perhaps I missed something, but—is there a connection between what we were discussing before and lunar theory?"

"Bear with me for a few moments, Dr. King," Harrington apologized. "There is a connection—at least, I'm *afraid* there is a connection—but I would rather present my points in their proper order before making my conclusions." They granted him an alert silence; he went on:

"Although we are in the habit of referring to the 'craters' of the Moon, we know they are not volcanic craters. Superficially, they follow none of the rules of terrestrial volcanoes in appearance or distribution, but when Rutter came out in 1952 with his monograph on the dynamics of vulcanology, he proved rather conclusively that the lunar craters could not be caused by anything that we know as volcanic action.

"That left the bombardment theory as the simplest hypothesis. It looks good, on the face of it, and a few minutes spent throwing pebbles into a patch of mud will convince anyone that the lunar craters could have been formed by falling meteors.

"But there are difficulties. If the Moon was struck so repeatedly, why not the Earth? It hardly seems necessary to mention that the Earth's atmosphere would be no protection against masses big enough to form craters like Endymion or Plato. And if they fell after the Moon was a dead world while the Earth was still young enough to change its face and erase the marks of bombardment, why did the meteors avoid so nearly completely the great dry basins we call lunar seas?

"I want to cut this short; you'll find the data and the mathematical investigations from the data here in my notes. There is one other major objection to the meteor-bombardment theory: the great rays that spread from Tycho across almost the entire surface of the Moon. It makes the Moon look like a crystal ball that had been struck with a hammer, and impact from outside seems evident, but there are difficulties. The striking mass, our hypothetical meteor, must be small enough to have formed the crater of Tycho, but it must have the mass and speed to crack an entire planet.

"Work it out for yourself—you must either postulate a chunk out of the core of a dwarf star, or speeds such as we have never observed within the system. It's conceivable but a farfetched explanation."

He turned to King. "Doctor, does anything occur to you that might account for a phenomenon like Tycho?"

The Superintendent grasped the arms of his chair, then glanced at his palms. He fumbled for a handkerchief, and wiped them. "Go ahead," he said, almost inaudibly.

"Very well then." Harrington drew out of his briefcase a large photograph of the Moon—a beautiful full-Moon portrait made at Lick. "I want you to imagine the Moon as she might have been some-time in the past. The dark areas we call the 'seas' are actual oceans. It has an atmosphere, perhaps a heavier gas than oxygen and nitrogen, but an active gas, capable of supporting some conceivable form of life.

"For this is an inhabited planet, inhabited by intelligent beings, beings capable of discovering atomic power and exploiting it!"

He pointed out on the photograph, near the southern limb, the lime-white circle of Tycho, with its shining, incredible, thousand-mile-long rays spreading, thrusting, jutting out from it. "Here ... here at Tycho was located their main power plant." He moved his fin-gers to a point near the equator and somewhat east of meridian—the point where three great dark areas merged, *Mare Nubium, Mare Imbrium, Oceanus Procellarum*—and picked out two bright splotches surrounded, also, by rays, but shorter, less distinct, and wavy. "And here at Copernicus and at Kepler, on islands at the middle of a great ocean, were secondary power stations."

He paused, and interpolated soberly: "Perhaps they knew the danger they ran, but wanted power so badly that they were willing to gamble the life of their race. Perhaps they were ignorant of the ruin-ous possibilities of their little machines, or perhaps their mathemati-cians assured them that it could not happen.

"But we will never know—no one can ever know. For it blew up and killed them—and it killed their planet.

"It whisked off the gassy envelope and blew it into outer space. It blasted great chunks off the planet's crust. Perhaps some of that escaped completely, too, but all that did not reach the speed of escape fell back down in time and splashed great ring-shaped craters in the land.

"The oceans cushioned the shock; only the more massive frag-ments formed craters through the water. Perhaps some life still re-mained in those ocean depths. If so, it was doomed to die—for the water, unprotected by atmospheric pressure, could not remain liquid and must inevitably escape in time to outer space. Its life-blood drained away. The planet was dead—dead by suicide!"

He met the grave eyes of his two silent listeners with an expression almost of appeal. "Gentlemen ... this is only a theory, I realize ... only a theory, a dream, a nightmare ... but it has kept me awake so many nights that I had to come tell you about it, and see if you saw it the same way I do. As for the mechanics of it, it's all in there in my notes. You can check it—and I pray that you find some error! But it is the only lunar theory I have examined which included all of the known data and accounted for all of them."

He appeared to have finished. Lentz spoke up. "Suppose, Captain, suppose we check your mathematics and find no flaw—what then?"

Harrington flung out his hands. "That's what I came here to find out!"

Although Lentz had asked the question, Harrington directed the appeal to King. The Superintendent looked up; his eyes met the astronomer's, wavered and dropped again. "There's nothing to be done," he said dully, "nothing at all."

Harrington stared at him in open amazement. "But good God, man!" he burst out. "Don't you see it? That bomb has *got* to be disassembled—at once!"

"Take it easy, Captain." Lentz's calm voice was a spray of cold water. "And don't be too harsh on poor King—this worries him even more than it does you. What he means is this: We're not faced with a problem in physics, but with a political and economic situation. Let's put it this way: King can no more dump the bomb than a peasant with a vineyard on the slopes of Mount Vesuvius can abandon his holdings and pauperize his family simply because there will be an eruption some day.

"King doesn't own that bomb out there; he's only the custodian. If he dumps it against the wishes of the legal owners, they'll simply oust him and put in someone more amenable. No, we have to convince the owners."

"The President could do it," suggested Harrington. "I could get to the President—"

"No doubt you could, through the Navy Department. And you might even convince him. But could he help much?"

"Why, of course he could. He's the *President*!"

"Wait a minute. You're Director of the Naval Observatory; suppose you took a sledge hammer and tried to smash the big telescope—how far would you get?"

"Not very far," Harrington conceded. "We guard the big fellow pretty closely."

"Nor can the President act in an arbitrary manner," Lentz persisted. "He's not an unlimited monarch. If he shuts down this plant without due process of law, the Federal courts will tie him in knots. I admit that Congress isn't helpless but—would you like to try to give a congressional committee a course in the mechanics of infinitesimals?"

Harrington readily stipulated the point. "But there is another way," he pointed out. "Congress is responsive to public opinion. What we need to do is to convince the public that the bomb is a menace to everybody. That could be done without ever trying to explain things in terms of higher mathematics."

"Certainly it could," Lentz agreed. "You could go on the air with it and scare everybody half to death. You could create the damnedest panic this slightly slug-nutty country has ever seen. No, thank you. I, for one, would rather have us all take the chance of being quietly killed than bring on a mass psychosis that would destroy the culture we are building up. I think one taste of the Crazy Years is enough."

"Well, then, what do *you* suggest?"

Lentz considered shortly, then answered: "All I see is a forlorn hope. We've got to work on the Board of Directors and try to beat some sense into their heads."

King, who had been following the discussion with attention in spite of his tired despondence, interjected a remark: "How would you go about that?"

"I don't know," Lentz admitted. "It will take some thinking. But it seems the most fruitful line of approach. If it doesn't work, we can always fall back on Harrington's notion of publicity—I don't insist that the world commit suicide to satisfy my criteria of evaluation."

Harrington glanced at his wristwatch—a bulky affair—and whistled. "Good heavens!" he exclaimed. "I forgot the time! I'm supposed officially to be at the Flagstaff Observatory."

King had automatically noted the time shown by the Captain's watch as it was displayed. "But it can't be that late," he had objected. Harrington looked puzzled, then laughed.

"It isn't—not by two hours. We are in zone plus-seven; this shows zone plus-five—it's radio-synchronized with the master clock at Washington."

"Did you say radio-synchronized?"

"Yes. Clever, isn't it?" He held it out for inspection. "I call it a telechronometer; it's the only one of its sort to date. My nephew designed it for me. He's a bright one, that boy. He'll go far. That is"—his face clouded, as if the little interlude had only served to emphasize the tragedy that hung over them—"if any of us live that long!"

A signal light glowed at King's desk, and Steinke's face showed on the communicator screen. King answered him, then said, "Your car is ready, Dr. Lentz."

"Let Captain Harrington have it."

"Then you're not going back to Chicago?"

"No. The situation has changed. If you want me, I'm stringing along."

The following Friday, Steinke ushered Lentz into King's office. King looked almost happy as he shook hands. "When did you ground, Doctor? I didn't expect you back for another hour or so."

"Just now. I hired a cab instead of waiting for the shuttle."

"Any luck?"

"None. The same answer they gave you: 'The Company is assured by independent experts that Destry's mechanics is valid, and sees no reason to encourage an hysterical attitude among its employees.'"

King tapped on his desk top, his eyes unfocused. Then, hitching himself around to face Lentz directly, he said, "Do you suppose the Chairman is right?"

"How?"

"Could the three of us—you, me and Harrington—have gone off the deep end—slipped mentally?"

"No."

"You're sure?"

"Certainly. I looked up some independent experts of my own, not retained by the Company, and had them check Harrington's work. It checks." Lentz purposely neglected to mention that he had done so partly because he was none too sure of King's present mental stability.

King sat up briskly, reached out and stabbed a push button. "I am going to make one more try," he explained, "to see if I can't throw a scare into Dixon's thick head. Steinke," he said to the communicator, "get me Mr. Dixon on the screen."

"Yes, sir."

In about two minutes the visiphone screen came to life and showed the features of Chairman Dixon. He was transmitting, not from his office, but from the board room of the Company in Jersey City. "Yes?" he said. "What is it, Superintendent?" His manner was somehow both querulous and affable.

"Mr. Dixon," King began, "I've called to try to impress on you the seriousness of the Company's action. I stake my scientific reputation that Harrington has proved completely that—"

"Oh, that? Mr. King, I thought you understood that that was a closed matter."

"But, Mr. Dixon—"

"Superintendent, please! If there were any possible legitimate cause to fear, do you think I would hesitate? I have children, you know, and grandchildren."

"That is just why—"

"We try to conduct the affairs of the company with reasonable wisdom and in the public interest. But we have other responsibilities, too. There are hundreds of thousands of little stockholders who expect us to show a reasonable return on their investment. You must not expect us to jettison a billion-dollar corporation just because you've taken up astrology! Moon theory!" He sniffed.

"Very well, Mr. Chairman." King's tone was stiff.

"Don't take it that way, Mr. King. I'm glad you called—the Board has just adjourned a special meeting. They have decided to accept you for retirement—with full pay, of course."

"I did not apply for retirement!"

"I know, Mr. King, but the Board feels that—"

"I understand. Good-by!"

"Mr. King—"

"Good-by!" He switched him off, and turned to. Lentz. "'—with full pay,'" he quoted, "which I can enjoy in any way that I like for the rest of my life—just as happy as a man in the death house!"

"Exactly," Lentz agreed. "Well, we've tried our way. I suppose we should call up Harrington now and let him try the political and publicity method."

"I suppose so," King seconded absentmindedly. "Will you be leaving for Chicago now?"

"No," said Lentz. "No ... I think I will catch the shuttle for Los Angeles and take the evening rocket for the antipodes."

King looked surprised, but said nothing. Lentz answered the unspoken comment. "Perhaps some of us on the other side of the Earth will survive. I've done all that I can here. I would rather be a live sheepherder in Australia than a dead psychiatrist in Chicago."

King nodded vigorously. "That shows horse sense. For two cents, I'd dump the bomb now and go with you."

"Not horse sense, my friend—a horse will run back into a burning barn, which is exactly *not* what I plan to do. Why don't you do it and come along? If you did, it would help Harrington to scare 'em to death."

"I believe I will!"

Steinke's face appeared again on the screen. "Harper and Erickson are here, chief."

"I'm busy."

"They are pretty urgent about seeing you."

"Oh ... all right," King said in a tired voice. "Show them in. It doesn't matter."

They breezed in, Harper in the van. He commenced talking at once, oblivious to the Superintendent's morose preoccupation. "We've got it, chief, we've got it—and it all checks out to the umpteenth decimal!"

"You've got what? Speak English."

Harper grinned. He was enjoying his moment of triumph, and was stretching it out to savor it. "Chief, do you remember a few weeks back when I asked for an additional allotment—a special one without specifying how I was going to spend it?"

"Yes. Come on—get to the point."

"You kicked at first, but finally granted it. Remember? Well, we've got something to show for it, all tied up in pink ribbon. It's the greatest advance in radioactivity since Hahn split the nucleus. Atomic fuel, chief, atomic fuel, safe, concentrated, and controllable. Suitable for rockets, for power plants, for any damn thing you care to use it for."

King showed alert interest for the first time. "You mean a power source that doesn't require the bomb?"

"The bomb? Oh, no. I didn't say that. You use the bomb to make the fuel, then you use the fuel anywhere and anyhow you like, with something like ninety-two percent recovery of the energy of the bomb. But you could junk the mercury-steam sequence, if you wanted to."

King's first wild hope of a way out of his dilemma was dashed; he subsided. "Go ahead. Tell me about it."

"Well—it's a matter of artificial radioactives. Just before I asked for that special research allotment, Erickson and I—Dr. Lentz had a finger in it, too—found two isotopes of a radioactive that seemed to be mutually antagonistic. That is, when we goosed 'em in the presence of each other they gave up their latent energy all at once—blew all to hell. The important point is, we were using just a gnat's whisker of mass of each—the reaction didn't require a big mass like the bomb to maintain it."

"I don't see," objected King, "how that could—"

"Neither do we, quite—but it works. We've kept it quiet until we were sure. We checked on what we had, and we found a dozen other fuels. Probably we'll be able to tailormake fuels for any desired purpose. But here it is." Harper handed King a bound sheaf of typewritten notes which he had been carrying under the arm. "That's your copy. Look it over."

King started to do so. Lentz joined him, after a look that was a silent request for permission, which Erickson had answered with his only verbal contribution, "Sure, Doc."

As King read, the troubled feeling of an acutely harassed executive left him. His dominant personality took charge, that of the scientist. He enjoyed the controlled and cerebral ecstasy of the impersonal seeker for the elusive truth. The emotions felt in the throbbing thalamus were permitted only to form a sensuous obligato for the cold flame of cortical activity. For the time being, he was sane, more nearly completely sane than most men ever achieve at any time.

For a long period there was only an occasional grunt, the clatter of turned pages, a nod of approval. At last he put it down.

"It's the stuff," he said. "You've done it, boys. It's great; I'm proud of you."

Erickson glowed a bright pink and swallowed. Harper's small, tense figure gave the ghost of a wriggle, reminiscent of a wire-haired terrier receiving approval. "That's fine, chief. We'd rather hear you say that than get the Nobel Prize."

"I think you'll probably get it. However"—the proud light in his eyes died down—"I'm not going to take any action in this matter."

"Why not, chief?" Harper's tone was bewildered.

"I'm being retired. My successor will take over in the near future; this is too big a matter to start just before a change in administration."

"*You* being retired! What the hell! *Why?*"

"About the same reason I took you off the bomb—at least, the Directors think so."

"But that's nonsense! You were right to take me off the bomb; I *was* getting jumpy. But you're another matter—we all depend on you."

"Thanks, Cal—but that's how it is; there's nothing to be done about it." He turned to Lentz. "I think this is the last ironical touch needed to make the whole thing pure farce," he observed bitterly. "This thing is big, bigger than we can guess at this stage—and I have to give it a miss."

"Well," Harper burst out, "I can think of something to do about it!" He strode over to King's desk and snatched up the manuscript. "Either you superintend the exploitation or the company will damn well get along without our discovery!" Erickson concurred belligerently.

"Wait a minute." Lentz had the floor. "Dr. Harper, have you already achieved a practical rocket fuel?"

"I said so. We've got it on hand now."

"An escape-speed fuel?" They understood his verbal shorthand—a fuel that would lift a rocket free of the Earth's gravitational pull.

"Sure. Why, you could take any of the Clipper rockets, refit them a trifle, and have breakfast on the Moon."

"Very well. Bear with me—" He obtained a sheet of paper from King and commenced to write. They watched in mystified impatience. He continued briskly for some minutes, hesitating only momentarily. Presently he stopped and spun the paper over to King. "Solve it!" he demanded.

King studied the paper. Lentz had assigned symbols to a great number of factors, some social, some psychological, some physical, some economical. He had thrown them together into a structural relationship, using the symbols of calculus of statement. King understood the paramathematical operations indicated by the symbols, but he was not as used to them as he was to the symbols and operations of mathematical physics. He plowed through the equations, moving his lips slightly in unconscious subvocalization.

He accepted a pencil from Lentz and completed the solution. It required several more lines, a few more equations, before the elements canceled out, or rearranged themselves, into a definite answer.

He stared at this answer while puzzlement gave way to dawning comprehension and delight.

He looked up. "Erickson! Harper!" he rapped out. "We will take your new fuel, refit a large rocket, install the bomb in it, and throw it into an orbit around the Earth, far out in space. There we will use it to make more fuel, safe fuel, for use on Earth, with the danger from the bomb itself limited to the operators actually on watch!"

There was no applause. It was not that sort of an idea; their minds were still struggling with the complex implications.

"But, chief," Harper finally managed, "how about your retirement? We're still not going to stand for it."

"Don't worry," King assured him. "It's all in there, implicit in those equations, you two, me, Lentz, the Board of Directors—and just what we all have to do to accomplish it."

"All except the matter of time," Lentz cautioned.

"Eh?"

"You'll note that elapsed time appears in your answer as an undetermined unknown."

"Yes … yes, of course. That's the chance we have to take. Let's get busy!"

Chairman Dixon called the Board of Directors to order. "This being a special meeting, we'll dispense with minutes and reports," he announced. "As set forth in the call we have agreed to give the retiring superintendent three hours of our time."

"Mr. Chairman—"

"Yes, Mr. Thornton?"

"I thought we had settled that matter."

"We have, Mr. Thornton, but in view of Superintendent King's long and distinguished service, if he asks a hearing, we are honor bound to grant it. You have the floor, Dr. King."

King got up and stated briefly, "Dr. Lentz will speak for me." He sat down.

Lentz had to wait till coughing, throat clearing and scraping of chairs subsided. It was evident that the board resented the outsider.

Lentz ran quickly over the main points in the argument which contended that the bomb presented an intolerable danger anywhere on the face of the Earth. He moved on at once to the alternative proposal that the bomb should be located in a rocketship, an artificial moonlet flying in a free orbit around the Earth at a convenient distance—say, fifteen thousand miles—while secondary power stations on earth burned a safe fuel manufactured by the bomb.

He announced the discovery of the Harper-Erickson technique and dwelt on what it meant to them commercially. Each point was presented as persuasively as possible, with the full power of his engaging personality. Then he paused and waited for them to blow off steam.

They did. "Visionary—" "Unproved—" "No essential change in the situation—" The substance of it was that they were very happy to hear of the new fuel, but not particularly impressed by it. Perhaps in another twenty years, after it had been thoroughly tested and proved commercially, and provided enough uranium had been mined to build another bomb, they might consider setting up another power station outside the atmosphere. In the meantime there was no hurry.

Lentz patiently and politely dealt with their objections. He emphasized the increasing incidence of occupational psychoneurosis among the engineers and grave danger to everyone near the bomb even under the orthodox theory. He reminded them of their insurance and indemnity-bond costs, and of the "squeeze" they paid State politicians.

Then he changed his tone and let them have it, directly and brutally. "Gentlemen," he said, "we believe that we are fighting for our lives—our own lives, our families and every life on the globe. If you refuse this compromise, we will fight as fiercely and with as little regard for fair play as any cornered animal." With that he made his first move in attack.

It was quite simple. He offered for their inspection the outline of a propaganda campaign on a national scale, such as any major advertising firm should carry out as matter of routine. It was complete to the last detail, television broadcasts, spot plugs, newspaper and magazine coverage and—most important—a supporting whispering campaign and a letters-to-Congress organization. Every businessman there knew from experience how such things worked.

But its object was to stir up fear of the bomb and to direct that fear, not into panic, but into rage against the Board of Directors personally, and into a demand that the government take action to have the bomb removed to outer space.

"This is blackmail! We'll stop you!"

"I think not," Lentz replied gently. "You may be able to keep us out of some of the newspapers, but you can't stop the rest of it. You can't even keep us off the air—ask the Federal Communications Commission." It was true. Harrington had handled the political end and had performed his assignment well; the President was convinced.

Tempers were snapping on all sides; Dixon had to pound for order. "Dr. Lentz," he said, his own temper under taut control, "you plan to make every one of us appear a blackhearted scoundrel with no other thought than personal profit, even at the expense of the lives of others. You know that is not true; this is a simple difference of opinion as to what is wise."

"I did not say it was true," Lentz admitted blandly, "but you will admit that I can convince the public that you are deliberate villains. As to it being a difference of opinion—you are none of you atomic physicists; you are not entitled to hold opinions in this matter.

"As a matter of fact," he went on callously, "the only doubt in my mind is whether or not an enraged public will destroy your precious power plant before Congress has time to exercise eminent domain and take it away from you!"

Before they had time to think up arguments in answer and ways of circumventing him, before their hot indignation had cooled and set as stubborn resistance, he offered his gambit. He produced another layout for a propaganda campaign—an entirely different sort.

This time the Board of Directors was to be built up, not torn down. All of the same techniques were to be used; behind-the-scenes feature articles with plenty of human interest would describe the functions of the company, describe it as a great public trust, administered by patriotic, unselfish statesmen of the business world. At the proper point in the campaign, the Harper-Erickson fuel would be announced, not as a semi-accidental result of the initiative of two employees, but as the long-expected end product of years of systematic research conducted under a fixed policy growing naturally out of their humane determination to remove forever the menace of explosion from even the sparsely settled Arizona desert.

No mention was to be made of the danger of complete, planet-embracing catastrophe.

Lentz discussed it. He dwelt on the appreciation that would be due them from a grateful world. He invited them to make a noble sacrifice and, with subtle misdirection, tempted them to think of themselves as heroes. He deliberately played on one of the most deep-rooted of simian instincts, the desire for approval from one's kind, deserved or not.

All the while he was playing for time, as he directed his attention from one hard case, one resistant mind, to another. He soothed and he tickled and he played on personal foibles. For the benefit of the timorous and the devoted family men, he again painted a picture of the suffering, death and destruction that might result from their well-meant reliance on the unproved and highly questionable predictions of Destry's mathematics. Then he described in glowing detail a picture of a world free from worry but granted almost unlimited power, safe power from an invention which was theirs for this one small concession.

It worked. They did not reverse themselves all at once, but a committee was appointed to investigate the feasibility of the proposed spaceship power plant. By sheer brass Lentz suggested names for the committee and Dixon confirmed his nominations, not because he wished to, particularly, but because he was caught off guard and could not think of a reason to refuse without affronting the colleagues.

The impending retirement of King was not mentioned by either side. Privately, Lentz felt sure that it never would be mentioned.

It worked, but there was left much to do. For the first few days after the victory in committee, King felt much elated by the prospect of an early release from the soul-killing worry. He was buoyed up by pleasant demands of manifold new administrative duties. Harper and Erickson were detached to Goddard Field to collaborate with the rocket engineers there in design of firing chambers, nozzles, fuel stowage, fuel metering and the like. A schedule had to be worked out with the business office to permit as much power of the bomb as possible to be diverted to making atomic fuel, and a giant combustion chamber for atomic fuel had to be designed and ordered to replace the bomb itself during the interim between the time it was shut down on Earth and the later time when sufficient local, smaller plants could be built to carry the commercial load. He was busy.

When the first activity had died down and they were settled in a new routine, pending the shutting down of the bomb and its removal to outer space, King suffered an emotional reaction. There was, by then, nothing to do but wait, and tend the bomb, until the crew at Goddard Field smoothed out the bugs and produced a space-worthy rocketship.

They ran into difficulties, overcame them, and came across more difficulties. They had never used such high reaction velocities; it took many trials to find a nozzle shape that would give reasonably high efficiency. When that was solved, and success seemed in sight, the jets burned out on a time-trial ground test. They were stalemated for weeks over that hitch.

Back at the power plant Superintendent King could do nothing but chew his nails and wait. He had not even the release of running over to Goddard Field to watch the progress of the research, for, urgently as he desired to, he felt an even stronger, an overpowering compulsion to watch over the bomb lest it—heart-breakingly!—blow up at the last minute.

He took to hanging around the control room. He had to stop that; his unease communicated itself to his watch engineers; two of them cracked up in a single day—one of them on watch.

He must face the fact—there had been a grave upswing in psychoneurosis among his engineers since the period of watchful waiting had commenced. At first, they had tried to keep the essential facts of the plan a close secret, but it had leaked out, perhaps through some member of the investigating committee. He admitted to himself now that it had been a mistake ever to try to keep it secret—Lentz had advised against it, and the engineers not actually engaged in the change-over were bound to know that something was up.

He took all of the engineers into confidence at last, under oath of secrecy. That had helped for a week or more, a week in which they were all given a spiritual lift by the knowledge, as he had been. Then it had worn off, the reaction had set in, and psychological observers had started disqualifying engineers for duty almost daily. They were even reporting each other as mentally unstable with great frequency; he might even be faced with a shortage of psychiatrists if that kept up, he thought to himself with bitter amusement. His engineers were already standing four hours in every sixteen. If one more dropped out, he'd put himself on watch. That would be a relief, to tell himself the truth.

Somehow, some of the civilians around about and the nontechnical employees were catching on to the secret. That mustn't go on—if it spread any farther there might be a nationwide panic. But how the hell could he stop it? He couldn't.

He turned over in bed, rearranged his pillow, and tried once more to get to sleep. No soap. His head ached, his eyes were balls of pain, and his brain was a ceaseless grind of useless, repetitive activity, like a disk recording stuck in one groove.

God! This was unbearable! He wondered if he were cracking up—if he already had cracked up. This was worse, many times worse, than the old routine when he had simply acknowledged the danger and tried to forget it as much as possible. Not that the bomb was any different—it was this five-minutes-to-armistice feeling, this waiting for the curtain to go up, this race against time with nothing to do to help.

He sat up, switched on his bed lamp, and looked at the clock. Three thirty. Not so good. He got up, went into his bathroom, and dissolved a sleeping powder in a glass of whiskey and water, half and half. He gulped it down and went back to bed. Presently he dozed off.

He was running, fleeing down a long corridor. At the end lay safety—he knew that, but he was so utterly exhausted that he doubted his ability to finish the race. The thing pursuing him was catching up; he forced his leaden, aching legs into greater activity. The thing behind him increased its pace, and actually touched him. His heart stopped, then pounded again. He became aware that he was screaming, shrieking in mortal terror.

But he had to reach the end of that corridor; more depended on it than just himself. He had to. He had to! *He had to!*

Then the sound hit him, and he realized that he had lost, realized it with utter despair and utter, bitter defeat. He had failed; the bomb had blown up.

The sound was the alarm going off; it was seven o'clock. His pajamas were soaked, dripping with sweat, and his heart still pounded. Every ragged nerve throughout his body screamed for release. It would take more than a cold shower to cure this case of the shakes.

He got to the office before the janitor was out of it. He sat there, doing nothing, until Lentz walked in on him, two hours later. The psychiatrist came in just as he was taking two small tablets from a box in his desk.

"Easy … easy, old man," Lentz said in a slow voice. "What have you there?" He came around and gently took possession of the box.

"Just a sedative."

Lentz studied the inscription on the cover. "How many have you had today?"

"Just two, so far."

"You don't need a sedative; you need a walk in the fresh air. Come, take one with me."

"You're a fine one to talk—you're smoking a cigarette that isn't lighted!"

"Me? Why, so I am! We both need that walk. Come."

Harper arrived less than ten minutes after they had left the office. Steinke was not in the outer office. He walked on through and pounded on the door of King's private office, then waited with the man who accompanied him—a hard young chap with an easy confidence to his bearing. Steinke let them in.

Harper brushed on past him with a casual greeting, then checked himself when he saw that there was no one else inside.

"Where's the chief?" he demanded.

"Gone out. Should be back soon."

"I'll wait. Oh—Steinke, this is Greene. Greene—Steinke."

The two shook hands. "What brings you back, Cal?" Steinke asked, turning back to Harper.

"Well ... I guess it's all right to tell you—"

The communicator screen flashed into sudden activity, and cut him short. A face filled most of the frame. It was apparently too close to the pickup, as it was badly out of focus. "Superintendent!" it yelled in an agonized voice. "The bomb—"

A shadow flashed across the screen, they heard a dull *smack*, and the face slid out of the screen. As it fell it revealed the control room behind it. Someone was down on the floor plates, a nameless heap. Another figure ran across the field of pickup and disappeared.

Harper snapped into action first. "That was Silard!" he shouted, "In the control room! Come, on, Steinke!" He was already in motion himself.

Steinke went dead-white, but hesitated only an unmeasurable instant. He pounded sharp on Harper's heels. Greene followed without invitation, in a steady run that kept easy pace with them.

They had to wait for a capsule to unload at the tube station. Then all three of them tried to crowd into a two-passenger capsule. It refused to start, and moments were lost before Greene piled out and claimed another car.

The four-minute trip at heavy acceleration seemed an interminable crawl. Harper was convinced that the system had broken down, when the familiar click and sigh announced their arrival at the station under the bomb. They jammed each other trying to get out at the same time.

The lift was up; they did not wait for it. That was unwise; they gained no time by it, and arrived at the control level out of breath. Nevertheless, they speeded up when they reached the top, zigzagged frantically around the outer shield, and burst into the control room.

The limp figure was still on the floor, and another, also inert, was near it. The second's helmet was missing.

The third figure was bending over the trigger. He looked up as they came in, and charged them. They hit him together, and all three went down. It was two to one, but they got in each other's way. The man's heavy armor protected him from the force of their blows. He fought with senseless, savage violence.

Harper felt a bright, sharp pain; his right arm went limp and useless. The armored figure was struggling free of them.

There was a shout from somewhere behind them, "Hold still!"

Harper saw a flash with the corner of one eye, a deafening crack hurried on top of it, and re-echoed painfully in the restricted space.

The armored figure dropped back to his knees, balanced there, and then fell heavily on his face. Greene stood in the entrance, a service pistol balanced in his hand.

Harper got up and went over to the trigger. He tried to reduce the dampening adjustment, but his right hand wouldn't carry out his orders, and his left was too clumsy. "Steinke," he called, "come here! Take over."

Steinke hurried up, nodded as he glanced at the readings, and set busily to work.

It was thus that King found them when he bolted in a very few minutes later.

"Harper!" he shouted,, while his quick glance was still taking in the situation. "What's happened?"

Harper told him briefly. He nodded. "I saw the tail end of the fight from my office—Steinke!" He seemed to grasp for the first time who was on the trigger. "He can't manage the controls—" He hurried toward him.

Steinke looked up at his approach. "Chief!" he called out. "Chief! *I've got my mathematics back!*"

King looked bewildered, then nodded vaguely, and let him be. He turned back to Harper. "How does it happen you're here?"

"Me? I'm here to report—we've done it, chief!"

"Eh?"

"We've finished; it's all done. Erickson stayed behind to complete the power-plant installation on the big ship. I came over in the ship we'll use to shuttle between Earth and the big ship, the power plant. Four minutes from Goddard Field to here in her. That's the pilot over there." He pointed to the door, where Greene's solid form partially hid Lentz.

"Wait a minute. You say that everything is ready to install the bomb in the ship? You're sure?"

"Positive. The big ship has already flown with our fuel—longer and faster than she will have to fly to reach station in her orbit; I was in it—out in space, chief! We're all set, six ways from zero."

King stared at the dumping switch, mounted behind glass at the top of the instrument board. "There's fuel enough," he said softly, as if he were alone and speaking only to himself; "there's been fuel enough for weeks."

He walked swiftly over to the switch, smashed the glass with his fist, and pulled it.

The room rumbled and shivered as two and a half tons of molten, massive metal, heavier than gold, coursed down channels, struck against baffles, split into a dozen streams, and plunged to rest in leaden receivers—to rest, safe and harmless, until it could be reassembled far out in space.

AFTERWORD

December 1979, exactly 40 years after I researched BLOWUPS HAPPEN (Dec. '39): I had some doubt about republishing this because of the current ignorant fear of fission power, recently enhanced by the harmless flap at Three Mile Island. When I wrote this, there was not a full gram of purified U-235 on this planet, and no one knew its hazards in detail, most especially the mass and geometry and speed of assembly necessary to make "blowups happen." But we now know from long experience and endless tests that the "tons" used in this story could never be assembled—no explosion, melt-down possible, melt-down being the worst that can happen at a power plant; to cause U-235 to explode is very difficult and requires very different design. Yes, radiation is hazardous BUT—

RADIATION EXPOSURE

*Half a mile from Three-Mile
     plant during the flap.* . . . . *83 millirems*

At the power plant. . . . . *1,100 millirems*

*During heart catheterization
     for angiogram.* . . . . *45,000 millirems*
     —which I underwent 18 months ago. I feel fine.

R.A.H.

"Anything you get free costs
more than [it's] worth—but you
don't find it out until later."

—Bernardo de la Paz

FOREWORD

I had always planned to quit the writing business as soon as that mortgage was paid off. I had never had any literary ambitions, no training for it, no interest in it—backed into it by accident and stuck with it to pay off debt, I being always firmly resolved to quit the silly business once I had my chart squared away.

At a meeting of the Mañana Literary Society—an amorphous dis-organization having as its avowed purpose "to permit young writers to talk out their stories to each other in order to get them off their minds and thereby save themselves the trouble of writing them down"—at a gather-ing of this noble group I was expounding my determination to retire from writing once my bills were paid—in a few weeks, during 1940, if the tripe continued to sell.

William A. P. White ("Anthony Boucher") gave me a sour look. "Do you know any retired writers?"

"How could I? All the writers I've ever met are in this room."

"Irrelevant. You know retired school teachers, retired naval officers, re-tired policemen, retired farmers. Why don't you know at least one retired writer?"

"What are you driving at?"

"Robert, there are no retired writers. There are writers who have stopped selling ... but they have not stopped writing."

I pooh-poohed Bill's remarks—possibly what he said applied to writers in general ... but I wasn't really a writer; I was just a chap who needed money and happened to discover that pulp writing offered an easy way to grab some without stealing and without honest work. ("Honest work"—a euphemism for underpaid bodily exertion, done standing up or on your knees, often in bad weather or other nasty circumstances, and frequently involving shovels, picks, hoes, assembly lines, tractors, and unsympathetic supervisors. It has never appealed to me. Sitting at a typewriter in a nice warm room, with no boss, cannot possibly be described as "honest work.")

"Blowups Happen" sold and I gave a mortgage-burning party. But I did not quit writing at once (24 Feb. 1940) because, while I had the Old Man of the Sea (that damned mortgage) off my back, there were still some other items. I needed a new car; the house needed paint and some repairs; I wanted to make a trip to New York; and it would not hurt to have a couple of hundred extra in the bank as a cushion—and I had a dozen-odd stories in file, planned and ready to write.

So I wrote "Magic, Incorporated" and started east on the proceeds, and wrote "They" and Sixth Column *while I was on that trip. The latter was the only story of mine ever influenced to any marked degree by John W. Campbell, Jr. He had in file an unsold story he had written some years earlier. JWC did not show me his manuscript; instead he told me the story line orally and stated that, if I would write it, he would buy it.*

He needed a serial; I needed an automobile. I took the brass check.

Writing Sixth Column *was a job I sweated over. I had to reslant it to remove racist aspects of the original story line. And I didn't really believe the pseudoscientific rationale of Campbell's three spectra—so I worked especially hard to make it sound realistic.*

It worked out all right. The check for the serial, plus 35¢ in cash, bought me that new car ... and the book editions continue to sell and sell and sell, and have earned more than forty times as much as I was paid for the serial. So it was a financial success ... but I do not consider it to be an artistic success.

While I was back east I told Campbell of my plans to quit writing later that year. He was not pleased as I was then his largest supplier of copy. I finally said, "John, I am not going to write any more stories against deadlines. But I do have a few more stories on tap that I could write. I'll send you a story from time to time ... until the day comes when you bounce one. At that point we're through. Now that I know you personally, having a story rejected by you would be too traumatic."

So I went back to California and sold him "Crooked House" and "Logic of Empire" and "Universe" and "Solution Unsatisfactory" and Methuselah's Children *and "By His Bootstraps" and "Common Sense" and "Goldfish Bowl" and* Beyond This Horizon *and "Waldo" and "The Unpleasant Profession of Jonathan Hoag"—which brings us smack up against World War II.*

Campbell did bounce one of the above (and I shan't say which one) and I promptly retired—put in a new irrigation system—built a garden terrace—resumed serious photography, etc. This went on for about a month when I found that I was beginning to be vaguely ill: poor appetite, loss of weight, insomnia, jittery, absent-minded—much like the early symptoms of pulmonary tuberculosis, and I thought, "Damn it, am I going to have still a third *attack?"*

Campbell dropped me a note and asked why he hadn't heard from me—I reminded him of our conversation months past: He had rejected one of my stories and that marked my retirement from an occupation that I had never planned to pursue permanently.

He wrote back and asked for another look at the story he had bounced. I sent it to him, he returned it promptly with the recommendation that I take out this comma, speed up the 1st half of page umpteen, delete that adjective—fiddle changes that Katie Tarrant would have done if told to.

I sat down at my typewriter to make the suggested changes ... and suddenly realized that I felt good *for the first time in weeks.*

Bill "Tony Boucher" White had been dead right. Once you get the monkey on your back there is no cure short of the grave. I can leave the typewriter alone for weeks, even months, by going to sea. I can hold off for any necessary time if I am strenuously engaged in some other full-time, worthwhile occupation such as a construction job, a political campaign, or (damn it!) recovering from illness.

But if I simply loaf for more than two or three days, that monkey starts niggling at me. Then nothing short of a few thousand words will soothe my nerves. And as I get older the attacks get worse; it is beginning to take 300,000 words and up to produce that feeling of warm satiation. At that I don't have it in its most virulent form; two of my colleagues are reliably reported not to have missed their daily fix in more than forty years.

The best that can be said for "Solution Unsatisfactory" is that the solution is still unsatisfactory and the dangers are greater than ever. There is little satisfaction in having called the turn forty years ago; being a real-life Cassandra is not happy-making.

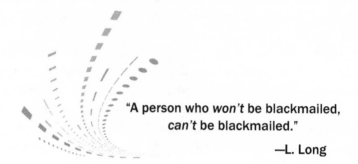

"A person who *won't* be blackmailed, *can't* be blackmailed."

—L. Long

SOLUTION UNSATISFACTORY

In 1903 the Wright brothers flew at Kitty Hawk.

In December, 1938, in Berlin, Dr. Hahn split the uranium atom.

In April, 1943, Dr. Estelle Karst, working under the Federal Emergency Defense Authority, perfected the Karst-Obre technique for producing artificial radioactives.

So American foreign policy had to change.

Had to. *Had to.* It is very difficult to tuck a bugle call back into a bugle. Pandora's Box is a one-way proposition. You can turn pig into sausage, but not sausage into pig. Broken eggs stay broken. "All the King's horses and all the King's men can't put Humpty together again."

I ought to know—I was one of the King's men.

By rights I should not have been. I was not a professional military man when World War II broke out, and when Congress passed the draft law I drew a high number, high enough to keep me out of the army long enough to die of old age.

Not that very many died of old age that generation!

But I was the newly appointed secretary to a freshman congressman; I had been his campaign manager and my former job had left me. By profession, I was a high-school teacher of economics and sociology—school boards don't like teachers of social subjects actually to deal with social problems—and my contract was not renewed. I jumped at the chance to go to Washington.

97

My congressman was named Manning. Yes, *the* Manning, Colonel Clyde C. Manning, U.S. Army retired—Mr. Commissioner Manning. What you may not know about him is that he was one of the Army's No. 1 experts in chemical warfare before a leaky heart put him on the shelf. I had picked him, with the help of a group of my political associates, to run against the two-bit chiseler who was the incumbent in our district. We needed a strong liberal candidate and Manning was tailor-made for the job. He had served one term in the grand jury, which cut his political eye teeth, and had stayed active in civic matters thereafter.

Being a retired army officer was a political advantage in vote-getting among the more conservative and well-to-do citizens, and his record was O.K. for the other side of the fence. I'm not primarily concerned with vote-getting; what I liked about him was that, though he was liberal, he was tough-minded, which most liberals aren't. Most liberals believe that water runs downhill, but, praise God, it'll never reach the bottom.

Manning was not like that. He could see a logical necessity and act on it, no matter how unpleasant it might be.

We were in Manning's suite in the House Office Building, taking a little blow from that stormy first session of the Seventy-eighth Congress and trying to catch up on a mountain of correspondence, when the War Department called. Manning answered it himself.

I had to overhear, but then I was his secretary. "Yes," he said, "speaking. Very well, put him on: Oh … hello, General … Fine, thanks. Yourself?" Then there was a long silence. Presently, Manning said, "But I can't do that, General, I've got this job to take care of. … What's that? … Yes, who is to do my committee work and represent my district? … I think so." He glanced at his wrist watch. "I'll be right over."

He put down the phone, turned to me, and said, "Get your hat, John. We are going over to the War Department."

"So?" I said, complying.

"Yes," he said with a worried look, "the Chief of Staff thinks I ought to go back to duty." He set off at a brisk walk, with me hanging back to try to force him not to strain his bum heart. "It's impossible, of course." We grabbed a taxi from the stand in front of the office building and headed for the Department.

But it *was* possible, and Manning agreed to it, after the Chief of Staff presented his case. Manning had to be convinced, for there is no way on earth for anyone, even the President himself, to order a congressman to leave his post, even though he happens to be a member of the military service, too.

The Chief of Staff had anticipated the political difficulty and had been forehanded enough to have already dug up an opposition congressman with whom to pair Manning's vote for the duration of the emergency. This other congressman, the Honorable Joseph T. Brigham, was a reserve officer who wanted to go to duty himself—or was willing to; I never found out which. Being from the opposite political party, his vote in the House of Representatives could be permanently paired against Manning's and neither party would lose by the arrangement.

There was talk of leaving me in Washington to handle the political details of Manning's office, but Manning decided against it, judging that his other secretary could do that, and announced that I must go along as his adjutant. The Chief of Staff demurred, but Manning was in a position to insist, and the Chief had to give in.

A chief of staff can get things done in a hurry if he wants to. I was sworn in as a temporary officer before we left the building; before the day was out I was at the bank, signing a note to pay for the sloppy service uniforms the Army had adopted and to buy a dress uniform with a beautiful shiny belt—a dress outfit which, as it turned out, I was never to need.

We drove over into Maryland the next day and Manning took charge of the Federal nuclear research laboratory, known officially by the hush-hush title of War Department Special Defense Project No. 347. I didn't know a lot about physics and nothing about modern atomic physics, aside from the stuff you read in the Sunday supplements. Later, I picked up a smattering, mostly wrong, I suppose, from associating with the heavyweights with whom the laboratory was staffed.

Colonel Manning had taken an Army p.g. course at Massachusetts Tech and had received a master of science degree for a brilliant thesis on the mathematical theories of atomic structure. That was why the Army had to have him for this job. But that had been some years before; atomic theory had turned several cartwheels in the meantime; he admitted to me that he had to bone like the very devil to try to catch up to the point where he could begin to understand what his highbrow charges were talking about in their reports.

I think he overstated the degree of his ignorance; there was certainly no one else in the United States who could have done the job. It required a man who could direct and suggest research in a highly esoteric field, but who saw the problem from the standpoint of urgent military necessity. Left to themselves, the physicists would have reveled in the intellectual luxury of an unlimited research expense account, but, while they undoubtedly would have made major advances in human knowledge, they might never have developed anything of military usefulness, or the military possibilities of a discovery might be missed for years.

It's like this: It takes a smart dog to hunt birds, but it takes a hunter behind him to keep him from wasting time chasing rabbits. And the hunter needs to know nearly as much as the dog.

No derogatory reference to the scientists is intended—by no means! We had all the genius in the field that the United States could produce, men from Chicago, Columbia, Cornell, M.I.T., Cal Tech, Berkeley, every radiation laboratory in the country, as well as a couple of broad-A boys lent to us by the British. And they had every facility that ingenuity could think up and money could build. The five-hundred-ton cyclotron which had originally been intended for the University of California was there, and was already obsolete in the face of the new gadgets these brains had thought up, asked for, and been given. Canada supplied us with all the uranium we asked for—tons of the treacherous stuff—from Great Bear Lake, up near the Yukon, and the fractional-residues technique of separating uranium isotope 235 from the commoner isotope 238 had already been worked out, by the same team from Chicago that had worked up the earlier expensive mass spectrograph method.

Someone in the United States government had realized the terrific potentialities of uranium 235 quite early and, as far back as the summer of 1940, had rounded up every atomic research man in the country and had sworn them to silence. Atomic power, if ever developed, was planned to be a government monopoly, at least till the war was over. If might turn out to be the most incredibly powerful explosive ever dreamed of, and it might be the source of equally incredible power. In any case, with Hitler talking about secret weapons and shouting hoarse insults at democracies, the government planned to keep any new discoveries very close to the vest.

Hitler had lost the advantage of a first crack at the secret of uranium through not taking precautions. Dr. Hahn, the first man to break open the uranium atom, was a German. But one of his laboratory assistants had fled Germany to escape a pogrom. She came to this country, and told us about it.

We were searching, there in the laboratory in Maryland, for a way to use U235 in a controlled explosion. We had a vision of a one-ton bomb that would be a whole air raid in itself, a single explosion that would flatten out an entire industrial center. Dr. Ridpath, of Continental Tech, claimed that he could build such a bomb, but that he could not guarantee that it would not explode as soon as it was loaded and as for the force of the explosion—well, he did not believe his own figures; they ran out to too many ciphers.

The problem was, strangely enough, to find an explosive which would be weak enough to blow up only one county at a time, and stable enough to blow up only on request. If we could devise a really practical rocket fuel at the same time, one capable of driving a war rocket at a thousand miles an hour, or more, then we would be in a position to make most anybody say "uncle" to Uncle Sam.

We fiddled around with it all the rest of 1943 and well into 1944. The war in Europe and the troubles in Asia dragged on. After Italy folded up, England was able to release enough ships from her Mediterranean fleet to ease the blockade of the British Isles. With the help of the planes we could now send her regularly and with the additional over-age destroyers we let her have, England hung on somehow, digging in and taking more and more of her essential defense industries underground. Russia shifted her weight from side to side as usual, apparently with the policy of preventing either side from getting a sufficient advantage to bring the war to a successful conclusion. People were beginning to speak of "permanent war."

I was killing time in the administrative office, trying to improve my typing—a lot of Manning's reports had to be typed by me personally—when the orderly on duty stepped in and announced Dr. Karst. I flipped the interoffice communicator. "Dr. Karst is here, chief. Can you see her?"

"Yes," he answered, through his end.

I told the orderly to show her in.

Estelle Karst was quite a remarkable old girl and, I suppose, the first woman ever to hold a commission in the Corps of Engineers. She was an M.D. as well as an Sc.D. and reminded me of the teacher I had had in fourth grade. I guess that was why I always stood up instinctively when she came into the room—I was afraid she might look at me and sniff. It couldn't have been her rank; we didn't bother much with rank.

She was dressed in white coveralls and a shop apron and had simply thrown a hooded cape over herself to come through the snow. I said, "Good morning, ma'am," and led her into Manning's office.

The Colonel greeted her with the urbanity that had made him such a success with women's clubs, seated her, and offered her a cigarette.

"I'm glad to see you, Major," he said. "I've been intending to drop around to your shop."

I knew what he was getting at; Dr. Karst's work had been primarily physiomedical; he wanted her to change the direction of her research to something more productive in a military sense.

"Don't call me 'major,'" she said tartly.

"Sorry, Doctor—"

"I came on business, and must get right back. And I presume you are a busy man, too. Colonel Manning, I need some help."

"That's what we are here for."

"Good. I've run into some snags in my research. I think that one of the men in Dr. Ridpath's department could help me, but Dr. Ridpath doesn't seem disposed to be cooperative."

"So? Well, I hardly like to go over the head of a departmental chief, but tell me about it; perhaps we can arrange it. Whom do you want?"

"I need Dr. Obre."

"The spectroscopist. Hm-m-m. I can understand Dr. Ridpath's reluctance, Dr. Karst, and I'm disposed to agree with him. After all, the high-explosives research is really our main show around here."

She bristled and I thought she was going to make him stay in after school at the very least. "Colonel Manning, do you realize the importance of artificial radioactives to modern medicine?"

"Why, I believe I do. Nevertheless, Doctor, our primary mission is to perfect a weapon which will serve as a safeguard to the whole country in time of war—"

She sniffed and went into action. "Weapons—fiddlesticks! Isn't there a medical corps in the Army? Isn't it more important to know how to heal men than to know how to blow them to bits? Colonel Manning, you're not a fit man to have charge of this project! You're a … you're a, a warmonger, that's what you are!"

I felt my ears turning red, but Manning never budged. He could have raised Cain with her, confined her to her quarters, maybe even have court-martialed her, but Manning isn't like that. He told me once that every time a man is court-martialed, it is a sure sign that some senior officer hasn't measured up to his job.

"I am sorry you feel that way, Doctor," he said mildly, "and I agree that my technical knowledge isn't what it might be. And, believe me, I do wish that healing were all we had to worry about. In any case, I have not refused your request. Let's walk over to your laboratory and see what the problem is. Likely there is some arrangement that can be made which will satisfy everybody."

He was already up and getting out his greatcoat. Her set mouth relaxed a trifle and she answered, "Very well. I'm sorry I spoke as I did."

"Not at all," he replied. "These are worrying times. Come along, John."

I trailed after them, stopping in the outer office to get my own coat and to stuff my notebook in a pocket.

By the time we had trudged through mushy snow the eighth of a mile to her lab they were talking about gardening!

Manning acknowledged the sentry's challenge with a wave of his hand and we entered the building. He started casually on into the inner lab, but Karst stopped him. "Armor first, Colonel."

We had trouble finding overshoes that would fit over Manning's boots, which he persisted in wearing, despite the new uniform regulations, and he wanted to omit the foot protection, but Karst would not hear of it. She called in a couple of her assistants who made jury-rigged moccasins out of some soft-lead sheeting.

The helmets were different from those used in the explosives lab, being fitted with inhalers. "What's this?" inquired Manning.

"Radioactive dust guard," she said. "It's absolutely essential."

We threaded a lead-lined meander and arrived at the workroom door which she opened by combination. I blinked at the sudden bright illumination and noticed the air was filled with little shiny motes.

"Hm-m-m—it *is* dusty," agreed Manning. "Isn't there some way of controlling that?" His voice sounded muffled from behind the dust mask.

"The last stage has to be exposed to air," explained Karst. "The hood gets most of it. We could control it, but it would mean a quite expensive new installation."

"No trouble about that. We're not on a budget, you know. It must be very annoying to have to work in a mask like this."

"It is," acknowledged Karst. "The kind of gear it would take would enable us to work without body armor, too. That would be a comfort."

I suddenly had a picture of the kind of thing these researchers put up with. I am a fair-sized man, yet I found that armor heavy to carry around. Estelle Karst was a small woman, yet she was willing to work maybe fourteen hours, day after day, in an outfit which was about as comfortable as a diving suit. But she had not complained.

Not all the heroes are in the headlines. These radiation experts not only ran the chance of cancer and nasty radioaction burns, but the men stood a chance of damaging their germ plasm and then having their wives present them with something horrid in the way of off-spring—no chin, for example, and long hairy ears. Nevertheless, they went right ahead and never seemed to get irritated unless something held up their work.

Dr. Karst was past the age when she would be likely to be concerned personally about progeny, but the principle applies.

I wandered around, looking at the unlikely apparatus she used to get her results, fascinated as always by my failure to recognize much that reminded me of the physics laboratory I had known when I was an undergraduate, and being careful not to touch anything. Karst started explaining to Manning what she was doing and why, but I knew that it was useless for me to try to follow that technical stuff. If Manning wanted notes, he would dictate them. My attention was caught by a big boxlike contraption in one corner of the room. It had a hopperlike gadget on one side and I could hear a sound from it like the whirring of a fan with a background of running water. It intrigued me.

I moved back to the neighborhood of Dr. Karst and the Colonel and heard her saying, "The problem amounts to this, Colonel: I am getting a much more highly radioactive end product than I want, but there is considerable variation in the half-life of otherwise equivalent samples. That suggests to me that I am using a mixture of isotopes, but I haven't been able to prove it. And frankly, I do not know enough about that end of the field to be sure of sufficient refinement in my methods. I need Dr. Obre's help on that."

I think those were her words, but I may not be doing her justice, not being a physicist. I understood the part about "half-life." All radioactive materials keep right on radiating until they turn into something else, which takes theoretically forever. As a matter of practice their periods, or "lives," are described in terms of how long it takes the original radiation to drop to one-half strength. That time is called a "half-life" and each radioactive isotope of an element has its own specific characteristic half-lifetime.

One of the staff—I forget which one—told me once that any form of matter can be considered as radioactive in some degree; it's a question of intensity and period, or half-life.

"I'll talk to Dr. Ridpath," Manning answered her, "and see what can be arranged. In the meantime you might draw up plans for what you want to reequip your laboratory."

"Thank you, Colonel."

I could see that Manning was about ready to leave, having pacified her; I was still curious about the big box that gave out the odd noises.

"May I ask what that is, Doctor?"

"Oh, that? That's an air conditioner."

"Odd-looking one. I've never seen one like it."

"It's not to condition the air of this room. It's to remove the radioactive dust before the exhaust air goes outdoors. We wash the dust out of the foul air."

"Where does the water go?"

"Down the drain. Out into the bay eventually, I suppose."

I tried to snap my fingers, which was impossible because of the lead mittens. "That accounts for it, Colonel!"

"Accounts for what?"

"Accounts for those accusing notes we've been getting from the Bureau of Fisheries. This poisonous dust is being carried out into Chesapeake Bay and is killing the fish."

Manning turned to Karst. "Do you think that possible, Doctor?"

I could see her brows draw together through the window in her helmet. "I hadn't thought about it," she admitted. "I'd have to do some figuring on the possible concentrations before I could give you a definite answer. But it is possible—yes. However," she added anxiously, "it would be simple enough to divert this drain to a sink hole of some sort."

"Hm-m-m—yes." He did not say anything for some minutes, simply stood there, looking at the box.

Presently he said, "This dust is pretty lethal?"

"Quite lethal, Colonel." There was another long silence.

At last I gathered he had made up his mind about something for he said decisively, "I am going to see to it that you get Obre's assistance, Doctor—"

"Oh, good!"

"—but I want you to help me in return. I am very much interested in this research of yours, but I want it carried on with a little broader scope. I want you to investigate for maxima both in period and intensity as well as for minima. I want you to drop the strictly utilitarian approach and make an exhaustive research along lines which we will work out in greater detail later."

She started to say something but he cut in ahead of her. "A really thorough program of research should prove more helpful in the long run to your original purpose than a more narrow one. And I shall make it my business to expedite every possible facility for such a research. I think we may turn up a number of interesting things."

He left immediately, giving her no time to discuss it. He did not seem to want to talk on the way back and I held my peace. I think he had already gotten a glimmering of the bold and drastic strategy this was to lead to, but even Manning could not have thought out that early the inescapable consequences of a few dead fish—otherwise he would never have ordered the research.

No, I don't really believe that. He would have gone right ahead, knowing that if he did not do it, someone else would. He would have accepted the responsibility while bitterly aware of its weight.

1944 wore along with no great excitement on the surface. Karst got her new laboratory equipment and so much additional help that her department rapidly became the largest on the grounds. The explosives research was suspended after a conference between Manning and Ridpath, of which I heard only the end, but the meat of it was that there existed not even a remote possibility at that time of utilizing U235 as an explosive. As a source of power, yes, sometime in the distant future when there had been more opportunity to deal with the extremely ticklish problem of controlling the nuclear reaction. Even then it seemed likely that it would not be a source of power in prime movers such as rocket motors or mobiles, but would be used in vast power plants at least as large as the Boulder Dam installation.

After that Ridpath became a sort of co-chairman of Karst's department and the equipment formerly used by the explosives department was adapted or replaced to carry on research on the deadly artificial radioactives. Manning arranged a division of labor and Karst stuck to her original problem of developing techniques for tailor-making radioactives. I think she was perfectly happy, sticking with a one-track mind to the problem at hand. I don't know to this day whether or not Manning and Ridpath ever saw fit to discuss with her what they intended to do.

As a matter of fact, I was too busy myself to think much about it. The general elections were coming up and I was determined that Manning should have a constituency to return to, when the emergency was over. He was not much interested, but agreed to let his name be filed as a candidate for re-election. I was trying to work up a campaign by remote control and cursing because I could not be in the field to deal with the thousand and one emergencies as they arose.

I did the next best thing and had a private line installed to permit the campaign chairman to reach me easily. I don't think I violated the Hatch Act, but I guess I stretched it a little. Anyhow, it turned out all right; Manning was elected as were several other members of the citizen-military that year. An attempt was made to smear him by claiming that he was taking two salaries for one job, but we squelched that with a pamphlet entitled "For Shame!" which explained that he got *one* salary for *two* jobs. That's the Federal law in such cases and people are entitled to know it.

It was just before Christmas that Manning first admitted to me how much the implications of the Karst-Obre process were preying on his mind. He called me into his office over some inconsequential matter, then did not let me go. I saw that he wanted to talk.

"How much of the K-O dust do we now have on hand?" he asked suddenly.

"Just short of ten thousand units," I replied. "I can look up the exact figures in half a moment." A unit would take care of a thousand men, at normal dispersion. He knew the figure as well as I did, and I knew he was stalling.

We had shifted almost imperceptibly from research to manufacture, entirely on Manning's initiative and authority. Manning had never made a specific report to the Department about it, unless he had done so orally to the Chief of Staff.

"Never mind," he answered to my suggestion, then added, "Did you see those horses?"

"Yes," I said briefly.

I did not want to talk about it. I like horses. We had requisitioned six broken-down old nags, ready for the bone yard, and had used them experimentally. We knew now what the dust would do. After they had died, any part of their carcasses would register on a photographic plate and tissue from the apices of their lungs and from the bronchia glowed with a light of its own.

Manning stood at the window, staring out at the dreary Maryland winter for a minute or two before replying, "John, I wish that radioactivity had never been discovered. Do you realize what that devilish stuff amounts to?"

"Well," I said, "it's a weapon, about like poison gas—maybe more efficient."

"Rats!" he said, and for a moment I thought he was annoyed with me personally. "That's about like comparing a sixteen-inch gun with a bow and arrow. We've got here the first weapon the world has ever seen against which there is no defense, none whatsoever. It's death itself, C.O.D."

"Have you seen Ridpath's report?" he went on.

I had not. Ridpath had taken to delivering his reports by hand to Manning personally.

"Well," he said, "ever since we started production I've had all the talent we could spare working on the problem of a defense against the dust. Ridpath tells me and I agree with him that there is no means whatsoever to combat the stuff, once it's used."

"How about armor," I asked, "and protective clothing?"

"Sure, sure," he agreed irritatedly, "provided you never take it off to eat, or to drink or for any purpose whatever, until the radioaction has ceased, or you are out of the danger zone. That is all right for laboratory work; I'm talking about war."

I considered the matter. "I still don't see what you are fretting about, Colonel. If the stuff is as good as you say it is, you've done just exactly what you set out to do—develop a weapon which would give the United States protection against aggression."

He swung around. "John, there are times when I think you are downright stupid!"

I said nothing. I knew him and I knew how to discount his moods. The fact that he permitted me to see his feelings is the finest compliment I have ever had.

"Look at it this way," he went on more patiently; "this dust, as a weapon, is not just simply sufficient to safeguard the United States, it amounts to a loaded gun held at the head of every man, woman, and child on the globe!"

"Well," I answered, "what of that? It's our secret, and we've got the upper hand. The United States can put a stop to this war, and any other war. We can declare a *Pax Americana*, and enforce it."

"Hm-m-m—I wish it were that easy. But it won't remain our secret; you can count on that. It doesn't matter how successfully we guard it; all that anyone needs is the hint given by the dust itself and then it is just a matter of time until some other nation develops a technique to produce it. You can't stop brains from working, John; the reinvention of the method is a mathematical certainty, once they know what it is they are looking for. And uranium is a common enough substance, widely distributed over the globe—don't forget that!

"It's like this; Once the secret is out—and it will be out if we ever use the stuff!—the whole world will be comparable to a room full of men, each armed with a loaded .45. They can't get out of the room and each one is dependent on the good will of every other one to stay alive. All offense and no defense. See what I mean?"

I thought about it, but I still didn't guess at the difficulties. It seemed to me that a peace enforced by us was the only way out, with precautions taken to see that we controlled the sources of uranium. I had the usual American subconscious conviction that our country would never use power in sheer aggression. Later, I thought about the Mexican War and the Spanish-American War and some of the things we did in Central America, and I was not so sure—

—◆—

It was a couple of weeks later, shortly after inauguration day, that Manning told me to get the Chief of Staff's office on the telephone. I heard only the tail end of the conversation. "No, General, I won't," Manning was saying. "I won't discuss it with you, or the Secretary, either. This is a matter the Commander in Chief is going to have to decide in the long run. If he turns it down, it is imperative that no one else ever knows about it. That's my considered opinion. ... What's that? ... I took this job under the condition that I was to have a free hand. You've got to give me a little leeway this time. ... Don't go brass hat on me. I knew you when you were a plebe. ... O.K., O.K., sorry. ... If the Secretary of War won't listen to reason, you tell him I'll be in my seat in the House of Representatives tomorrow, and that I'll get the favor I want from the majority leader. ... All right. Good-bye."

Washington rang up again about an hour later. It was the Secretary of War. This time Manning listened more than he talked. Toward the end, he said, "All I want is thirty minutes alone with the President. If nothing comes of it, no harm has been done. If I convince him, then you will know all about it. ... No, sir, I did not mean that you would avoid responsibility. I intended to be helpful. ... Fine! Thank you, Mr. Secretary."

The White House rang up later in the day and set a time.

We drove down to the District the next day through a nasty cold rain that threatened to turn to sleet. The usual congestion in Washington was made worse by the weather; it very nearly caused us to be late in arriving. I could hear Manning swearing under his breath all the way down Rhode Island Avenue. But we were dropped at the west wing entrance to the White House with two minutes to spare. Manning was ushered into the Oval Office almost at once and I was left cooling my heels and trying to get comfortable in civilian clothes. After so many months of uniform they itched in the wrong places.

The thirty minutes went by.

The President's reception secretary went in, and came out very promptly indeed. He stepped on out into the outer reception room and I heard something that began with, "I'm sorry, Senator, but—"

He came back in, made a penciled notation, and passed it out to an usher.

Two more hours went by.

Manning appeared at the door at last and the secretary looked relieved. But he did not come out, saying instead, "Come in, John. The President wants to take a look at you."

I fell over my feet getting up.

Manning said, "Mr. President, this is Captain DeFries." The President nodded, and I bowed, unable to say anything. He was standing on the hearth rug, his fine head turned toward us, and looking just like his pictures—but it seemed strange for the President of the United States not to be a tall man.

I had never seen him before, though, of course, I knew something of his record the two years he had been in the Senate and while he was Mayor before that.

The President said, "Sit down, DeFries. Care to smoke?" Then to Manning, "You think he can do it?"

"I think he'll have to. It's Hobson's choice."

"And you are sure of him?"

"He was my campaign manager."

"I see."

The President said nothing more for a while and God knows I didn't!—though I was bursting to know what they were talking about. He commenced again with, "Colonel Manning, I intend to follow the procedure you have suggested, with the changes we discussed. But I will be down tomorrow to see for myself that the dust will do what you say it will. Can you prepare a demonstration?"

"Yes, Mr. President."

"Very well, we will use Captain DeFries unless I think of a better procedure." I thought for a moment that they planned to use me for a guinea pig! But he turned to me and continued, "Captain, I expect to send you to England as my representative."

I gulped. "Yes, Mr. President." And that is every word I had to say in calling on the President of the United States.

—◈—

After that, Manning had to tell me a lot of things he had on his mind. I am going to try to relate them as carefully as possible, even at the risk of being dull and obvious and of repeating things that are common knowledge.

We had a weapon that could not be stopped. Any type of K-O dust scattered over an area rendered that area uninhabitable for a length of time that depended on the half-life of the radioactivity.

Period. Full stop.

Once an area was dusted there was nothing that could be done about it until the radioactivity had fallen off to the point where it was no longer harmful. The dust could not be cleaned out; it was everywhere. There was no possible way to counteract it—burn it, combine it chemically; the radioactive isotope was still there, still radioactive, still deadly. Once used on a stretch of land, for a predetermined length of time that piece of earth *would not tolerate life.*

It was extremely simple to use. No complicated bomb-sights were needed, no care need be taken to hit "military objectives." Take it aloft in any sort of aircraft, attain a position more or less over the area you wish to sterilize, and drop the stuff. Those on the ground in the contaminated area are dead men, dead in an hour, a day, a week, a month, depending on the degree of the infection—but *dead.*

Manning told me that he had once seriously considered, in the middle of the night, recommending that every single person, including himself, who knew the Karst-Obre technique be put to death, in the interests of all civilization. But he had realized the next day that it had been sheer funk; the technique was certain in time to be rediscovered by someone else.

Furthermore, it would not do to wait, to refrain from using the grisly power, until someone else perfected it and used it. The only possible chance to keep the world from being turned into one huge morgue was for us to use the power first and drastically—get the upper hand and keep it.

We were not at war, legally, yet we had been in the war up to our necks with our weight on the side of democracy since 1940. Manning had proposed to the President that we turn a supply of the dust over to Great Britain, under conditions we specified, and enable them thereby to force a peace. But the terms of the peace would be dictated by the United States—for we were not turning over the secret.

After that, the *Pax Americana.*

The United States was having power thrust on it, willy-nilly. We had to accept it and enforce a worldwide peace, ruthlessly and drastically, or it would be seized by some other nation. There could not be co-equals in the possession of this weapon. The factor of time predominated.

I was selected to handle the details in England because Manning insisted, and the President agreed with him, that every person technically acquainted with the Karst-Obre process should remain on the laboratory reservation in what amounted to protective custody—imprisonment. That included Manning himself. I could go because I did not have the secret—I could not even have acquired it without years of schooling—and what I did not know I could not tell, even under, well, drugs. We were determined to keep the secret as long as we could to consolidate the *Pax*; we did not distrust our English cousins, but they were Britishers, with a first loyalty to the British Empire. No need to tempt them.

I was picked because I understood the background if not the science, and because Manning trusted me. I don't know why the President trusted me, too, but then my job was not complicated.

We took off from the new field outside Baltimore on a cold, raw afternoon which matched my own feelings. I had an all-gone feeling in my stomach, a runny nose, and, buttoned inside my clothes, papers appointing me a special agent of the President of the United States. They were odd papers, papers without precedent; they did not simply give me the usual diplomatic immunity; they made my person very nearly as sacred as that of the President himself.

At Nova Scotia we touched ground to refuel, the F.B.I. men left us, we took off again, and the Canadian transfighters took their stations around us. All the dust we were sending was in my plane; if the President's representative were shot down, the dust would go to the bottom with him.

No need to tell of the crossing. I was airsick and miserable, in spite of the steadiness of the new six-engined jobs. I felt like a hang-man on the way to an execution, and wished to God that I were a boy again, with nothing more momentous than a debate contest, or a track meet, to worry me.

There was some fighting around us as we neared Scotland, I know, but I could not see it, the cabin being shuttered. Our pilot-captain ignored it and brought his ship down on a totally dark field, using a beam, I suppose, though I did not know nor care. I would have wel-comed a crash. Then the lights outside went on and I saw that we had come to rest in an underground hangar.

I stayed in the ship. The Commandant came to see me to his quarters as his guest. I shook my head. "I stay here," I said. "Orders. You are to treat this ship as United States soil, you know."

He seemed miffed, but compromised by having dinner served for both of us in my ship.

There was a really embarrassing situation the next day. I was com-manded to appear for a Royal audience. But I had my instructions and I stuck to them. I was sitting on that cargo of dust until the President told me what to do with it. Late in the day I was called on by a member of Parliament—nobody admitted out loud that it was the Prime Minister—and a Mr. Windsor. The M.P. did most of the talking and I answered his questions. My other guest said very little and spoke slowly with some difficulty. But I got a very favorable impression of him. He seemed to be a man who was carrying a load beyond human strength and carrying it heroically.

There followed the longest period in my life. It was actually only a little longer than a week, but every minute of it had that split-second intensity of imminent disaster that comes just before a car crash. The President was using the time to try to avert the need to use the dust. He had two face-to-face television conferences with the new Fuehrer. The President spoke German fluently, which should have helped. He spoke three times to the warring peoples themselves, but it is doubt-ful if very many on the Continent were able to listen, the police regu-lations there being what they were.

The Ambassador from the Reich was given a special demonstration of the effect of the dust. He was flown out over a deserted stretch of Western prairie and allowed to see what a single dusting would do to a herd of steers. It should have impressed him and I think that it did—*nobody* could ignore a visual demonstration!—but what report he made to his leader we never knew.

The British Isles were visited repeatedly during the wait by bombing attacks as heavy as any of the war. I was safe enough but I heard about them, and I could see the effect on the morale of the officers with whom I associated. Not that it frightened them—it made them coldly angry. The raids were not directed primarily at dockyards or factories, but were ruthless destruction of anything, particularly villages.

"I don't see what you chaps are waiting for," a flight commander complained to me. "What the Jerries need is a dose of their own *shrecklichkeit*, a lesson in their own Aryan culture."

I shook my head. "We'll have to do it our own way."

He dropped the matter, but I knew how he and his brother officers felt. They had a standing toast, as sacred as the toast to the King: "Remember Coventry!"

Our President had stipulated that the R.A.F. was not to bomb during the period of negotiation, but their bombers were busy nevertheless. The continent was showered, night after night, with bales of leaflets, prepared by our own propaganda agents. The first of these called on the people of the Reich to stop a useless war and promised that the terms of peace would not be vindictive. The second rain of pamphlets showed photographs of that herd of steers. The third was a simple direct warning to get out of cities and to stay out.

As Manning put it, we were calling "Halt!" three times before firing. I do not think that he or the President expected it to work, but we were morally obligated to try.

The Britishers had installed for me a televisor, of the Simonds-Yarley nonintercept type, the sort whereby the receiver must "trigger" the transmitter in order for the transmission to take place at all. It made assurance of privacy in diplomatic rapid communication for the first time in history, and was a real help in the crisis. I had brought along my own technician, one of the F.B.I.'s new corps of specialists, to handle the scrambler and the trigger.

He called to me one afternoon. "Washington signaling."

I climbed tiredly out of the cabin and down to the booth on the hangar floor, wondering if it were another false alarm.

It was the President. His lips were white. "Carry out your basic instructions, Mr. DeFries."

"Yes, Mr. President!"

The details had been worked out in advance and, once I had accepted a receipt and token payment from the Commandant for the dust, my duties were finished. But, at our insistence, the British had invited military observers from every independent nation and from the several provisional governments of occupied nations. The United States Ambassador designated me as one at the request of Manning.

Our task group was thirteen bombers. One such bomber could have carried all the dust needed, but it was split up to insure most of it, at least, reaching its destination. I had fetched forty percent more dust than Ridpath calculated would be needed for the mission and my last job was to see to it that every canister actually went on board a plane of the flight. The extremely small weight of dust used was emphasized to each of the military observers.

We took off just at dark, climbed to twenty-five thousand feet, refueled in the air, and climbed again. Our escort was waiting for us, having refueled thirty minutes before us. The flight split into thirteen groups, and cut the thin air for middle Europe. The bombers we rode had been stripped and hiked up to permit the utmost maximum of speed and altitude.

Elsewhere in England, other flights had taken off shortly before us to act as a diversion. Their destinations were every part of Germany; it was the intention to create such confusion in the air above the Reich that our few planes actually engaged in the serious work might well escape attention entirely, flying so high in the stratosphere.

The thirteen dust carriers approached Berlin from different directions, planning to cross Berlin as if following the spokes of a wheel. The night was appreciably clear and we had a low moon to help us.

Berlin is not a hard city to locate, since it has the largest square-mile area of any modern city and is located on a broad flat alluvial plain. I could make out the River Spree as we approached it, and the Havel. The city was blacked out, but a city makes a different sort of black from open country. Parachute flares hung over the city in many places, showing that the R.A.F. had been busy before we got there and the A.A. batteries on the ground helped to pick out the city.

There was fighting below us, but not within fifteen thousand feet of our altitude as nearly as I could judge.

The pilot reported to the captain, "On line of bearing!" The chap working the absolute altimeter steadily fed his data into the fuse pots of the canister. The canisters were equipped with a light charge of black powder, sufficient to explode them and scatter the dust at a time after release predetermined by the fuse pot setting. The method used was no more than an efficient expedient. The dust would have been almost as effective had it simply been dumped out in paper bags, although not as well distributed.

The Captain hung over the navigator's board, a slight frown on his thin sallow face. "Ready one!" reported the bomber.

"Release!"

"Ready two!"

The Captain studied his wristwatch. "Release!"

"Ready three!"

"Release!"

When the last of our ten little packages was out of the ship we turned tail and ran for home.

No arrangements had been made for me to get home; nobody had thought about it. But it was the one thing I wanted to do. I did not feel badly; I did not feel much of anything. I felt like a man who has at last screwed up his courage and undergone a serious operation; it's over now, he is still numb from shock but his mind is relaxed. But I wanted to go home.

The British Commandant was quite decent about it; he serviced and manned my ship at once and gave me an escort for the offshore war zone. It was an expensive way to send one man home, but who cared? We had just expended some millions of lives in a desperate attempt to end the war; what was a money expense? He gave the necessary orders absentmindedly.

I took a double dose of nembutal and woke up in Canada. I tried to get some news while the plane was being serviced, but there was not much to be had. The government of the Reich had issued one official news bulletin shortly after the raid, sneering at the much vaunted "secret weapon" of the British and stating that a major air attack had been made on Berlin and several other cities, but that the raiders had been driven off with only minor damage. The current Lord Haw-Haw started one of his sarcastic speeches but was unable to continue it. The announcer said that he had been seized with a heart attack, and substituted some recordings of patriotic music. The station cut off in the middle of the "Horst Wessel" song. After that there was silence.

I managed to promote an Army car and a driver at the Baltimore field which made short work of the Annapolis speedway. We almost overran the turnoff to the laboratory.

Manning was in his office. He looked up as I came in, said, "Hello, John," in a dispirited voice, and dropped his eyes again to the blotter pad. He went back to drawing doodles.

I looked him over and realized for the first time that the chief was an old man. His face was gray and flabby, deep furrows framed his mouth in a triangle. His clothes did not fit.

I went up to him and put a hand on his shoulder. "Don't take it so hard, chief. It's not your fault. We gave them all the warning in the world."

He looked up again. "Estelle Karst suicided this morning."

Anybody could have anticipated it, but nobody did. And somehow I felt harder hit by her death than by the death of all those strangers in Berlin. "How did she do it?" I asked.

"Dust. She went into the canning room, and took off her armor."

I could picture her—head held high, eyes snapping, and that set look on her mouth which she got when people did something she disapproved of. One little old woman whose lifetime work had been turned against her.

"I wish," Manning added slowly, "that I could explain to her why we *had* to do it."

We buried her in a lead-lined coffin, then Manning and I went on to Washington.

While we were there, we saw the motion pictures that had been made of the death of Berlin. You have not seen them; they never were made public, but they were of great use in convincing the other nations of the world that peace was a good idea. I saw them when Congress did, being allowed in because I was Manning's assistant.

They had been made by a pair of R.A.F. pilots, who had dodged the *Luftwaffe* to get them. The first shots showed some of the main streets the morning after the raid. There was not much to see that would show up in telephoto shots, just busy and crowded streets, but if you looked closely you could see that there had been an excessive number of automobile accidents.

The second day showed the attempt to evacuate. The inner squares of the city were practically deserted save for bodies and wrecked cars, but the streets leading out of town were boiling with people, mostly on foot, for the trams were out of service. The pitiful creatures were fleeing, not knowing that death was already lodged inside them. The plane swooped down at one point and the cinematographer had his telephoto lens pointed directly into the face of a young woman for several seconds. She stared back at it with a look too woebegone to forget, then stumbled and fell.

She may have been trampled. I hope so. One of those six horses had looked like that when the stuff was beginning to hit his vitals.

The last sequence showed Berlin and the roads around it a week after the raid. The city was dead; there was not a man, a woman, a child—nor cats, nor dogs, not even a pigeon. Bodies were all around, but they were safe from rats. There were no rats.

The roads around Berlin were quiet now. Scattered carelessly on shoulders and in ditches, and to a lesser extent on the pavement itself, like coal shaken off a train, were the quiet heaps that had been the citizens of the capital of the Reich. There is no use in talking about it.

But, so far as I am concerned, I left what soul I had in that projection room and I have not had one since.

The two pilots who made the pictures eventually died—systemic, cumulative infection, dust in the air over Berlin. With precautions it need not have happened, but the English did not believe, as yet, that our extreme precautions were necessary.

The Reich took about a week to fold up. It might have taken longer if the new Fuehrer had not gone to Berlin the day after the raid to "prove" that the British boasts had been hollow. There is no need to recount the provisional governments that Germany had in the following several months; the only one we are concerned with is the so-called restored monarchy which used a cousin of the old Kaiser as a symbol, the one that sued for peace.

Then the trouble started.

When the Prime Minister announced the terms of the private agreement he had had with our President, he was met with a silence that was broken only by cries of "Shame! Shame! Resign!" I suppose it was inevitable; the Commons reflected the spirit of a people who had been unmercifully punished for four years. They were in a mood to enforce a peace that would have made the Versailles Treaty look like the Beatitudes.

The vote of no confidence left the Prime Minister no choice. Forty-eight hours later the King made a speech from the throne that violated all constitutional precedent, for it had not been written by a Prime Minister. In this greatest crisis in his reign, his voice was clear and unlabored; it sold the idea to England and a national coalition government was formed.

I don't know whether we would have dusted London to enforce our terms or not; Manning thinks we would have done so. I suppose it depended on the character of the President of the United States, and there is no way of knowing about that since we did not have to do it.

The United States, and in particular the President of the United States, was confronted by two inescapable problems. First, we had to consolidate our position at once, use our temporary advantage of an overwhelmingly powerful weapon to insure that such a weapon would not be turned on us. Second, some means had to be worked out to stabilize American foreign policy so that it could handle the tremendous power we had suddenly had thrust upon us.

The second was by far the most difficult and serious. If we were to establish a reasonably permanent peace—say a century or so—through a monopoly on a weapon so powerful that no one dare fight us, it was imperative that the policy under which we acted be more lasting than passing political administrations. But more of that later—

The first problem had to be attended to at once—time was the heart of it. The emergency lay in the very simplicity of the weapon. It required nothing but aircraft to scatter it and the dust itself, which was easily and quickly made by anyone possessing the secret of the Karst-Obre process and having access to a small supply of uranium-bearing ore.

But the Karst-Obre process was simple and might be independently developed at any time. Manning reported to the President that it was Ridpath's opinion, concurred in by Manning, that the staff of any modern radiation laboratory should be able to work out an equivalent technique in six weeks, working from the hint given by the events in Berlin alone, and should then be able to produce enough dust to cause major destruction in another six weeks.

Ninety days—ninety days *provided* they started from scratch and were not already halfway to their goal. Less than ninety days—perhaps no time at all—

By this time Manning was an unofficial member of the Cabinet; "Secretary of Dust," the President called him in one of his rare jovial moods. As for me, well, I attended Cabinet meetings, too. As the only layman who had seen the whole show from beginning to end, the President wanted me there.

I am an ordinary sort of man who, by a concatenation of improbabilities, found himself shoved into the councils of the rulers. But I found that the rulers were ordinary men, too, and frequently as bewildered as I was.

But Manning was no ordinary man. In him ordinary hard sense had been raised to the level of genius. Oh, yes, I know that it is popular to blame everything on him and to call him everything from traitor to mad dog, but I still think he was both wise and benevolent. I don't care how many second-guessing historians disagree with me.

"I propose," said Manning, "that we begin by immobilizing all aircraft throughout the world."

The Secretary of Commerce raised his brows. "Aren't you," he said, being a little fantastic, Colonel Manning?"

"No, I'm not," answered Manning shortly. "I'm being realistic. The key to this problem is aircraft. Without aircraft the dust is an inefficient weapon. The only way I see to gain time enough to deal with the whole problem is to ground all aircraft and put them out of operation. All aircraft, that is, not actually in the service of the United States Army. After that we can deal with complete world disarmament and permanent methods of control."

"Really now," replied the Secretary, "you are not proposing that commercial airlines be put out of operation. They are an essential part of world economy. It would be an intolerable nuisance."

"Getting killed is an intolerable nuisance, too," Manning answered stubbornly. "I do propose just that. All aircraft. *All.*"

The President had been listening without comment to the discussion. He now cut in. "How about aircraft on which some groups depend to stay alive, Colonel, such as the Alaskan lines?"

"If there are such, they must be operated by American Army pilots and crews. No exceptions."

The Secretary of Commerce looked startled. "Am I to infer from that last remark that you intended this prohibition to apply to the *United States* as well as other nations?"

"Naturally."

"But that's impossible. It's unconstitutional. It violates civil rights."

"Killing a man violates his civil rights, too," Manning answered stubbornly.

"You can't do it. Any Federal Court in the country would enjoin you in five minutes."

"It seems to me," said Manning slowly, "that Andy Jackson gave us a good precedent for that one when he told John Marshall to go fly a kite." He looked slowly around the table at faces that ranged from undecided to antagonistic. "The issue is sharp, gentlemen, and we might as well drag it out in the open. We can be dead men, with everything in due order, constitutional, and technically correct; or we can do what has to be done, stay alive, and try to straighten out the legal aspects later." He shut up and waited.

The Secretary of Labor picked it up. "I don't think the Colonel has any corner on realism. I think I see the problem, too, and I admit it is a serious one. The dust must never be used again. Had I known about it soon enough, it would never have been used on Berlin. And I agree that some sort of worldwide control is necessary. But where I differ with the Colonel is in the method. What he proposes is a military dictatorship imposed by force on the whole world. Admit it, Colonel. Isn't that what you are proposing?"

Manning did not dodge it. "That is what I am proposing."

"Thanks. Now we know where we stand. I, for one, do not regard democratic measures and constitutional procedure as of so little importance that I am willing to jettison them any time it becomes convenient. To me, democracy is more than a matter of expediency, it is a faith. Either it works, or I go under with it."

"What do you propose?" asked the President.

"I propose that we treat this as an opportunity to create a worldwide democratic commonwealth! Let us use our present dominant position to issue a call to all nations to send representatives to a conference to form a world constitution."

"League of Nations," I heard someone mutter.

"No!" he answered the side remark. "Not a League of Nations. The old League was helpless because it had no real existence, no power. It was not implemented to enforce its decisions; it was just a debating society, a sham. This would be different *for we would turn over the dust to it!*"

Nobody spoke for some minutes. You could see them turning it over in their minds, doubtful, partially approving, intrigued but dubious.

"I'd like to answer that," said Manning.

"Go ahead," said the President.

"I will. I'm going to have to use some pretty plain language and I hope that Secretary Larner will do me the honor of believing that I speak so from sincerity and deep concern and not from personal pique.

"I think a world democracy would be a very fine thing and I ask that you believe me when I say I would willingly lay down my life to accomplish it. I also think it would be a very fine thing for the lion to lie down with the lamb, but I am reasonably certain that only the lion would get up. If we try to form an actual world democracy, we'll be the lamb in the setup.

"There are a lot of good, kindly people who are internationalists these days. Nine out of ten of them are soft in the head and the tenth is ignorant. If we set up a worldwide democracy, what will the electorate be? Take a look at the facts: Four hundred million Chinese with no more concept of voting and citizen responsibility than a flea; three hundred million Hindus who aren't much better indoctrinated; God knows how many in the Eurasian Union who believe in God knows what; the entire continent of Africa only semicivilized; eighty million Japanese who really believe that they are Heaven-ordained to rule; our Spanish-American friends who might trail along with us and might not, but who don't understand the Bill of Rights the way we think of it; a quarter of a billion people of two dozen different nationalities in Europe, all with revenge and black hatred in their hearts.

"No, it won't wash. It's preposterous to talk about a world democracy for many years to come. If you turn the secret of the dust over to such a body, you will be arming the whole world to commit suicide."

Larner answered at once. "I could resent some of your remarks, but I won't. To put it bluntly, I consider the source. The trouble with you, Colonel Manning, is that you are a professional soldier and have no faith in people. Soldiers may be necessary, but the worst of them are martinets and the best are merely paternalistic." There was quite a lot more of the same.

Manning stood it until his turn came again. "Maybe I am all those things, but you haven't met my argument. *What are you going to do about the hundreds of millions of people who have no experience in, nor love for, democracy?* Now, perhaps, I don't have the same concept of democracy as yourself, but I do know this: Out West there are a couple of hundred thousand people who sent me to Congress; I am *not* going to stand quietly by and let a course be followed which I think will result in their deaths or utter ruin.

"Here is the probable future, as I see it, potential in the smashing of the atom and the development of lethal artificial radioactives. Some power makes a supply of the dust. They'll hit us first to try to knock us out and give them a free hand. New York and Washington overnight, then all of our industrial areas while we are still politically and economically disorganized. But our army would not be in those cities; we would have planes and a supply of dust somewhere where the first dusting wouldn't touch them. Our boys would bravely and righteously proceed to poison their big cities. Back and forth it would go until the organization of each country had broken down so completely that they were no longer able to maintain a sufficiently high level of industrialization to service planes and manufacture dust. That presupposes starvation and plague in the process. You can fill in the details.

"The other nations would get in the game. It would be silly and suicidal, of course, but it doesn't take brains to take a hand in this. All it takes is a very small group, hungry for power, a few airplanes and a supply of dust. *It's a vicious circle that cannot possibly be stopped until the entire planet has dropped to a level of economy too low to support the techniques necessary to maintain it.* My best guess is that such a point would be reached when approximately three-quarters of the world's population were dead of dust, disease, or hunger, and culture reduced to the peasant-and-village type.

"Where is your Constitution and your Bill of Rights if you let that happen?

I've shortened it down, but that was the gist of it. I can't hope to record every word of an argument that went on for days.

The Secretary of the Navy took a crack at him next. "Aren't you getting a bit hysterical, Colonel? After all, the world has seen a lot of weapons which were going to make war an impossibility too horrible to contemplate. Poison gas, and tanks, and airplanes—even firearms, if I remember my history."

Manning smiled wryly. "You've made a point, Mr. Secretary. 'And when the wolf *really* came, the little boy shouted in vain.' I imagine the Chamber of Commerce in Pompeii presented the same reasonable argument to any early vulcanologist so timid as to fear Vesuvius. I'll try to justify my fears. The dust differs from every earlier weapon in its deadliness and ease of use, but most importantly in that we have developed no defense against it. For a number of fairly technical reasons, I don't think we ever will, at least not this century."

"Why not?"

"Because there is no way to counteract radioactivity short of putting a lead shield between yourself and it, an *airtight* lead shield. People might survive by living in sealed underground cities, but our characteristic American culture could not be maintained."

"Colonel Manning," suggested the Secretary of State, "I think you have overlooked the obvious alternative."

"Have I?"

"Yes—to keep the dust as our own secret, go our own way, and let the rest of the world look out for itself. That is the only program that fits our traditions." The Secretary of State was really a fine old gentleman, and not stupid, but he was slow to assimilate new ideas.

"Mr. Secretary," said Manning respectfully, "I wish we could afford to mind our own business. I do wish we could. But it is the best opinion of all the experts that we can't maintain control of this secret except by rigid policing. The Germans were close on our heels in nuclear research; it was sheer luck that we got there first. I ask you to imagine Germany a year hence—with a supply of dust."

The Secretary did not answer, but I saw his lips form the word Berlin.

They came around. The President had deliberately let Manning bear the brunt of the argument, conserving his own stock of goodwill to coax the obdurate. He decided against putting it up to Congress; the dusters would have been overhead before each senator had finished his say. What he intended to do might be unconstitutional, but if he failed to act there might not be any Constitution shortly. There was precedent—the Emancipation Proclamation, the Monroe Doctrine, the Louisiana Purchase, suspension of habeas corpus in the War between the States, the Destroyer Deal.

On February 22nd the President declared a state of full emergency internally and sent his Peace Proclamation to the head of every sovereign state. Divested of its diplomatic surplusage, it said: *The United States is prepared to defeat any power, or combination of powers, in jig time. Accordingly, we are outlawing war and are calling on every nation to disarm completely at once. In other words, "Throw down your guns, boys; we've got the drop on you!"*

A supplement set forth the procedure: All aircraft capable of flying the Atlantic were to be delivered in one week's time to a field, or rather a great stretch of prairie, just west of Fort Riley, Kansas. For lesser aircraft, a spot near Shanghai and a rendezvous in Wales were designated. Memoranda would be issued later with respect to other war equipment. Uranium and its ores were not mentioned; that would come later.

No excuses. Failure to disarm would be construed as an act of war against the United States.

There were no cases of apoplexy in the Senate; why not, I don't know.

There were only three powers to be seriously worried about, England, Japan, and the Eurasian Union. England had been forewarned, we had pulled her out of a war she was losing, and she—or rather her men in power—knew accurately what we could and would do.

Japan was another matter. They had not seen Berlin and they did not really believe it. Besides, they had been telling each other for so many years that they were unbeatable, they believed it. It does not do to get too tough with a Japanese too quickly, for they will die rather than lose face. The negotiations were conducted very quietly indeed, but our fleet was halfway from Pearl Harbor to Kobe, loaded with enough dust to sterilize their six biggest cities, before they were concluded. Do you know what did it? This never hit the newspapers but it was the wording of the pamphlets we proposed to scatter before dusting.

The Emperor was pleased to declare a New Order of Peace. The official version, built up for home consumption, made the whole matter one of collaboration between two great and friendly powers, with Japan taking the initiative.

The Eurasian Union was a puzzle. After Stalin's unexpected death in 1941, no western nation knew very much about what went on in there. Our own diplomatic relations had atrophied through failure to replace men called home nearly four years before. Everybody knew, of course, that the new group in power called themselves Fifth Internationalists, but what that meant, aside from ceasing to display the pictures of Lenin and Stalin, nobody knew.

But they agreed to our terms and offered to cooperate in every way. They pointed out that the Union had never been warlike and had kept out of the recent world struggle. It was fitting that the two remaining great powers should use their greatness to insure a lasting peace.

I was delighted; I had been worried about the E.U.

They commenced delivery of some of their smaller planes to the receiving station near Shanghai at once. The reports on the number and quality of the planes seemed to indicate that they had stayed out of the war through necessity; the planes were mostly of German make and in poor condition, types that Germany had abandoned early in the war.

Manning went west to supervise certain details in connection with immobilizing the big planes, the transoceanic planes, which were to gather near Fort Riley. We planned to spray them with oil, then dust from a low altitude, as in crop dusting, with a low concentration of one-year dust. Then we could turn our backs on them and forget them, while attending to other matters.

But there were hazards. The dust must not be allowed to reach Kansas City, Lincoln, Wichita—any of the nearby cities. The smaller towns roundabout had been temporarily evacuated. Testing stations needed to be set up in all directions in order that accurate tab on the dust might be kept. Manning felt personally responsible to make sure that no bystander was poisoned.

We circled the receiving station before landing at Fort Riley. I could pick out the three landing fields which had hurriedly been graded. Their runways were white in the sun, the twenty-four-hour cement as yet undirtied. Around each of the landing fields were crowded dozens of parking fields, less perfectly graded. Tractors and bulldozers were still at work on some of them. In the easternmost fields, the German and British ships were already in place, jammed wing to body as tightly as planes on the flight deck of a carrier—save for a few that were still being towed into position, the tiny tractors looking from the air like ants dragging pieces of leaf many times larger than themselves.

Only three flying fortresses had arrived from the Eurasian Union. Their representatives had asked for a short delay in order that a supply of high-test aviation gasoline might be delivered to them. They claimed a shortage of fuel necessary to make the long flight over the Arctic safe. There was no way to check the claim and the delay was granted while a shipment was routed from England.

We were about to leave, Manning having satisfied himself as to safety precautions, when a dispatch came in announcing that a flight of E.U. bombers might be expected before the day was out. Manning wanted to see them arrive; we waited around for four hours. When it was finally reported that our escort of fighters had picked them up at the Canadian border, Manning appeared to have grown fidgety and stated that he would watch them from the air. We took off, gained altitude and waited.

There were nine of them in the flight, cruising in column of echelons and looking so huge that our little fighters were hardly noticeable. They circled the field and I was admiring the stately dignity of them when Manning's pilot, Lieutenant Rafferty, exclaimed, "What the devil! They are preparing to land downwind!"

I still did not tumble, but Manning shouted to the copilot, "Get the field!"

He fiddled with his instruments and announced, "Got 'em, sir!"

"General alarm! Armor!"

We could not hear the sirens, naturally, but I could see the white plumes rise from the big steam whistle on the roof of the Administration Building—three long blasts, then three short ones. It seemed almost at the same time that the first cloud broke from the E.U. planes.

Instead of landing, they passed low over the receiving station, jampacked now with ships from all over the world. Each echelon picked one of three groups centered around the three landing fields and streamers of heavy brown smoke poured from the bellies of the E.U. ships. I saw a tiny black figure jump from a tractor and run toward the nearest building. Then the smoke screen obscured the field.

"Do you still have the field?" demanded Manning.

"Yes, sir."

"Cross connect to the chief safety technician. Hurry!"

The copilot cut in the amplifier so that Manning could talk directly. "Saunders? This is Manning. How about it?"

"Radioactive, chief. Intensity seven point four."

They had paralleled the Karst-Obre research.

Manning cut him off and demanded that the communication office at the field raise the Chief of Staff. There was nerve-stretching delay, for it had to be routed over land wire to Kansas City, and some chief operator had to be convinced that she should commandeer a trunk line that was in commercial use. But we got through at last and Manning made his report. "It stands to reason," I heard him say, "that other flights are approaching the border by this time. New York, of course, and Washington. Probably Detroit and Chicago as well. No way of knowing."

The Chief of Staff cut off abruptly, without comment. I knew that the U.S. air fleets, in a state of alert for weeks past, would have their orders in a few seconds, and would be on their way to hunt out and down the attackers, if possible before they could reach the cities.

I glanced back at the field. The formations were broken up. One of the E.U. bombers was down, crashed, half a mile beyond the station. While I watched, one of our midget dive bombers screamed down on a behemoth E.U. ship and unloaded his eggs. It was a center hit, but the American pilot had cut it too fine, could not pull out, and crashed before his victim.

There is no point in rehashing the newspaper stories of the Four-Days War. The point is that we should have lost it, and we would have, had it not been for an unlikely combination of luck, foresight, and good management. Apparently, the nuclear physicists of the Eurasian Union were almost as far along as Ridpath's crew when the destruction of Berlin gave them the tip they needed. But we had rushed them, forced them to move before they were ready, because of the deadline for disarmament set forth in our Peace Proclamation.

If the President had waited to fight it out with Congress before issuing the proclamation, there would not be any United States.

Manning never got credit for it, but it is evident to me that he anticipated the possibility of something like the Four-Days War and prepared for it in a dozen different devious ways. I don't mean military preparation; the Army and the Navy saw to that. But it was no accident that Congress was adjourned at the time. I had something to do with the vote-swapping and compromising that led up to it, and I know.

But I put it to you—would he have maneuvered to get Congress out of Washington at a time when he feared that Washington might be attacked if he had had dictatorial ambitions?

Of course, it was the President who was back of the ten-day leaves that had been granted to most of the civil-service personnel in Washington and he himself must have made the decision to take a swing through the South at that time, but it must have been Manning who put the idea in his head. It is inconceivable that the President would have left Washington to escape personal danger.

And then, there was the plague scare. I don't know how or when Manning could have started that—it certainly did not go through my notebook—but I simply do not believe that it was accidental that a completely unfounded rumor of bubonic plague caused New York City to be semideserted at the time the E.U. bombers struck.

At that, we lost over eight hundred thousand people in Manhattan alone.

Of course, the government was blamed for the lives that were lost and the papers were merciless in their criticism at the failure to anticipate and force an evacuation of all the major cities.

If Manning anticipated trouble, why did he not ask for evacuation? Well, as I see it, for this reason:

A big city will not be, never has been, evacuated in response to rational argument. London never was evacuated on any major scale and we failed utterly in our attempt to force the evacuation of Berlin. The people of New York City had considered the danger of air raids since 1940 and were long since hardened to the thought.

But the fear of a nonexistent epidemic of plague caused the most nearly complete evacuation of a major city ever seen.

And don't forget what we did to Vladivostok and Irkutsk and Moscow—those were innocent people, too. War isn't pretty.

I said luck played a part. It was bad navigation that caused one of our ships to dust Ryazan instead of Moscow, but that mistake knocked out the laboratory and plant which produced the only supply of military radioactives in the Eurasian Union. Suppose the mistake had been the other way around—suppose that one of the E.U. ships in attacking Washington, D.C., by mistake had included Ridpath's shop forty-five miles away in Maryland?

Congress reconvened at the temporary capital in St. Louis, and the American Pacification Expedition started the job of pulling the fangs of the Eurasian Union. It was not a military occupation in the usual sense; there were two simple objectives: to search out and dust all aircraft, aircraft plants, and fields, and to locate and dust radiation laboratories, uranium supplies, and lodes of carnotite and pitchblende. No attempt was made to interfere with, or to replace, civil government.

We used a two-year dust, which gave a breathing spell in which to consolidate our position. Liberal rewards were offered to informers, a technique which worked remarkably well not only in the E.U., but in most parts of the world.

The "weasel," an instrument to smell out radiation, based on the electroscope-discharge principle and refined by Ridpath's staff, greatly facilitated the work of locating uranium and uranium ores. A grid of weasels, properly spaced over a suspect area, could locate any important mass of uranium almost as handily as a direction-finder can spot a radio station.

But, notwithstanding the excellent work of General Bulfinch and the Pacification Expedition as a whole, it was the original mistake of dusting Ryazan that made the job possible of accomplishment.

Anyone interested in the details of the pacification work done in 1945-6 should see the "Proceedings of the American Foundation for Social Research" for a paper entitled *A Study of the Execution of the American Peace Policy from February, 1945*. The *de facto* solution of the problem of policing the world against war left the United States with the much greater problem of perfecting a policy that would insure that the deadly power of the dust would never fall into unfit hands.

The problem is as easy to state as the problem of squaring the circle and almost as impossible of accomplishment. Both Manning and the President believed that the United States must of necessity keep the power for the time being, until some permanent institution could be developed fit to retain it. The hazard was this: Foreign policy is lodged jointly in the hands of the President and the Congress. We were fortunate at the time in having a good President and an adequate Congress, but that was no guarantee for the future. We have had unfit Presidents and power-hungry Congresses—oh, yes! Read the history of the Mexican War.

We were about to hand over to future governments of the United States the power to turn the entire globe into an empire, our empire. And it was the sober opinion of the President that our characteristic and beloved democratic culture would not stand up under the temptation. Imperialism degrades both oppressor and oppressed.

The President was determined that our sudden power should be used for the absolute minimum of maintaining peace in the world— the simple purpose of outlawing war and nothing else. It must not be used to protect American investments abroad, to coerce trade agreements, for any purpose but the simple abolition of mass killing.

There is no science of sociology. Perhaps there will be, some day, when a rigorous physics gives a finished science of colloidal chemistry and that leads in turn to a complete knowledge of biology, and from there to a definitive psychology. After that we may begin to know something about sociology and politics. Sometime around the year 5000 A.D., maybe—if the human race does not commit suicide before then.

Until then, there is only horse sense and rule of thumb and observational knowledge of probabilities. Manning and the President played by ear.

The treaties with Great Britain, Germany and the Eurasian Union, whereby we assumed the responsibility for world peace and at the same time guaranteed the contracting nations against our own misuse of power, were rushed through in the period of relief and goodwill that immediately followed the termination of the Four-Days War. We followed the precedents established by the Panama Canal treaties, the Suez Canal agreements, and the Philippine Independence policy.

But the purpose underneath was to commit future governments of the United States to an irrevocable benevolent policy.

The act to implement the treaties by creating the Commission of World Safety followed soon after, and Colonel Manning became Mr. Commissioner Manning. Commissioners had a life tenure and the intention was to create a body with the integrity, permanence and freedom from outside pressure possessed by the Supreme Court of the United States. Since the treaties contemplated an eventual joint trust, commissioners need not be American citizens—and the oath they took was *to preserve the peace of the world.*

There was trouble getting the clause past the Congress! Every other similar oath had been to the Constitution of the United States.

Nevertheless the Commission was formed. It took charge of world aircraft, assumed jurisdiction over radioactives, natural and artificial, and commenced the long slow task of building up the Peace Patrol.

Manning envisioned a corps of world policemen, an aristocracy which, through selection and indoctrination, could be trusted with unlimited power over the life of every man, every woman, every child on the face of the globe. For the power *would* be unlimited; the precautions necessary to insure the unbeatable weapon from getting loose in the world again made it axiomatic that its custodians would wield power that is safe only in the hands of Deity. There would be no one to guard those selfsame guardians. Their own characters and the watch they kept on each other would be all that stood between the race and disaster.

For the first time in history, supreme political power was to be exerted with no possibility of checks and balances from the outside. Manning took up the task of perfecting it with a dragging subconscious conviction that it was too much for human nature. The rest of the Commission was appointed slowly, the names being sent to the Senate after long joint consideration by the President and Manning. The director of the Red Cross, an obscure little professor of history from Switzerland, Dr. Igor Rimski who had developed the Karst-Obre technique independently and whom the A.P.F. had discovered in prison after the dusting of Moscow—those three were the only foreigners. The rest of the list is well known.

Ridpath and his staff were of necessity the original technical crew of the Commission; United States Army and Navy pilots its first patrolmen. Not all of the pilots available were needed; their records were searched, their habits and associates investigated, their mental processes and emotional attitudes examined by the best psychological research methods available—which weren't good enough. Their final acceptance for the Patrol depended on two personal interviews, one with Manning, one with the President.

Manning told me that he depended more on the President's feeling for character than he did on all the association and reaction tests the psychologists could think up. "It's like the nose of a bloodhound," he said. "In his forty years of practical politics he has seen more phonies than you and I will ever see and each one was trying to sell him something. He can tell one in the dark."

The long-distance plan included the schools for the indoctrination of cadet patrolmen, schools that were to be open to youths of any race, color, or nationality, and from which they would go forth to guard the peace *of every country but their own.* To that country a man would never return during his service. They were to be a deliberately expatriated band of Janizaries, with an obligation only to the Commission and to the race, and welded together with a carefully nurtured esprit de corps.

It stood a chance of working. Had Manning been allowed twenty years without interruption, the original plan might have worked.

The President's running mate for reelection was the result of a political compromise. The candidate for Vice President was a confirmed isolationist who had opposed the Peace Commission from the first, but it was he or a party split in a year when the opposition was strong. The President sneaked back in but with a greatly weakened Congress; only his power of veto twice prevented the repeal of the Peace Act. The Vice President did nothing to help him, although he did not publicly lead the insurrection. Manning revised his plans to complete the essential program by the end of 1952, there being no way to predict the temper of the next administration.

We were both overworked and I was beginning to realize that my health was gone. The cause was not far to seek; a photographic film strapped next to my skin would cloud in twenty minutes. I was suffering from cumulative minimal radioactive poisoning. No well-defined cancer that could be operated on, but a systemic deterioration of function and tissue. There was no help for it, and there was work to be done. I've always attributed it mainly to the week I spent sitting on those canisters before the raid on Berlin.

February 17, 1951. I missed the televue flash about the plane crash that killed the President because I was lying down in my apartment. Manning, by that time, was requiring me to rest every afternoon after lunch, though I was still on duty. I first heard about it from my secretary when I returned to my office, and at once hurried into Manning's office.

There was a curious unreality to that meeting, It seemed to me that we had slipped back to that day when I returned from England, the day that Estelle Karst died. He looked up. "Hello, John," he said.

I put my hand on his shoulder. "Don't take it so hard, chief," was all I could think of to say.

Forty-eight hours later came the message from the newly sworn-in President for Manning to report to him. I took it in to him, an official despatch which I decoded. Manning read it, face impassive.

"Are you going, chief?" I asked.

"Eh? Why, certainly."

I went back into my office, and got my topcoat, gloves, and briefcase.

Manning looked up when I came back in. "Never mind, John," he said. "You're not going." I guess I must have looked stubborn, for he added, "You're not to go because there is work to do here. Wait a minute."

He went to his safe, twiddled the dials, opened it and removed a sealed envelope which he threw on the desk between us. "Here are your orders. Get busy."

He went out as I was opening them. I read them through and got busy. There was little enough time.

The new President received Manning standing and in the company of several of his bodyguards and intimates. Manning recognized the senator who had led the movement to use the Patrol to recover expropriated holdings in South America and Rhodesia, as well as the chairman of the committee on aviation with whom he had had several unsatisfactory conferences in an attempt to work out a *modus operandi* for reinstituting commercial airlines.

"You're prompt, I see," said the President. "Good."

Manning bowed.

"We might as well come straight to the point," the Chief Executive went on. "There are going to be some changes of policy in the administration. I want your resignation."

"I am sorry to have to refuse, sir."

"We'll see about that. In the meantime, Colonel Manning, you are relieved from duty."

"Mr. Commissioner Manning, if you please."

The new President shrugged. "One or the other, as you please. You are relieved, either way."

"I am sorry to disagree again. My appointment is for life."

"That's enough," was the answer. "This is the United States of America. There can be no higher authority. You are under arrest."

I can visualize Manning staring steadily at him for a long moment, then answering slowly, "You are physically able to arrest me, I will concede, but I advise you to wait a few minutes." He stepped to the window. "Look up into the sky."

Six bombers of the Peace Commission patrolled over the Capitol. "None of those pilots is American born," Manning added slowly. "If you confine me, none of us here in this room will live out the day."

There were incidents thereafter, such as the unfortunate affair at Fort Benning three days later, and the outbreak in the wing of the Patrol based in Lisbon and its resultant wholesale dismissals, but for practical purposes, that was all there was to the *coup d'etat*.

Manning was the undisputed military dictator of the world.

Whether or not any man as universally hated as Manning can perfect the Patrol he envisioned, make it self-perpetuating and trustworthy, I don't know, and—because of that week of waiting in a buried English hangar—I won't be here to find out. Manning's heart disease makes the outcome even more uncertain—he may last another twenty years; he may keel over dead tomorrow—and there is no one to take his place. I've set this down partly to occupy the short time I have left and partly to show there is another side to any story, even world dominion.

Not that I would like the outcome, either way. If there is anything to this survival-after-death business, I am going to look up the man who invented the bow and arrow and take him apart with my bare hands. For myself, I can't be happy in a world where any man, or group of men, has the power of death over you and me, our neighbors, every human, every animal, every living thing. I don't like anyone to have that kind of power.

And neither does Manning.

FOREWORD

After World War II I resumed writing with two objectives: first, to explain the meaning *of atomic weapons through popular articles; second, to break out from the limitations and low rates of pulp science-fiction magazines into anything and everything: slicks, books, motion pictures, general fiction, specialized fiction not intended for SF magazines, and nonfiction.*

My second objective I achieved in every respect, but in my first and much more important objective I fell flat on my face.

Unless you were already adult in August 1945 it is almost impossible for me to convey emotionally to you how people felt about the A-bomb, how many different ways they felt about it, how nearly totally ignorant 99.9% of our citizens were on the subject, including almost all of our military leaders and governmental officials.

And including editors!

(The general public is just as dangerously ignorant as to the significance of nuclear weapons today, 1979, as in 1945—but in different ways. In 1945 we were smugly ignorant; in 1979 we have the Pollyannas, and the Ostriches, and the Jingoists who think we can "win" a nuclear war, and the group—a majority?—who regard World War III as of no importance compared with inflation, gasoline rationing, forced school-busing, or you name it. There is much excuse for the ignorance of 1945; the citizenry had been hit by ideas utterly new and strange. But there is no *excuse for the ignorance of 1979. Ignorance today can be charged only to stupidity and laziness—both capital offences.)*

I wrote nine articles intended to shed light on the post-Hiroshima age, and I have never worked harder on any writing, researched the back-

ground more thoroughly, tried harder to make the (grim and horrid) message entertaining and readable. I offered them to commercial markets, not to make money, but because the only propaganda that stands any chance of influencing people is packaged so attractively that editors will buy it in the belief that the cash customers will be entertained by it.

Mine was not packaged that attractively.

I was up against some heavy tonnage:

General Groves, in charge of the Manhattan District (code name for A-bomb R & D), testified that it would take from twenty years to forever for another country to build an A-bomb. (U.S.S.R. did it in 4 years.)

The Chief of Naval Operations testified that the "only" way to deliver the bomb to a target across an ocean was by ship.

A very senior Army Air Force general testified that "blockbuster" bombs were just as effective and cheaper.

The chairman of NACA (shortly to become NASA) testified (Science News Letter 25 May 1946) that intercontinental rockets were impossible.

Ad nauseum—the old sailors want wooden ships, the old soldiers want horse cavalry.

But I continued to write these articles until the U.S.S.R. rejected the United States' proposals for controlling and outlawing atomic weapons through open skies and mutual on-the-ground inspection,. i.e., every country in the world to surrender enough of its sovereignty to the United Nations that mass-weapons war would become impossible (and lesser war unnecessary).

The U.S.S.R. rejected inspection—and I stopped trying to peddle articles based on tying the Bomb down through international policing.

I wish that I could say that thirty-three years of "peace" (i.e., no A- or H- or C- or N- or X- bombs dropped) indicates that we really have nothing to fear from such weapons, because the human race has sense enough not to commit suicide. But I am sorry to say that the situation is even more dangerous, even less stable, than it was in 1946.

Here are three short articles, each from a different approach, with which I tried (and failed) to beat the drum for world peace.

Was I really so naif that I thought that I could change the course of history this way? No, not really. But, damn it, I had to try!

—— THE LAST DAYS OF THE UNITED STATES ——————

"Here lie the bare bones of the United States of America, conceived in freedom, died in bondage. 1776-1986. Death came mercifully, in one stroke, during senility.

"Rest in Peace!"

No expostulations, please. Let us not kid ourselves. The next war can destroy us, utterly, as a nation—and World War III is staring us right in the face. So far, we have done little to avert it and less to prepare for it. Once upon a time the United Nations Organization stood a fair chance of preventing World War III. Now, only a major operation can equip the UNO to cope with the horrid facts of atomics and rocketry—a major operation which would take away the veto power of the Big Five and invest the world organization with the sole and sovereign power to possess atomic weapons.

Are we, as a people, prepared to make the necessary sacrifices to achieve a world authority?

Take a look around you. Many of your friends and neighbors believe that the mere possession of the atomic bomb has rendered us immune to attack. So—the country settles back with a sigh of relief, content to leave foreign affairs to William Randolph Hearst, the *Denver Post*, and the *Chicago Tribune*. We turn our backs on world responsibility and are now hell-bent on new washing machines and new cars.

From such an attitude, with dreadful certainty, comes World War III, the Twenty Minute War, the Atomic War, the War of Final Destruction. The "secret" of the atomic bomb cannot be kept, the experts have told us repeatedly, for the "secret" is simply engineering know-how which can be developed by any industrial nation.

From this fact it can be predicted that any industrial nation, even though small and comparatively weak, will in a few years be able to create the means to destroy the United States at will in one all-out surprise attack. What constitutes a strong power in the Atomic Era? Scientific knowledge, engineering skill, and access to the ores of uranium—no more is needed. Under such circumstances the pretensions of the Big Five to veto powers over the affairs of this planet are preposterous. At the moment there is only the Big One, the United States, through its temporary exclusive possession of the Bomb. Tomorrow—five to ten years—the list might include any of the many nations with the two requirements.

Belgium and Canada have the greatest known deposits of uranium. Both are small but both possess science and skill in abundance. Potentially they are more powerful than any of the so-called Big Five, more powerful than the United States or Russia. Will they stand outside indefinitely, hat in hand, while the "Big Five" determine the fate of the human race? The developments of atomic weapons and of rocketry are analogous to the development of the revolver in individual affairs—it has made the little ones and the big ones all the same size. Some fine day some little nation may decide she is tired of having us around, give us one twenty-minute treatment with atomic rocket bombs, and accept our capitulation.

We have reason to fear such an attack. We have been through one Pearl Harbor; we *know* that it can happen to us. Our present conduct breeds fear and distrust in the hearts of men all over the globe. No matter how we think of ourselves, no matter how peaceful and good hearted we think ourselves to be, two facts insure that we will be hated by many. We have the Bomb—it is like a loaded revolver pointed at the heads of all men. Oh, we won't pull the trigger! Nevertheless, do you suppose they love us for it?

Our other unforgivable sin is being rich while they are poor. Never mind our rationalizations—they see our wasteful luxury while much of the globe starves. Hungry men do not reason calmly. We are getting ourselves caught in a situation which should lead us to expect attack from any quarter, from whoever first produces atomic weapons and long-distance rockets.

Knowing these things, the professional gentlemen who are charged with the defense of this country, the generals and the admirals and the members of the military and naval affairs committees of both houses, are cudgelling their brains in a frenzied but honest attempt to persuade the rest of the country to follow this course or that, which, in their several opinions, will safeguard the country in any coming debacle.

But there is a tragic sameness to their proposals. With few exceptions, they favor preparedness for the *last* war. Thusly:

Conscription in peacetime to build up a reserve;

Emphasis on aircraft carriers rather than battleships;

Decentralization of cities;

An armaments race to keep our head start in atomic weapons;

Agreements to "outlaw" atomic weapons;

Consolidation of the Army and the Navy;

Buying enough war planes each year to insure new development;

An active military and foreign affairs intelligence corps;

Moving the aircraft industry inland;

Placing essential war industry underground.

These are the *progressive* proposals. (Some still favor infantry and battleships!) In contrast, General Arnold says to expect war in which *space ships* cruise outside the atmosphere and launch super-high-speed, atomic-armed rockets on cities below. Hap Arnold tells his boys to keep their eyes on Buck Rogers. Somebody is wrong—is it Hap Arnold or his more conservative colleagues?

Compulsory military training—France had that, for both wars. The end was Vichy.

Aircraft carriers *vs.* battleships. Look, pals, the aircraft carrier was the weapon of *this* war, before Hiroshima. Carriers don't look so good against space ships. Let's build galleons instead; they are cheaper, prettier, and just as useful.

Decentralization of large cities—let's table this one for a moment. There is some sense to it, if carried to its logical conclusion. But not with half measures and not for $250,000,000,000, the sum mentioned by Sumner Spaulding, its prime proponent.

Bigger and better atomic weapons for the United States—this has a reasonable and reassuring sound. We've got the plant and the trained men; let's stay ahead in the race. Dr. Robert Wilson says that atomic bombs a hundred or a thousand times as powerful as the Hiroshima bomb are now in prospect. Teddy Roosevelt advised us to "Speak softly but carry a big stick."

It is a tempting doctrine, but the great-hearted Teddy died long before Hiroshima; his day was the day of the charge up San Juan Hill. A hundred obsolete atomic bombs could destroy the United States— if the enemy struck first. Our super bombs would not save us, unless we were willing to strike first, without declaring war. If two men are locked in a basement, one armed with a 50-calibre machine gun, the other with an 18th century ball-and-powder pistol, victory goes to the man who shoots first, not to the one with the better weapon. That is the logic of atomics and now is the time to learn it by heart.

Agreements to "outlaw" atomic weapons? Swell! Remember the Kellogg Pact? It "outlawed" war.

Consolidation of the armed forces: A proposition sensible in itself, but disastrously futile unless we realize that *all* previous military art is obsolete in the atomic age. The best pre-Hiroshima weapons are now no more than the sidearms of the occupying military police. Buck Rogers must be the new chief of staff. Otherwise we will find ourselves with the most expensive luxury in the world—a second-best military establishment.

Purchase of military aircraft in quantities to insure new development—we bought sailing ships-of-the-line in the 1880's. This makes the same sort of pseudo-sense. Airplanes are already obsolete—slow, clumsy, and useless. The V-2 is credited with a speed of 3600 miles per hour. Here is a simple problem in proportion: The Wright Brothers crate at Kitty Hawk bears the same relation to the B-29 that the V-2 bears to the rocket ship of the coming war. Complete the equation by visualizing the coming rocket ship. Then stop wasting taxes on airplanes.

An efficient intelligence system—Fine! But no answer in itself. The British intelligence was quite efficient before this war. Mr. Chamberlain's desk was piled high with intelligence reports, reports which showed that Munich need never have happened. This has since been confirmed by high German General Staff officers. But Mr. Chamberlain did not read the reports. *Intelligence reports are useful only to the intelligent.*

Moving the aircraft industry inland—excellent preparation for World War II. Move an industry which we don't need for World War III inland where it will be safe from the weapons of World War II. While we are about it let's put stockades around them to keep the Indians out. In the meantime our potential enemies will have plenty of time to perfect long-range rockets.

Placing key war industry underground—assembly lines underground are all very well, but blast furnaces and many other things simply won't fit. Whatever digging in we do, be sure we do it so secretly that the enemy will never suspect, lest he drop an earthquake-type atomic bomb somewhere nearby and bury all hands. Let us be certain, too, that he does not introduce a small atomic bomb inside the underground works, disguised as a candy vending machine, a lunch pail, or a fire extinguisher. The age of atomics is a field day for saboteurs; underground works could be colossal death traps.

No one wants this new war, no sane men anywhere. Yet we are preparing for it and a majority, by recent Gallup polls, believe it will come. We have seen the diplomats and prime ministers and presidents and foreign affairs committees and state departments manage to get things messed up in the past; from where we sit it looks as if they were hell-bent on messing them up again. We hear the rumble of the not-so-distant drum.

What we want, we little men everywhere, is planetary organization so strong that it can enforce peace, forbid national armaments, atomic or otherwise, and in general police the globe so that a decent man can raise his kids and his dog and smoke his pipe free from worry of sudden death. But we see the same old messing around with half measures.

(If you want to help to try to stop the messing-up process, you might write Congressman Jerry Voorhis, or Senator Fulbright, or Senator Ball, or Beardsley Ruml, or Harold Stassen. Or even the President himself.)

If things go from bad to worse and we have to fight a war, can we prepare to win it? First let us try to grasp what kind of a war it will be. Look at LIFE, Nov. 19, 1945, page 27: *THE 36-HOUR WAR: Arnold Report Hints at the Catastrophe of the Next Great Conflict.* The first picture shows Washington, D.C., being destroyed by an atomic rocket bomb. The text and pictures go on to show 13 U.S. cities being destroyed the same way, enemy airborne troops attempting to occupy, the U.S. striking back with its own rockets from underground emplacements, and eventually winning—at a cost of 13 cities and at least 10,000,000 American lives.

Horrible as the picture is, it is much too optimistic. There is no reason at all to assume that the enemy will attack in too little force, destroying only 13 cities, or to assume that he will attempt to occupy until we have surrendered, or to assume that we will be able to strike back after we are attacked.

It is not safe to assume that the enemy will be either faint-hearted or foolish. If he follows our example with Japan, he will smash us until we surrender, then land. If his saboteurs are worth their blood money, our own rocket emplacements may be blown up by concealed atomic bombs just in advance of the attack.

Atomic rocket warfare has still another drawback—it is curiously anonymous. We might think we knew who had attacked us but be entirely mistaken.

You can think of at least three nations which dislike both us and Russia. What better joke for them than to select a time when suspicion has been whipped up between the two giants to lob just a few atomic rockets from a ship in the North Atlantic, or from a secret emplacement in the frozen north of Greenland—half at us, half at Russia, and with the attack in each case apparently coming from the other, and then sit back while we destroyed each other!

A fine joke! You would die laughing.

Don't think it can't be done, to us and to Russia.

What *can* we do?

The first thing is to get Congress to take a realistic view of the situation. The most certain thing about LIFE's description of the coming war was the destruction of Washington. Washington is the prime military target on earth today for it is the center of the nervous system of the nation that now has the Bomb. It must be destroyed first and it will be destroyed, if war ever comes. Your congressman has the most dangerous job in the world today. You may live through World War III—he can't. Make yours realize this; he may straighten up and fly right.

What we want him to work for is world order and world peace. But we may not get it. The other nations may be fed up with our shilly-shallying and may not go along with us, particularly any who believe they are close to solving the problems of atomic weapons. We may have to go it alone. In such cases, is there anything we can do to preserve ourselves?

Yes, probably—but the price is high.

We can try for another Buck Rogers weapon with which to ward off atomic bomb rockets. It would need to be better than anything we have now or can foresee. To be 100% effective (with atom bombs, anything less is hardly good enough!) it should be something which acts with much greater speed than guns or anti-aircraft rockets. There is a bare possibility that science could cook up some sort of a devastatingly powerful beam of energy, acting with the speed of light, which would be a real anti-aircraft weapon, even against rockets. But the scientists don't promise it.

We would need the best anti-aircraft devices possible, in the meantime. A robot hook-up of target-seeking rockets, radar, and computing machines might give considerable protection, if extensive enough, but there is a lot of research and test and production ahead before any such plan is workable. Furthermore, it could not be air tight and it would be very expensive—and very annoying, for it would end civilian aviation. If we hooked the thing up to ignore civilian planes, we would leave ourselves wide open to a Trojan Horse tactic in which the enemy would use ordinary planes to deliver his atomic bombs.

Such a defense, although much more expensive and much more trouble than all our pre-War military establishment, would be needed. If we are not willing to foot the bill, we can at least save money by not buying flame throwers, tanks, or battleships.

We can prepare to attack. We can be so bristlingly savage that other nations may fear to attack us. If we are not to have a super-state and a world police, then the United States needs the fastest and the most long-range rockets, the most powerful atomic blasts, and every other dirty trick conceived in comic strip or fantastic fiction. We must have space ships and we must have them first. We must land on the Moon and take possession of it in order to forbid its use to other nations as a base against us and in order to have it as a base against any enemy of ours. We must set up, duplicate, and reduplicate rocket installations intended to destroy almost automatically any spot on earth; we must let the world know that we have them and that we are prepared to use them at the drop of a diplomat's silk hat. We must be prepared to tell uncooperative nations that there are men sitting in front of switches, day and night, and that an attack on Washington would cause those switches to be thrown.

And we must guard the secrets of the locations and natures of our weapons in a fashion quite impossible for a normal democracy in peace time. More of that later.

Decentralization we would have to have. Not the picayune $250,000,000,000 job which has been proposed—

("Wait a minute! Why should we disperse our cities if we are going to have that Buck Rogers super-dooper death ray screen?")

We haven't *got* such a screen. Nor is it certain that we will ever have such a screen, no matter how much money we spend. Such a screen is simply the one remote possibility which modern physics admits. It may turn out to be impossible to develop it; we simply don't know.

We must disperse thoroughly, so thoroughly that no single concentration of population in the United States is an inviting target. Mr. Sumner Spaulding's timid proposal of a quarter of a trillion dollars was based on the pleasant assumption that Los Angeles was an example of a properly dispersed city for the Atomic Age. This is an incredible piece of optimism which is apparently based on the belief that Hiroshima is the pattern for all future atomic attacks. Hiroshima was destroyed with *one* bomb. Will the enemy grace the city of the Angels with only *one* bomb? Why not a dozen?

The Hiroshima bomb was the gentlest, least destructive atomic bomb ever likely to be loosed. Will the enemy favor us with a love tap such as that?

Within twenty miles of the city hall of Los Angeles lives half the population of the enormous state of California. An atomic bomb dropped on that City Hall would not only blast the swarming center of the city, it would set fire to the surrounding mountains ("WARN-ING! No Smoking, In or Out of Cars—$500 fine and six months imprisonment") from Mount Wilson Observatory to the sea. It would destroy the railroad terminal half a dozen blocks from the City Hall and play hob with the water system, water fetched clear from the State of Arizona.

If that is dispersion, I'll stay in Manhattan.

Los Angeles is a modern miracle, an enormous city kept alive in a desert by a complex and vulnerable concatenation of technical expedients. The first three colonies established there by the Spaniards starved to death to the last man, woman, and child. If the fragile structure of that city were disrupted by a single atomic bomb, those who survived the blast would in a few short days be reduced to a starving, thirst-crazed mob, ready for murder and cannibalism.

No, if we are to defend ourselves we must not assume that Los Angeles is "dispersed" despite the jokes about her far-flung city line. The Angelenos must be relocated from Oregon to Mexico, in the Mojave Desert, in Imperial Valley, in the great central valley, in the Coast Range, and in the High Sierras.

The same principles apply everywhere. Denver must be scattered out toward Laramie and Boulder, while Colorado Springs must flow around Pike's Peak to Cripple Creek. Kansas City and Des Moines must meet at the Iowa-Missouri line, while Joplin flows up toward Kansas City and on down into the Ozarks. As for Manhattan, that is almost too much to describe—from Boston to Baltimore all the great east coast cities must be abandoned and the population scattered like leaves.

The cities must go. Only villages must remain. If we are to rely on dispersion as a defense in the Atomic Age, then we must spread ourselves out so thin that the enemy cannot possibly destroy us with one bingo barrage, so thin that we will be too expensive and too difficult to destroy.

It would be difficult. It would be incredibly difficult and expensive—Mr. Spaulding's estimate would not cover the cost of new housing alone, but new housing would be the least of our problems. We would have to rebuild more than half of our capital plant—shops, warehouses, factories, railroads, highways, power plants, mills, garages, telephone lines, pipe lines, aqueducts, granaries, universities. We would have to take the United States apart and put it back together again according to a new plan and for a new purpose. The financial cost would be unimportant, because we could not buy it, we would have to *do* it, with our own hands, our own sweat. It would mean a sixty-hour week for everyone, no luxury trades, and a bare minimum standard of living for all for some years. Thereafter the standard of living would be permanently depressed, for the new United States would be organized for defense, not for mass production, nor efficient marketing, nor convenient distribution. We would have to pay for our village culture in terms of lowered consumption. Worse, a large chunk of our lowered productivity must go into producing and supporting the atomic engines of war necessary to strike back against an aggressor—for dispersion alone would not protect us from invasion.

If the above picture is too bleak, let us not prate about dispersion. There are only three real alternatives open to us: One, to form a truly sovereign superstate to police the globe; two, to prepare realistically for World War III in which case dispersion, real and thorough dispersion, is utterly necessary, or, third, to sit here, fat, dumb, and happy, wallowing in our luxuries, until the next Hitler annihilates us!

The other necessary consequences of defense by dispersion are even more chilling than the economic disadvantages. If we go it alone and depend on ourselves to defend ourselves we must be prepared permanently to surrender that democratic freedom of action which we habitually enjoyed in peace time. We must resign ourselves to becoming a socialistic, largely authoritarian police state, with freedom of speech, freedom of occupation, and freedom of movement subordinated to military necessity, as defined by those in charge.

Oh, yes! I dislike the prospect quite as much as you do, but I dislike still more the idea of being atomized, or of being served up as a roast by my starving neighbors. Here is what you can expect:

The front door bell rings. Mr. Joseph Public, solid citizen, goes to answer it. He recognizes a neighbor. "Hi, Jack! What takes you out so late?"

"Got some dope for you, Joe. Relocation orders—I was appointed an emergency deputy, you know."

"Hadn't heard, but glad to hear. Come in and sit down and tell me about it. How do the orders read? We stay, don't we?"

"Can't come in—thanks. I've got twenty-three more stops to make tonight. I'm sorry to say you don't stay. Your caravan will rendezvous at Ninth and Chelsea, facing west, and gets underway at noon tomorrow."

"What!"

"That's how it is. Sorry."

"Why, this is a damned outrage! I put in to stay here—with my home town as second choice."

The deputy shrugged. "So did everybody else. But you weren't even on the list of essential occupations from which the permanent residents were selected. Now, look—I've got to hurry. Here are your orders. Limit yourself to 150 pounds of baggage, each, and take food for three days. You are to go in your own car—you're getting a break—and you will be assigned two more passengers by the convoy captain, two more besides your wife I mean."

Joe Public shoved his hands in his pockets and looked stubborn. "I won't be there."

"Now, Joe, don't take that attitude. I admit it's kinda rough, being in the first detachment, but you've had lots of notice. The newspapers have been full of it. It's been six months since the President's proclamation."

"I won't go. There's some mistake. I saw the councilman last week and he said he thought I would be all right. He—"

"He told everybody that, Joe. This is a *Federal* order."

"I don't give a damn if it's from the Angel Gabriel. I tell you I won't go. I'll get an injunction."

"You can't, Joe. This has been declared a military area and protests have to go to the Provost Marshal. I'd hate to tell you what he does with them. Anyhow, you can't stay here—it's no business of mine to put you out; I just have to tell you—but the salvage crews will be here tomorrow morning to pull out your plumbing."

"They won't get in."

"Maybe not. But the straggler squads will go through all of these houses first."

"I'll shoot!"

"I wouldn't advise it. They're mostly ex-Marines."

Mr. Public was quiet for a long minute. Marines. "Look, Jack," he said slowly, "suppose I do go. I've got to have an exemption on this baggage limitation and I can't carry passengers. My office files alone will fill up the back seat."

"You won't need them. You are assigned as an apprentice carpenter. The barracks you are going to are only temporary."

"*Joseph! Joseph!* Don't stand there with the door open! Who is it?" His wife followed her voice in.

He turned to tell her; the deputy took that as a good time to leave.

At eleven the next morning he pulled out of the driveway, gears clashing. He had the white, drawn look of a man who has been up all night. His wife slept beside him, her hysteria drowned in a triple dose of phenobarbital.

That is dispersion. If you don't believe it, ask any native-born citizen of Japanese blood. Nothing less than force and police organization will drive the peasants off the slopes of Vesuvius. The bones of Pompeii and Herculaneum testify to that. Or, ask yourself—will you go willingly and cheerfully to any spot and any occupation the government assigns to you? If not, unless you are right now working frantically to make World War III impossible, you have not yet adjusted yourself to the horrid facts of the Atomic Age.

For these *are* the facts of the Atomic Age. If we are not to have a World State, then we must accept one of two grim alternatives: A permanent state of total war, even in "peace" time, with every effort turned to offense and defense, or relax to our fate, make our peace with God, and wait for death to come out of the sky. The time in which to form a World State is passing rapidly; it may be gone by the time this is printed. It is worthwhile to note that the publisher of the string of newspapers most bitterly opposed to "foreign entanglements," particularly with Russia, and most insistent on us holding on to the vanishing "secret" of the atomic bomb—this man, this publisher, lives on an enormous, self-sufficient ranch, already dispersed. Not for him is the peremptory knock on the door and the uprooting relocation order. Yet he presumes daily to tell our Congress what must be done with us and for us.

Look at the facts! Go to your public library and read the solemn statements of the men who built the atomic bomb. Do not let yourself be seduced into a false serenity by men who do not understand that the old world is dead. Regularly, in the past, our State Department has bungled us into wars and with equal regularity our military establishment has been unprepared for them. Then the lives and the strength of the common people have bought for them a victory.

Now comes a war which cannot be won after such mistakes.

If we are to die, let us die like men, eyes open, aware of our peril and striving to cope with it—not as fat and fatuous fools, smug in the belief that the military men and the diplomats have the whole thing under control.

"It is later than you think."

HOW TO BE A SURVIVOR

The Art of Staying Alive in the Atomic Age

Thought about your life insurance lately?

Wait a minute—sit back down! We don't want to sell you any insurance.

Let's put it another way: How's your pioneer blood these days? Reflexes in fine shape? Muscle tone good? Or do you take a taxi to go six blocks?

How are you at catching rabbits? The old recipe goes, "First, catch the rabbit—" Suppose your supper depended on catching a rabbit? Then on building a fire without matches? Then on cooking it? What kind of shape will you be in after the corner delicatessen is atomized?

When a committee of Senators asked Dr. J. Robert Oppenheimer whether or not a single attack on the United States could kill forty million people, he testified, "I am afraid it is true."

This is not an article about making the atom bomb safe for democracy. This is an article about *you*—and how you can avoid being one of the forty million knocked off in the first attack in World War III. How, if worst comes to worst, you can live through the next war, survive the aftermath, and build a new life.

If you have been reading the newspapers you are aware that World War III, if it ever comes, is expected to start with an all-out surprise attack by long-distance atomic bombing on the cities of America. General Marshall's final report included this assumption, General Arnold has warned us against such an attack, General Spaatz has described it and told us that it is almost impossible to ward it off if it

155

ever comes. Innumerable scientists, especially the boys who built the A-bomb, have warned us of it.

From the newspapers you may also have gathered that world affairs are not in the best of shape—the Balkans, India, Palestine, Iran, Argentina, Spain, China, the East Indies, etc., etc.—and the UNO does not seem as yet to have a stranglehold on all of the problems that could lead to another conflict.

Maybe so, maybe not—time will tell. Maybe we will form a real World State strong enough to control the atom bomb. If you are sure there will never be war again, don't let me waste your time. But if you think it possible that another Hitler or Tojo might get hold of the atomic bomb and want to try his luck, then bend an ear and we'll talk about how you and your kids can live through it. We'll start with the grisly assumption that the war will come fast and hard, when it comes, killing forty million or so at once, destroying the major cities, wrecking most of our industry and utterly disorganizing the rest. We will assume a complete breakdown of government and communication which will throw the survivors—that's you, chum!—on their own as completely as ever was Dan'l Boone.

No government—remember that. The United States will cease to be a fact except in the historical sense. You will be on your own, with no one to tell you what to do and no policeman on the corner to turn to for protection. And you will be surrounded with dangerous carnivores, worse than the grizzlies Daniel Boone tackled—the two-legged kind.

Perhaps we had better justify the assumption of complete breakdown in government. It might not happen, but, if the new Hitler has sense enough to write *Mein Kampf*, or even to read it as a textbook, he will do his very best to destroy and demoralize us by destroying our government—and his best could be quite efficient. If he wants to achieve political breakdown in his victim, Washington, D.C., will be his prime target, the forty-eight state capitals his secondary targets, and communication centers such as Kansas City his tertiary targets. The results should be roughly comparable to the effect on a man's organization when his head is chopped off.

Therefore, in this bad dream we are having, let us assume no government, no orders from Washington, no fireside chats, no reassurances. You won't be able to write to your congressman, because he, poor devil!, is marked for the kill. You can live through it, he can't. He will be radioactive dust. His profession is so hazardous that there is no need for him to study up on how to snare rabbits.

But *you* should—if you are smart, you can live through it.

Now as to methods—there is just one known way to avoid being killed by an atomic bomb. The formula is very simple:

Don't be there when it goes off!

Survival methods in the atomic age can be divided into two headings, strategical and tactical. The first or strategical aspect is entirely concerned with how not to be where the bomb is; the second, tactical part has to do with how to keep yourself and your family alive if you live through the destruction of the cities and the government.

Strategy first—the simplest way to insure long life for yourself and family is to move to Honduras or some other small and nonindustrialized country, establish yourself there, and quit worrying. It is most unlikely that such places will be subjected to atomic bombardment; if war comes, they will move into the economic and political sphere of the winner, to be sure, but probably without bloodshed, since resistance would be so obviously futile.

However, you probably cannot afford, or feel that you can't afford, any move as drastic as that. (Whether or not you can in truth afford it is a moot point, to be settled by your own notion of the degree of danger. The pre-War refugees from Nazi Germany could not "afford" to flee, either, but events proved the wisdom of doing so. There is an old Chinese adage, "In the course of a long life a wise man will be prepared to abandon his baggage several times." It has never been more true than it is today.)

There are several moves open to you which are less drastic. If you live on a farm or in a small village, several miles—fifty is a good figure—from the nearest large city, rail junction, power dam, auto factory, or other likely military target, strategy largely takes care of itself. If you are blasted, it will probably be an accident, a rocket gone wild, or something equally unforeseeable. If you are not in such a location, you had better make some plans.

Just a moment—a gentleman in the back row has a question. A little louder please. He asks, "Isn't it true that the government is planning to disperse the cities so we will be safe from atomic bombs?"

I don't know—is it? The only figure I have heard mentioned so far is $250,000,000,000. Quite aside from the question of whether or not large scale dispersion can be made effective, there is still the question as to whether or not Congress would appropriate a quarter of a trillion dollars in peacetime for any purpose. That is a political question, beyond the scope of this discussion. We are concerned here with how you, unassisted, with your two hands, your brain, and your ability to plan ahead, can keep yourself alive during and after any possible Next War.

If you have to live in a large city or other target area, your strategical planning has to be a good bit more detailed, alert, and shifty. You need an emergency home, perhaps an abandoned farm picked up cheaply or a cabin built on government land. What it is depends on the part of the country you live in and how much money you can put into it, but it should be chosen with a view to the possibilities it offers of eating off the country—fish, game, garden plot—and it should be near enough for you to reach it on one tank of gasoline. If the tank in your car is too small, have a special one built, or keep enough cans of reserve permanently in the trunk of your car. Your car should also be equipped with a survival kit, but that comes under tactics.

Having selected and equipped your emergency base, you must then, if you are to live in a target area, keep your ear to the ground and your eyes open with respect to world affairs. *There will be no time to get out after rockets are launched.* You will have to outguess events. This is a tricky assignment at best and is the principal reason why it is much better to live in the country in the first place, but you stand a fair chance of accomplishing it if you do not insist on being blindly optimistic and can overcome a natural reluctance to make a clean break with your past—business, home, clubs, friends, church—when it becomes evident that the storm clouds are gathering. Despite the tragic debacle at Pearl Harbor, quite a number of people, laymen among them, knew that a war with Japan was coming. If you think you can learn to spot the signs of trouble long enough in advance to jump, you may get away with living on the spot with the X mark.

Let us suppose that you were quick-witted, far sighted, and fast on your feet; you brought yourself and your family safely through the bombing and have them somewhere out in the country, away from the radioactive areas that were targets a short time before. The countryside is swarming with survivors from the edges of the bombed areas, survivors who are hungry, desperate, some of them armed, all of them free of the civilizing restrictions of organized living. Enemy troops, moving in to occupy, may already be present or may be dropping in from the skies any day.

How, on that day, will you feed and protect yourself and your family?

The tactical preparations for survival after the debacle fall mainly into three groups. First is the overhaul of your own bodily assets, which includes everything from joining the YMCA, to get rid of that paunch and increase your wind and endurance, to such things as getting typhoid and cholera shots, having that appendix out, and keeping your teeth in the best shape possible. If you wear glasses, you will need several pairs against the day when there will be no opticians in practice. Second is the acquisition of various materials and tools which you will be unable to make or grow in a sudden, synthetic stone age—items such as a pickax or a burning glass, for example, will be worth considerably more than two college degrees or a diamond bracelet. Third is training in various fundamental pioneer skills, not only how to snare and cook rabbits, but such things as where and when to plant potatoes, how to tell edible fungi from deadly toadstools without trying them on Junior, and how to walk silently.

All these things are necessary, but more important, much more important, is the acquiring of a survival point of view, the spiritual orientation which will enable you to face hardship, danger, cold, and hunger without losing your zest and courage and sense of humor. If you think it is going to be too hard to be worthwhile, if you can't face the prospect of coming back to the ruins of your cabin, burned down by drunken looters, other than with the quiet determination to build another, then don't bother to start. Move to a target area and wait for the end. It does not take any special courage or skill to accept the death that moves like lightning. You won't even have the long walk the steers have to make to get from the stockyard pens to the slaughterhouse.

But if your ancestors still move in your bones, you will know that it is worthwhile, just as they did. "The cowards never started and the weaklings died on the way." That was the spirit that crossed the plains, and such was the spirit of every emigrant who left Europe. There is good blood in your veins, *compadre!*

It is not possible to tell exactly what to do to prepare yourself best to survive, even if this were a book instead of a short article, for the details must depend on the nature of the countryside you must rely on, your opportunities for planning and preparing, the numbers, ages and sex of your dependents if any, your present skills, talents, and physical condition, and whether or not you are at present dispersed from target areas or must plan for such dispersal. But the principles under which you can make your plans and the easiest means by which to determine them can be indicated.

Start out by borrowing your son's copy of the *Boy Scout Manual.* It is a practical book of the sort of lore you will need. If you can't borrow it because he is not a member of the Scouts, send him down at once and make him join up. Then make him study. Get him busy on those merit badges—woodcraft, cooking, archery, carpentry. *Somebody* is going to have to make that fire without matches, if that rabbit is ever to be cooked and eaten. See to it that he learns how, from experts. Then make him teach you.

Can you fell a tree? Can you trim a stone? Do you know where to dig a cesspool? Where and how to dig a well? Can you pull a tooth? Can you shoot a rifle accurately and economically? Can you spot tularemia (we are back to that ubiquitous rabbit again!) in cleaning a rabbit? Do you know the rudiments of farming? Given simple tools, could you build a log, or adobe, or rammed-earth, or native-stone cabin from materials at hand and have it be weather-tight, varmint-proof, and reasonably comfortable?

You can't learn all the basic manual trades in your spare time in a limited number of years but you can acquire a jackleg but adequate knowledge of the more important ones, in the time we have left.

But how much time have we?

All we can do is estimate. How long will it be before other nations have the atomic bomb? Nobody knows—one estimate from the men who made it was "two to five years." Dr. Vannevar Bush spoke of "five to fifteen years" while another expert, equally distinguished, mentioned "five or ten years." Major General Leslie Groves, the atom general, thinks it will be a long time.

Let us settle on five years as a reasonable minimum working time. Of course, even if another nation, unfriendly to us, solved the production problems of atomic weapons in that length of time, there still might not be a war for a number of years, nor would there necessarily ever be one. However, since we don't know what world conditions will be like in five years, let's play it safe; let's try to be ready for it by 1950.

Four or five years is none too long to turn a specialized, soft, city dweller into a generalized, hardened pioneer. However, it is likely that you will find that you are enjoying it. It will be an interesting business and there is a deep satisfaction in learning how to do things with your own hands.

First get that *Scout Manual.* Look over that list of merit badges. Try to figure out what skills you are likely to need, what ones you now have, and what ones you need to study up on. The Manual will lead you in time to other books. Ernest Thompson Seton's *Two Little Savages* is full of ideas and suggestions.

Presently you will find that there are handbooks of various trades you have not time to master; books which contain information you could look up in an emergency if you have had the forethought to buy the book and hide it away in your out-of-town base. There are books which show how to build fireplaces, giving the exact dimensions of reflector, throat, ledge, and flue. You may not remember such details; being able to look them up may save you from a winter in a smoke-filled cabin. If there is any greater domestic curse than a smoking fireplace, I can't recall it, unless it be the common cold.

There are little handbooks which show, in colored pictures, the edible mushrooms and their inedible cousins. It is possible to live quite well on practically nothing but fungi, with comparatively little work; they exist in such abundance and variety.

You will need a medical reference book, selected with the advice of a wise and imaginative medical man. Tell him why you want it. Besides that, the best first-aid and nursing instruction you can get will not be too much. Before you are through with this subject you will find yourself selecting drugs, equipment, and supplies to be stored against the darkness, in your base as well as a lesser supply to go into the survival kit you keep in your automobile.

What goes into that survival kit, anyhow? You will have to decide; you won't take any present advice in any case. By the time you get to it you will think, quite correctly, that you are the best judge. But the contents of the survival kits supplied our aviators in this latest war will be very illuminating. The contents varied greatly, depending on climate and nature of mission—from pemmican to quinine, fish hooks to maps.

What to put in your cabin is still more difficult to state definitely. To start with, you might obtain a Sears Roebuck or Montgomery Ward catalog and go through it, item by item. Ask yourself "Do I have to have this?" then from the list that produces ask yourself "Could I make this item, or a substitute, in a pinch?"

If shoes wear out, it is possible to make moccasins—although shoes should be hoarded in preference to any other item of clothing. But you can't—unless you are Superman—make an ax. You will need an ax.

You will need certain drugs. Better be liberal here.

Salt is difficult to obtain, inland.

It is difficult to reject the idea of hoarding canned goods. A few hundred dollars worth, carefully selected, could supplement the diet of your family to the point of luxury for several years. It might save you from starvation, or the cannibalism that shamed the Donner Party, during your first winter of the Dark Ages, and it could certainly alleviate some of the sugar hunger you are sure to feel under most primitive conditions. But it is a very great risk to have canned goods. If you have them, you will be one of the hated rich if anybody finds out about them. We are assuming that there will be no government to protect you. To have canned goods—and have it known by anyone outside your own household—is to invite assassination. If you do not believe that a man will commit murder for one can of tomatoes, then you have never been hungry.

If you have canned goods, open them when the windows are shuttered and bury the cans. Resist the temptation to advertise your wealth by using the empty tins as receptacles.

Don't forget a can opener—two can openers.

You will have a rifle, high-powered and with telescopic sights, but you won't use it much. Cartridges are nearly irreplaceable. A deer or a man should be about the limit of the list of your targets … a deer when you need meat; a man when hiding or running is not enough.

That brings us to another subject and the most interesting of all. We have not talked much about the enemy, have we? And yet he was there, from the start. It was his atom bombs which reduced you to living off the country and performing your own amputations and accouchements. If you have laid your plans carefully, you won't see much of him for quite a while; this is a very, very big country. Where you are hidden out there never were very many people at any time; the chances of occupation forces combing all of the valleys, canyons, and hills of our back country in less than several years is negligible. It is entirely conceivable that an enemy could conquer or destroy our country, as a state, in twenty minutes, with atom bomb and rocket. Yet, when his occupation forces move in, they will be almost lost in this great continent. He may not find you for years.

There is your chance. It has been proved time and again, by the Fighting French, the recalcitrant Irish, the deathless Poles, yes and by our own Apache and Yaqui Indians, that you cannot conquer a free man; you can only kill him.

After the immediate problems of the belly, comes the Underground!

You'll need your rifle. You will need knives. You will need dynamite and fuses. You will need to know how to turn them into grenades. You must learn how to harry the enemy in the dark, how to turn his conquest into a mockery, too expensive to exploit. Oh, it can be done, it can be done! Once he *occupies*, his temporary advantage of the surprise attack with the atom bomb is over, for once his troops are scattered among you, *he cannot use the atom bomb.*

Then is your day. Then is the time for the neighborhood cell, the mountain hideout, the blow in the night. Yes, and then is the time for the martyr to freedom, the men and women who die painfully, with sealed lips.

Can we then win our freedom back? There is no way of telling. History has some strange quirks. It was a conflict between England and France that gave us our freedom in the first place. A quarrel in enemy high places, a young hopeful feeling his oats and anxious to displace the original dictator, might give us unexpected opportunity, opportunity we could exploit if we were ready.

There are ways to study for that day, too. There are books, many of them, which you may read to learn how other people have done it. One such book is Tom Wintringham's *New Ways of War.* It is almost a blueprint of what to do to make an invader wish he had stayed at home. It is available in a 25-cent Penguin-Infantry Journal edition. You can study up and become quite deadly, even though 4-F, or fifty.

If you plan for it, you can survive. If you study and plan and are ready to organize when the time comes, you can hope not only to survive but to play a part in winning back lost freedoms. General George Washington once quoted Scripture to describe what we were fighting for then—a time when "everyone shall sit in safety under his own vine and figtree, and none shall make him afraid!"

It is worth planning for.

PIE FROM THE SKY

Since we have every reason to expect a sudden rain of death from the sky sometime in the next few years, as a result of a happy combination of the science of atomics and the art of rocketry, it behooves the Pollyanna Philosopher to add up the advantages to be derived from the blasting of your apartment, row house, or suburban cottage.

It ain't all bad, chum. While you are squatting in front of your cave, trying to roast a rabbit with one hand while scratching your lice-infested hide with the other, there will be many cheerful things to think about, the assets of destruction, rather than torturing your mind with thoughts of the good old, easy days of taxis and tabloids and Charlie's Bar & Grill.

There are so many, many things in this so-termed civilization of ours which would be mightily improved by a once over lightly of the Hiroshima treatment. There is that dame upstairs, for instance, the one with the square bowling ball. Never again would she take it out for practice right over your bed at three in the morning. Isn't that some consolation?

No more soap operas. No more six minutes of good old Mom facing things bravely, interspersed with eight minutes of insistent, syrupy plugging for commercial junk you don't want and would be better off without. Never again will you have to wait breathlessly for "same time, same station" to find out what beautiful Mamie Jukes, that priceless moron, does about her nameless babe. She will be gone, along with the literary prostitute who brought her into being.

No more alarm clocks. *No more alarm clocks!* No more of the frenzied keeping of schedules, appointments, and deadlines that they imply. You won't have to gulp your coffee to run for the 8:19 commuters' special, nor keep your eye on the clock while you lunch. A few of the handy little plutonium pills dropped from the sky will end the senseless process of running for the bus to go to work to make the money to buy the food to get the strength to run for the bus. You will swap the pressure of minutes for the slow tide of eternity.

But best of all, you will be freed of the plague of the alarm that yanks you from the precious nirvana of sleep and sets you on your weary feet, with every nerve screaming protest. If you are snapped suddenly out of sleep in the Atomic Stone Age, it will be a mountain lion, a wolf, a man, or some other carnivore, not a mechanical monstrosity.

Westbrook Pegler will no longer exhibit to you his latest hate, nor will Lolly Parsons stuff you with her current girlish enthusiasm. (If your pet dislikes among the columnists are not these two, fill in names to suit yourself; none of them will bother you after the fission treatment.)

In fact, all the impact of world-wide troubles will fade away. Divorces, murders, and troubles in China will no longer smite from headline and radio. Your only worries will be your own worries.

No more John L. Lewis.

No more jurisdictional strikes.

No more "Hate-Roosevelt" clubs.

No more "Let's-Hate-Eleanor,-Too" clubs.

No more Petrillo.

No more damn fools who honk right behind your car while the lights are changing. I'll buy this one at a black market price right now.

No more Gerald L. K. Smith. ... and, conversely, no more people who think that the persecution of their particular minority is the only evil in the entire world worth talking about, or working to correct.

No more phony "days." You won't have to buy a red carnation to show that Mom is alive nor a white one to show that she's not. (It's even money that you will have lost track of her in the debacle and not know whether she is alive or dead.) No more "Boy's Day" in our city governments with pre-adolescent little stinkers handing out fines and puritanical speeches to tired street walkers while the elected judge smiles blandly for the photographers. No more "Eat More Citrus Fruit" or "Eat More Chocolate Candy" or "Read More Comic Books" weeks thought up by the advertising agents of industries.

While we are on the subject of phony buildups, let's give a cheer for the elimination of debutantes with press agents, for the blotting out of "cafe" society, for the consignment to oblivion of the whole notion of the "coming-out" party. The resumption of the coming-out party in the United States, with its attendant, incredibly callous, waste, at the very time that Europe starves, is a scandal to the jay birds. A few atom bombs would be no more than healthy fumigation of this imbecilic evil.

No more toothsome mammals built up by synthetic publicity into movie "stars" before they have played a part in a picture. This is probably a relatively harmless piece of idiocy in our whipped-cream culture, but the end of it, via A-bombs, may stop Sarah Bernhardt from spinning in her grave.

No more over-fed, under-worked, rapacious female tyrants. I won't say "mothers-in-law"; your mother-in-law may be a pretty good Joe. If not, you may have a chance to cut her up for steak.

There is actually nothing to prevent American women from being able, adult, useful citizens, and many of them are. But our society is so rigged that a worthless female can make a racket of it—but not after a brisk one-two with uranium! The parasites will starve when that day comes, from the cheerful idiots of the Helen Hokinson cartoons to the female dinosaurs who use sacrosanct sex as a club to bullyrag, blackmail, and dominate every man they can reach.

The parasite males will die out, too. Yes, pal, if you can manage to zig while the atomic rockets zag you will find society much changed and in many respects improved.

There are a lot of other minor advantages you should get firmly in mind now, lest you fall prey to a fatal nostalgia after this great, fantastic, incredible, somewhat glorious and very fragile technological culture crashes about your ears. Subway smell, for example. The guy who coughs on the back of your neck in the theater. Men who bawl out waitresses. The woman who crowds in ahead of you at the counter. The person who asks how much you paid for it. The preacher with the unctuous voice and the cash register heart. The millionairess who wills her money to found a home for orphan guppies. The lunkhead who dials a wrong number (your number) in the middle of the night and then is sore at you for not being the party he wanted. The sportsman who turns his radio up loud so that he can boo the Dodgers while out in his garden. The Dodgers. People who don't curb their dogs. People who spit on sidewalks. People who censor plays and suppress books. Breach-of-promise suits. People who stare at wounded veterans.

A blinding flash, a pillar of radioactive dust, and all this will be gone.

I don't mean to suggest that it will all be fun. Keeping alive after our cities have been smashed and our government disintegrated will be a grim business at best, as the survivors in central Europe could tell you. In spite of the endless list that could be made of the things we are better off without I do not think it will be very much fun to scrabble around in the woods for a bite to eat. For that reason I am thinking of liquidating, in advance, the next character who says to me, "Well, what difference does it make if we are atom-bombed—you gotta die sometime!"

I shall shoot him dead, blow through the barrel, and say, "You asked for it, chum."

Conceding that we will all die some day, is that a reason why I should let this grinning ape drag me along toward disaster just because he will take no thought of tomorrow?

Since there are so many of him the chances of us, as a nation, being able to avert disaster are not good. Perhaps some of us could form an association to live through World War III. Call it the *League for the Preservation of the Human Race*, or the *Doom's Day Men*, or something like that. Restrict the membership to survivor types, sound in tooth and wind, trained in useful trades or science, reasonably high I.Q.'s and proved fertility. Then set up two or three colonies remote from cities and other military targets.

It might work.

Maybe I will start it myself if I can find an angel to put up the dough for the original promotion. That should get me in as an *ex-*

officio member, I hope. I have looked over my own qualifications and I don't seem to measure up to the standards.

My ancestors got into America by a similar dodge. They got here early, when the immigration restrictions were pretty lax. Maybe I can repeat.

I am sure I shall not resign myself to death simply because Joe Chucklehead points out that atomization is quick and easy. Even if that were good I would not like it. Furthermore, it is not true. Death comes fast at the center of the blast; around the edges is a big area of the fatal burn and the slow death, with plenty of time to reconsider the disadvantages of chuckleheadness in the Atomic Age, before your flesh sloughs off and you give up the ghost. No, thank you, I plan to disperse myself to the country.

Of course, if you are so soft that you *like* inner-spring mattresses and clean water and regular meals, despite the numerous advantages of blowing us off the map, but are not too soft to try to do something to avoid the coming debacle, there is something you can do about it, other than forming Survival Leagues or cultivating an attitude of philosophical resignation.

If you really want to hang on to the advantages of our slightly wacky pseudo-civilization, there is just one way to do it, according to the scientists who know the most about the new techniques of war—and that is to form a sovereign world authority to prevent the Atomic War.

Run, do not walk, to the nearest Western Union, and telegraph your congressman to get off the dime and get on with the difficult business of forming an honest-to-goodness world union, with no jokers about Big Five vetoes or national armaments … to get on with it promptly, while there is still time, before Washington, D.C., is reduced to radioactive dust—and he with it, poor devil!

FOREWORD

While I was failing at World-Saving, I was beginning to achieve my second objective: to spread out, not limit myself to pulp science fiction. "They Do It With Mirrors" was my first attempt in the crime-mystery field, and from it I learned three things: a) whodunits are fairly easy to write and easy to sell; b) I was no threat to Raymond Chandler or Rex Stout as the genre *didn't interest me that much; and c) Crime Does Not Pay—Enough (the motto of the Mystery Writers of America).*

It may amuse you to know that this story was considered to be (in 1945) too risqué; the magazine editor laundered it before publication. You are seeing the original "dirty" version; try to find in it anything at all that *could bring a blush to the cheek of your maiden aunt.*

In late 1945 this magic mirror existed in a bar at (as I recall) the corner of Hollywood and Gower Gulch; the rest is fiction.

THEY DO IT WITH MIRRORS

An Edison Hill Crime Case

was there to see beautiful naked women. So was everybody else. It's a common failing.

I climbed on a stool at the end of the bar in Jack Joy's Joint and spoke to Jack himself, who was busy setting up two old-fashioneds. "Make it three," I said. "No, make it four and have one with me. What's the pitch, Jack? I hear you set up a peep show for the suckers."

"Hi, Ed. Nope, it's not a peep show—it's Art."

"What's the difference?"

"If they hold still, it's Art. If they wiggle around, it's illegal. That's the ruling. Here." He handed me a program.

It read:

THE JOY CLUB
PRESENTS

The Magic Mirror

Beautiful Models in a series of Entertaining and Artistic Pageants

10 p.m.	"Aphrodite"	Estelle
11 p.m.	"Sacrifice to the Sun"	Estelle and Hazel
12 p.m.	"The High Priestess"	Hazel
1 a.m.	"The Altar Victim"	Estelle
2 a.m.	"Invocation to Pan"	Estelle and Hazel

(Guests are requested to refrain stomping, whistling, or otherwise disturbing the artistic serenity of the presentations)

The last was a giggle. Jack's place was strictly a joint. But on the other side of the program I saw a new schedule of prices which informed me that the drink in my hand was going to cost me just twice what I had figured. And the place was jammed. By suckers—including me.

I was about to speak to Jack, in a kindly way, promising to keep my eyes closed during the show and then pay the old price for my drink, when I heard two sharp *beeps!*—a high tension buzzer sound, like radio code—from a spot back of the bar. Jack turned away from me, explaining, "That's the eleven o'clock show." He busied himself underneath the bar.

Being at the end of the bar I could see under the long side somewhat. He had enough electrical gear there to make a happy Christmas for a Boy Scout—switches, a rheostat dingus, a turntable for recordings, and a hand microphone. I leaned over and sized it up. I have a weakness for gadgets, from my old man. He named me Thomas Alva Edison Hill in hopes that I would emulate his idol. I disappointed him—I didn't invent the atom bomb, but I do sometimes try to repair my own typewriter.

Jack flipped a switch and picked up the hand mike. His voice came out of the juke box: "We now present the Magic Mirror." Then the turntable picked up with *Hymn to the Sun* from *Coq d'Or*, and he started turning the rheostat slowly.

The lights went down in the joint and came up slowly in the Magic Mirror. The "Mirror" was actually a sheet of glass about ten feet wide and eight high which shut off a little balcony stage. When the house lights were on bright and the stage was dark, you could not see through the glass at all; it looked like a mirror. As the house lights went out and the stage lights came on, you could see through the glass and a picture slowly built up in the "Mirror."

Jack had a single bright light under the bar which lighted him and the controls and which did not go out with the house lights. Because of my position at the end of the bar it hit me square in the eye. I had to block it with my hand to see the stage.

It was something to see.

Two girls, a blonde and a brunette. A sort of altar or table, with the blonde sprawled across it, volup'. The brunette standing at the end of the altar, grabbing the blonde by the hair with one hand while holding a fancy dagger upraised with the other. There was a backdrop in gold and dark blue—a sunburst in a phony Aztec or Egyptian design, but nobody was looking at it; they were looking at the girls.

The brunette was wearing a high show-girl head dress, silver sandals, and a G-string in glass jewels. Nothing more. No sign of a brassiere. The blonde was naked as an oyster, with her downstage knee drawn up just enough to get past sufficiently broad-minded censors.

But I was not looking at the naked blonde; I was looking at the brunette.

It was not just the two fine upstanding breasts nor the long graceful legs nor the shape of her hips and thighs; it was the overall effect. She was so beautiful it hurt. I heard somebody say, "Great jumping jeepers!" and was about to shush him when I realized it was me.

Then the lights went down and I remembered to breathe.

I paid the clip price for my drink without a quiver and Jack assured me: "They are hostesses between shows." When they showed up at the stairway leading down from the balcony he signalled them to come over and then introduced me.

"Hazel Dorn, Estelle d'Arcy—meet Eddie Hill."

Hazel, the brunette, said, "How do you do?" but the blonde said,

"Oh, I've met the Ghost before. How's business? Rattled any chains lately?"

I said, "Good enough," and let it pass. I knew her all right—but as Audrey Johnson, not as Estelle d'Arcy. She had been a steno at the City Hall when I was doing an autobiography of the Chief of Police. I had not liked her much; she had an instinct for finding a sore point and picking at it.

I am not ashamed of being a ghost writer, nor is it a secret. You will find my name on the title page of *Forty Years a Cop* as well as the name of the Chief—in small print but it is there: "with Edison Hill."

"How did you like the show?" Hazel asked, when I had ordered a round.

"I liked *you*," I said, softly enough to keep it private. "I can't wait for the next show to see more of you."

"You'll see more," she admitted and changed the subject. I gathered an impression that she was proud of her figure and liked to be told she was beautiful but was not entirely calloused about exhibiting it in public.

Estelle leaned across the bar to Jack. "Jackie Boy," she said in sweetly reasonable tones, "you held the lights too long again. It doesn't matter to me in that pose, but you had poor old Hazel trembling like a leaf before you doused the glim."

Jack set a three-minute egg timer, like a little hourglass on the bar. "Three minutes it says—three minutes you did."

"I don't think it was more than three minutes," Hazel objected. "I wasn't tired."

"You were trembling, dear. I saw you. You mustn't tire yourself—it makes lines. Anyhow," she added, "I'll just keep this," and she put the egg timer in her purse. "We'll time it ourselves."

"It was three minutes," Jack insisted.

"Never mind," she answered. "From now on it'll be three minutes, or mamma will have to lock Jackie in the dark closet."

Jack started to answer, thought better of it, then walked away to the other end of the bar. Estelle shrugged, then threw down the rest of her drink and left us. I saw her speak to Jack again, then join some customers at one of the tables.

Hazel looked at her as she walked away. "I'd paddle that chippie's pants," she muttered, "if she wore any."

"A bum beef?"

"Not exactly. Maybe Jack is a friend of yours—"

"Just an acquaintance."

"Well ... I've had worse bosses—but he is a bit of a jerk. Maybe he doesn't stretch the poses just out of meanness—I've never timed him—but some of those poses are too long for three minutes. Take Estelle's Aphrodite pose—you saw it?"

"No."

"She balances on the ball of one foot, no costume at all, but with one leg raised enough to furnish a fig leaf. Jack's got a blackout switch to cover her if she breaks, but, just the same, it's a strain."

"To cover himself with the cops, you mean."

"Well, yes. Jack wants us to make it just as strong as the vice squad will stand for."

"You ought not to be in a dive like this. You ought to have a movie contract."

She laughed without mirth. "Eddie, did you ever try to get a movie contract? I've tried."

"Just the same—oh, well! But why are you sore at Estelle? What you told me doesn't seem to cover it."

"She—skip it. She probably means well."

"You mean she shouldn't have dragged you into it?"

"Partly."

"What else?"

"Oh, nothing—look, do you think I need any wrinkle remover?" I examined her quite closely, until she actually blushed a little, then assured her that she did not.

"Thanks," she said. "Estelle evidently thinks so. She's been advising me to take care of myself lately and has been bringing me little presents of beauty preparations. I thank her for them and it appears to be sheer friendliness on her part … but it makes me squirm."

I nodded and changed the subject. I did not want to talk about Estelle; I wanted to talk about *her*—and me. I mentioned an agent I knew (my own) who could help her and that got her really interested, if not in me, at least in what I was saying.

Presently she glanced at the clock back of the bar and squealed. "I've got to peel for the customers. 'Bye now!" It was five minutes to twelve. I shifted from the end of the bar to the long side, just opposite Jack's Magic Mirror controls. I did not want that bright light of his interfering with me seeing Hazel.

It was just about twelve straight up when Jack came up from the rear of the joint, elbowed his other barman out of the way, and took his place near the controls. "Just about that time," he said to me. "Has she rung the buzzer?"

"Not a buzz."

"Okay, then." He cleared dirty glasses off the top of the bar while we waited, changed the platter on the turntable, and generally messed around. I kept my eyes on the mirror.

I heard the two *beeps!* sharp and clear. When he did not announce the show at once, I glanced around and saw that, while he had the mike in his hand, he was staring past it at the door, and looking considerably upset.

There were two cops just inside the door, Hannegan and Feinstein, both off the beat. I supposed he was afraid of a raid, which was silly. Pavement pounders don't pull raids. I knew what they were there for, even before Hannegan gave Jack a broad grin and waved him the okay sign—they had just slipped in for a free gander at the flesh under the excuse of watching the public morals.

"We now present the Magic Mirror," said Jack's voice out of the juke box. Somebody climbed on the stool beside me and slipped a hand under my arm. I looked around. It was Hazel.

"You're not here; you're up there," I said foolishly.

"Huh-uh. Estelle said—I'll tell you after the show."

The lights were coming up in the Mirror and the juke box was cranking out *Valse Triste*. The altar was in this scene, too, and Estelle was sprawled over it much as she had been before. As it got lighter you could see a red stain down her side and the prop dagger. Hazel had told me what each of the acts were; this was the one called "The Altar Victim," scheduled for the one o'clock show.

I was disappointed not to be seeing Hazel, but I had to admit it was good—good theater, of the nasty sort, sadism and sex combined. The red stuff—catsup I guessed—trickling down her bare side and the handle of the prop dagger sticking up as if she had been stabbed through—the customers liked it. It was a natural follow-up to the "Sacrifice to the Sun."

Hazel screamed in my ear.

Her first scream was solo. The next thing I can recall it seemed as if every woman in the place was screaming—soprano, alto, and some tenor, but mostly screeching soprano. Through it came the bull voice of Hannegan. "Keep your seats, folks! Somebody turn on the lights!"

I grabbed Hazel by the shoulders and shook her. "What's the matter? What's up?"

She looked dazed, then pointed at the Mirror. "She's dead ... she's dead ... she's dead!" she chanted. She scrambled down from the stool and took out for the back of the house. I started after her. The house lights came on abruptly, leaving the Mirror lights still on.

We finished one, two, three, up the stairway, through a little dressing room, and onto the stage. I almost caught up with Hazel, and Feinstein was close on my heels.

We stood there, jammed in the door, blinking at the flood lights, and not liking what we saw under them. She was dead all right. The dagger, which should have been faked between her arm and her breast with catsup spilled around to maintain the illusion—this prop dagger, this slender steel blade, was three inches closer to her breastbone than it should have been. It had been stabbed straight into her heart.

On the floor at the side of the altar away from the audience, close enough to Estelle to reach it, was the egg timer. As I looked at it the last of the sand ran out.

I caught Hazel as she fell—she was a big armful—and spread her on the couch. "Eddie," said Feinstein, "call the Station for me. Tell Hannegan not to let anyone out. I'm staying here." I called the station but did not have to tell Hannegan anything. He had them all seated again and was jollying them along. Jack was still standing back of the bar, shock on his face, and the bright light at the control board making him look like a death's head.

By twelve-fifteen Spade Jones, Lieutenant Jones of Homicide, showed up and from there on things slipped into a smooth routine. He knew me well, having helped me work up some of the book I did for the Chief, and he grabbed onto me at once for some of the background. By twelve-thirty he was reasonably sure that none of the customers could have done it. "I won't say one of them *didn't* do it, Eddie my boy—anybody could have done it who knew the exact second to slip upstairs, grab the knife, and slide it into her ribs. But the chances are against any of them knowing just when and how to do it."

"Anybody inside or outside," I corrected.

"So?"

"There's a fire exit at the foot of the stairs."

"You think I haven't noticed that?" He turned away and gave Hannegan instructions to let anybody go who could give satisfactory identification with a local address. The others would have to go downtown to have closer ties as material witnesses put on them by the night court. Perhaps some would land in the tank for further investigation, but in any case—clear 'em out!

The photographers were busy upstairs and so were the fingerprint boys. The Assistant Medical Examiner showed up, followed by reporters. A few minutes later, after the house was cleared, Hazel came downstairs and joined me. Neither of us said anything, but I patted her on the back. When they carried down the basket stretcher a little later, with a blanket-wrapped shape in it, I put my arm around her while she buried her eyes in my shoulders.

Spade talked to us one at a time. Jack was not talking. "It ain't smart to talk without a lawyer," was all Spade could get out of him. I thought to myself that it would be better to talk to Spade now than to be sweated and maybe massaged a little under the lights. My testimony would clear him even though it would show that there was a spat between him and Estelle. Spade would not frame a man. He was an honest cop, as cops go. I've known honest cops. Two, I think.

Spade took my story, then he took Hazel's, and called me back. "Eddie my boy," he said, "help me dig into this thing. As I understand it, this girl Hazel should have had the twelve o'clock show."

"That's right."

He studied one of the Joy Club's programs. "Hazel says she went upstairs to undress for the show about eleven-fifty-five."

"Exactly that time."

"Yeah. She was with you, wasn't she? She says she went up and that Estelle followed her in with a song-and-dance that the boss said to swap the two shows around."

"I wouldn't know about that."

"Naturally not. She says she beefed a little but gave in and came on downstairs, where she joined you. Correct?"

"Correct."

"Mmmm ... By the way, your remark about the fire door might lead to something. Hazel put me onto a boy friend for Estelle. Trumpeter in that rat race across the street. He could have ducked across and stabbed her. Wouldn't take long. Trumpet players can't be pushing wind all the time; they'd lose their lip."

"How would he know when to do it? It was supposed to be Hazel's show."

"Mmmm ... Well, maybe he did know. Swapping shows sounds like Estelle had made a date, and that sounds like a man. In which case he'd know about it. One of the boys is looking into it. Now about the way these shows worked—do you suppose you could show me how they were staged? Hannegan tried it but all he got was a shock."

"I'll try it," I said, getting up. "It's nothing very fancy. Did you ask Jack about Hazel's statement that Estelle had permission from him to swap the shows?"

"That's the one thing he cracked on. He states flatly that he didn't know that the shows were swapped. He says he expected to see Hazel in the Mirror."

The controls looked complicated but weren't. I showed Jones the rheostat and told him it enabled Jack to turn either set of lights down slowly while the other set went up. I found a bypass switch back of the rheostat which accounted for the present condition—all lights burning brightly, house and stage. There was a blackout switch and there was a switch that cut the hand microphone and the turntable in through the juke box. Near the latter was the buzzer—a small black case with two binding posts—which the girls used to signal Jack. Centered on the under side of the bar was a hundred-and-fifty watt bulb hooked in on its own line separate from the rheostat. Except for the line to this light all the wires from all the equipment disappeared into a steel conduit underneath the bar. It was this light which had dazzled me during the eleven o'clock show. It seemed excessive; a peanut bulb would have been more appropriate. Apparently Jack liked lots of light.

I explained the controls to Spade, then gave him a dry run. First I switched the rheostat back to "House" and threw off the bypass switch, leaving the room brightly lighted and the Magic Mirror dark. "The time is five minutes of twelve. Hazel leaves me to go upstairs. I shift around to the bar stool just opposite where I am now standing. At midnight Jack comes up and asks me if I've heard the buzzer. I say 'No.' He fiddles around a bit, clearing away glasses and the like. Then come two beeps on the buzzer. He picks up the microphone but he doesn't announce the show for a few seconds—he's just noticed Hannegan and Feinstein. Hannegan gives him the high sign and he goes ahead." Then I picked up the mike myself and spoke into it:

"We now present the Magic Mirror!"

I put down the mike and flipped on the turntable switch. The same platter was on and the juke box started playing *Valse Triste*. Ha-

179

zel looked up at me sharply, from where she had been resting her head on her arms a few tables away. She looked horrified, as if the reconstruction were too much for her stomach.

I turned the rheostat slowly from "House" to "Stage." The room darkened and the stage lit up. "That's all there was to it," I said. "Hazel sat down beside me just as Jack announced the show. As the lights came on she screamed."

Spade scratched his chin. "You say Joy was standing in front of you when the buzzer signal came from upstairs?"

"Positive."

"You gave him a motive—the war he was having with Estelle. But you've given him an alibi too."

"That's right. Either Estelle punched that buzzer herself, then lay-down and stabbed herself, or she was murdered and the murderer punched it to cover up, then ducked out while everybody had their eyes on the Mirror. Either way I had Jack Joy in sight."

"It's an alibi all right," he conceded. "Unless you were in cahoots with him," he said hopefully.

"Prove it," I answered, grinning. "Not with him. I think he's a jerk."

"We're all jerks, more or less, Eddie my boy. Let's look around upstairs."

I switched the bypass on, leaving both stage and house lighted, and followed him. I pointed out the buzzer to him, after searching for it myself. A conduit came up through the floor and ended in a junction box on the wall, from which cords ran to the flood lights. The button was on the junction box. I wondered why it was not on the "altar," then saw that the altar was a movable prop. Apparently the girls punched the button, then fell quickly into their poses. Spade tried the button meditatively, then wiped print powder off on his trousers. "I can't hear it," he said.

"Naturally not. This stage is almost a soundproof booth."

He had seen the egg timer but I had not told him until then about seeing the last of the sand run out. He pursed his lips. "You're sure?"

"Call it hallucination. *I* think I saw it. I'll testify to it."

He sat down on the altar, avoiding the blood stain, and said nothing for quite a long time. Finally he said, "Eddie my boy—"

"Yes?"

"You've not only given Jack Joy an alibi, you've damn near made it impossible for anyone to have done it."

"I know it. Could it have been suicide?"

"Could be. Could be. From the mechanics angle but not from the psychological angle. Would she have started that egg timer for her own suicide? Another thing. Take a look at that blood. Taste it."

"Huh?"

"Don't throw up. Smell it then."

I did, very gingerly. Then I smelled it again. Two smells. Tomato. Blood. Blood and tomato catsup. I thought I could detect differences in appearance as well. "You see, son? If she's going to have blood on her chest she won't bother with catsup. Aside from that and the timer it's a perfect, dramatic, female-style suicide. But it won't wash. It's murder, Eddie."

Feinstein stuck his head in. "Lieutenant—"

"What is it?"

"That musician punk. He had a date with her all right."

"Oh, he did, eh?"

"But he's clear. The band was on the air at midnight, in a number that features him in a trumpet solo."

"Damn! Get out of here."

"That ain't all. I called the Assistant Medical Examiner, like you said. The motive you suggested won't go—she not only wasn't expecting; she hadn't ever been had. *Virgo intacta*," he added in passable high school Latin.

"Feinstein, you'll be wanting to be a sergeant next," Spade answered placidly, "using big words like that. Get out."

"Okay, Lieutenant." I was more than a little surprised at the news. I would have picked Estelle as a case of round heels. Evidently she was a tease in more ways than one.

Spade sat a while longer, then said, "When it's light in here, it's dark out there; when it's light out there, it's dark in here."

"That's right. Ordinarily, that is. Right now we've got both sides lighted with the bypass."

"Ordinarily is what I mean. Light, dark; dark, light. Eddie my boy—"

"Yes?"

"Are you sweet on that Hazel girl?"

"I'm leaning that way," I admitted.

"Then keep an eye on her. The murderer was in here for just a few seconds—the egg timer and the buzzer prove that. He wasn't any of the few people who knew about the swap in the shows—not since the trumpet-playing boy friend got knocked out of the running. And it was dark. He murdered the wrong party, Eddie my boy. There's another murder coming up."

"Hazel," I said slowly.

"Yes, Hazel."

Spade Jones shooed us all home, me, Hazel, the two waiters, the other barman, and Jack Joy. I think he was tempted to hold Jack simply because he wouldn't talk but he compromised by telling him that if he stuck his head outside his hotel, he would find a nice policeman ready to take him down to a nice cell. He tipped me a wink and put a finger on his lips as he said good night to me.

But I didn't keep quiet. Hazel let me take her home readily enough. When I saw that she lived alone in a single apartment in a building without a doorman, I decided it called for an all night vigil and some explaining.

She stepped into the kitchenette and mixed me a drink. "One drink and out you go, Ed," she called to me. "You've been very sweet and I want to see you again and thank you, but tonight this girl goes to bed. I'm whipped."

"I'm staying all night," I announced firmly.

She came out with a drink in her hand and looked at me, both annoyed and a little puzzled. "Ed," she said, "aren't you working just a bit too fast? I didn't think you were that clumsy."

"Calm yourself, beautiful," I told her. "It's not necessarily a proposition. I'm going to watch over you. Somebody is trying to kill you."

She dropped the drink.

I helped her clean it up and explained the situation. "Somebody stabbed a girl in a dark room," I finished. "That somebody thought it was you. He knows better by now and he will be looking for a chance to finish the job. What you and I have got to figure out is: *Who wants to kill you?*"

She sat down and started to manhandle a handkerchief. "Nobody wants to kill me, Eddie. It was Estelle."

"No, it wasn't."

"But it couldn't have been me. I *know*."

"What do you know?"

"I—Oh, it's impossible. Stay all night if you want to. You can sleep on the couch." She got up and pulled the bed down out of the wall, went in the bath, closed the door, and splashed around for a while. "That bath is too small to dress and undress in," she stated flatly. "Anyhow I sleep raw. If you want to get undressed you won't scare me."

"Thanks," I said. "I'll take my coat and tie and shoes off."

"Suit yourself." Her voice was a little bit smothered as she was already wiggling her dress over her head.

She wore pants, whether Estelle ever did or not—a plain, white knit that looked clean and neat. She did not wear a brassiere and did not need to. The conception I had gotten of her figure in the Magic Mirror was entirely justified. She was simply the most magnificently beautiful thing I had ever seen in my life. In street clothes she was a beautiful, well-built woman; in her skin—wars have started over less.

I was beginning to doubt my ability to stay on the couch. I must have showed it, for she snorted, "Wipe the drool off your chin!" and stepped out of her pants.

"'Scuse, please," I answered and started unlacing my shoes. She stepped over and switched off the light, then went over to the one big window and raised the shade. It was closed but, with the light out, you could see outside easily. "Stand back from that window," I said. "You're too good a target."

"Huh? Oh, very well." She backed up a few steps but continued to stare thoughtfully out the window. I stared thoughtfully at her. There was a big neon sign across the street and the colored lights, pouring in the window, covered her from head to foot with a rosy liquid glow. She looked like something out of a dream of fairyland.

Presently I wasn't thinking how she looked; I was thinking about another room, where a girl had lain murdered, with the lights of a night club shining through a pane of glass, shining through like this neon.

My thoughts rearranged themselves rapidly and very painfully. I added them up a second time and still got the same answer. I did not like the answer. I was glad, damn glad, she was bare naked, with no way to conceal a gun, or a knife, or any other sort of deadly weapon. "Hazel," I said softly.

She turned to me. "Yes, Eddie?"

"I've just had a new idea … why should anyone want to kill you?"

"You said that before. There isn't any reason."

"I know. You're right; there isn't any. But put it this way—*why should you want to kill Estelle?*"

I thought she was going to faint again, but I didn't care—I wanted to shock her. Her lusciousness meant nothing to me now but a trap that had confused my thoughts. I had not wanted to think her guilty, so I had disregarded the fact that of all the persons involved she was the only one with the necessary opportunity, the knowledge of the swapped shows, and at least some motive. She had made it plain that she detested Estelle. She had covered it up but it was still evident.

But most important of all, the little stage had not been dark! True, it *looked* dark—from the outside. You can't see through glass when all the light comes from one side and you are on that same side—but light passes through the glass just the same. The neon on the street illuminated this room we were in fairly brightly; the brilliant lights of Jack's bar illuminated the little stage even when the stage floodlights were out.

She knew that. She knew it because she had been in there many times, getting ready to pose for the suckers. Therefore she knew that it was not a case of mistaken identity in the dark—there was no dark! And it would have to be nearly pitch black for anyone to mistake Hazel's blue-black mane for Estelle's peroxided mop.

She knew—why hadn't she said so? She was letting me stay all night, not wanting me around but risking her reputation and more, because I had propounded the wrong-girl-in-the-dark theory. She knew it would not hold water; why had she not said so?

"Eddie, have you gone crazy?" Her voice was frightened.

"No—gone sane. I'll tell you how you did it, my beautiful darling. You both were there—you admitted that. Estelle got in her pose, and asked you to punch the buzzer. You did—but first you grabbed the knife and slid it in her ribs. You wiped the handle, looked around, punched the buzzer, and lammed. About ten seconds later you were slipping your arm in mine. Me—your alibi!

"It *had* to be you," I went on, "for no one else would have had the guts to commit murder with nothing but glass between him and an audience. The stage was lighted—from the outside. You knew that, but it didn't worry you. You were used to parading around naked in front of that glass, certain you could not be seen while the house lights were on! No one else would have dared!"

She looked at me as if she could not believe her ears and her chin began to quiver. Then she squatted down on the floor and burst into tears. Real tears—they dripped. It was my cue to go soft, but I did not. I don't like killing.

I stood over her. "*Why did you kill her?* Why did you kill her?"

"Get out of here."

"Not likely. I'm going to see you fry, my big-busted angel." I headed for the telephone, keeping my eyes on her. I did not dare turn my back, even naked as she was.

She made a break, but it was not for me; it was for the door. How far she thought she could get in the buff I don't know.

I tripped her and fell on her. She was a big armful and ready to bite and claw, but I got a hammer lock on one arm and twisted it. "Be good," I warned her, "or I'll break it."

She lay still and I began to be aware that she was not only an armful but a very female armful. I ignored it. "Let me go, Eddie," she said in a tense whisper, "or I'll scream rape and get the cops in."

"Go right ahead, gorgeous," I told her. "The cops are just what I want, and quick."

"Eddie, Eddie, listen to reason—I didn't kill her, but *I know who did.*"

"Huh? Who?"

"I know ... I do know—but he *couldn't* have. That's why I haven't said anything."

"Tell me."

She didn't answer at once; I twisted her arm. "Tell me!"

"*Oh!* It was Jack."

"Jack? Nonsense—I was watching him."

"I know. But he did it, just the same. I don't know how—but he did it."

I held her down, thinking. She watched my face. "Ed?"

"Huh?"

"If I punched the buzzer, wouldn't my fingerprint be on it?"

"Should be."

"Why don't you find out?"

It stonkered me. I thought I was right but she seemed quite willing to make the test. "Get up," I said. "On your knees and then on your feet. But don't try to get your arm free and don't try any tricks, or, so help me, I'll kick you in the belly."

She was docile enough and I moved us over to the phone, dialled it with one hand and managed to get to Spade Jones through the police exchange. "Spade? This is Eddie—Eddie Hill. Was there a fingerprint on the buzzer button?"

"Now I wondered when you would be getting around to thinking of that. There was."

"Whose?"

"The corpse's."

"Estelle's?"

"The same. And Estelle's on the egg timer. None on the knife—wiped clean. Lots from both girls around the room, and a few odd ones—old, probably."

"Uh ... yes. ... well, thanks."

"Not at all. Call me if you get any bright ideas, son."

I hung up the phone and turned to Hazel. I guess I had let go her arm when Spade told me the print was not hers, but I don't remember doing so. She was standing there, rubbing her arm and looking at me in a very odd way. "Well," I said, "you can twist my arm, or kick me anywhere you like. I was wrong. I'm sorry. I'll try to prove it to you."

She started to speak and then started to leak tears again. It finished up with her accepting my apology in the nicest way possible, smearing me with lipstick and tears. I loved it and I felt like a heel.

Presently I wiped her face with my handkerchief and said, "You put on a robe or something and sit on the bed and I'll sit on the couch. We've got to dope this out and I can think better with that lovely chassis of yours covered up."

She trotted obediently and I sat down. "You say Jack killed her, but you admit you don't know how he could have done it. Then why do you think he did?"

"The music."

"Huh?"

"The music he played for the show was *Valse Triste*. That's Estelle's music, for Estelle's act. My act, the regular twelve o'clock act, calls for *Bolero*. He must have known that Estelle was up there; he used the right music."

"Then you figure he must have been lying when he claimed Estelle never arranged with him to swap the shows. But it's a slim reason to hang a man—he might have gotten that record by accident."

"Could, but not likely. The records were kept in order and were the same ones for the same shows every night. Nobody touched them but him. He would fire a man for touching anything around the control box. However," she went on, "I knew it had to be him before I noticed the music. Only it couldn't be."

"Only it couldn't be. Go ahead."

"He hated her."

"Why?"

"She teased him."

"'She teased him.' Suppose she did. Lots of people get teased. She teased lots of people. She teased you. She teased me. So what?"

"It's not the same thing," she insisted. "Jack was afraid of the dark."

It was a nasty story. The lunk was afraid of total darkness, really afraid, the way some kids are. Hazel told me he would not go back of the building to get his parked car at night without a flashlight. But that would not have given away his weakness, nor the fact that he was ashamed of it—lots of people use flashlights freely, just to be sure of their footing. But he had fallen for Estelle and apparently made a lot of progress—had actually gotten into bed with her. It never came to anything because she had snapped out the lights. Estelle had told Hazel about it, gloating over the fact that she had found out about what she termed his cowardice "soon enough."

"She needled him after that," Hazel went on. "Nothing that anyone could tumble to, if they didn't know. But *he* knew. He was afraid of her, afraid to fire her for fear she would tell. He hated her—at the same time he wanted her and was jealous of her. There was one time in the dressing room. I was there—" He had come in while they were dressing, or undressing, and had picked a fight with Estelle over one of the customers. She told him to get out. When he did not do it, she snapped out the light. "He went out of there like a jack rabbit, falling over his feet." She stopped. "How about it, Eddie? Motive enough?"

"Motive enough," I agreed. "You've got me thinking he did it. Only he couldn't."

"'Only he couldn't.' That's the trouble."

I told her to get into bed and try to get some sleep—that I planned to sit right where I was till the pieces fitted. I was rewarded with another sight of the contours as she chucked the robe, then I helped myself to a good-night kiss. I don't think she slept; at least she did not snore.

I started pounding my brain. The fact that the stage was not dark when it *seemed* dark changed the whole picture and eliminated, I thought, everyone not familiar with the mechanics of the Mirror. It left only Hazel, Jack, the other barman, the two waiters—and Estelle herself. It was physically possible for an Unknown Stranger to have slipped upstairs, slid the shiv in her, ducked downstairs, but psychologically—no. I made a mental note to find out what other models had worked in the Mirror.

The other barman and the two waiters Spade had eliminated—all of them had been fully alibied by one or more customers. *I* had alibied Jack. Estelle—but it wasn't suicide. And Hazel.

If Estelle's fingerprint meant what it seemed, Hazel was out—not time enough to commit a murder, arrange a corpse, wipe a handle, and get downstairs to my side before Jack started the show.

But in that case nobody could have done it—except a hypothetical sex maniac who did not mind a spot of butchery in front of a window full of people. Nonsense!

Of course the fingerprint was not conclusive. Hazel *could* have pushed the button with a coin or a bobby pin, without destroying an old print or making a new one. I hated to admit it but she was not clear yet.

Again, if Estelle did not push the button, then it looked still more like an insider; an outsider would not know where to find the button nor have any reason to push it.

For that matter, why should Hazel push it? It had not given her an alibi—it didn't make sense.

Round and round and round till my head ached.

It was a long time later that I went over and tugged at the covers. "Hazel—"

"Yes, Eddie?"

"Who punched the buzzer in the *eleven* o'clock show?"

She considered. "That show is both of us. She did—she always took charge."

"Mmmm. ... What other girls have worked in the Mirror?"

"Why, none. Estelle and I opened the show."

"Okay. Maybe I've got it. Let's call Spade Jones."

Spade assured me he would be only too happy to get out of a warm bed to play games with me and would I like a job waking the bugler, too? But he agreed to come to the Joy Club, with Joy in tow, and to fetch enough flat feet, firearms, and muscles to cope.

I was standing back of the bar in the Joy Club, with Hazel seated where she had been when she screamed and a cop from the Homicide Squad in my seat. Jack and Spade were at the end of the bar, where Spade could see.

"We will now show how a man can be two places at one time," I announced. "I am now Mr. Jack Joy. The time is shortly before midnight. Hazel has just left the dressing room and come downstairs. She stops off for a moment at the little girls room at the foot of the stairs, and thereby misses Jack, who is headed for those same stairs. He goes up and finds Estelle in the dressing room, peeled and ready for her act—probably."

I took a glance at Jack. His face was a taut mask, but he was a long way from breaking. "There was an argument—what about, I don't know, but it might have been over the trumpet boy she had swapped shows to meet. In any case, I am willing to bet that she stopped it by switching out the dressing room light to chase him out."

First blood. He flinched at that—his mask cracked. "He didn't stay out more than a few moments," I went on. "Probably he had a flashlight in his pocket—he's probably got one on him now—and that let him go back into that terrible, dark room, and switch on the light. Estelle was already on the stage, anointing herself with catsup, and almost ready to push the buzzer. She must have been about to do so, for she had started the egg timer. He grabbed the prop dagger and stabbed her, stabbed her dead."

I stopped. No blood from Jack this time. His mask was on firmly. "He arranges her in the pose—ten seconds, for that; it was nothing but a sprawl—wipes the handle and ducks out. Ten seconds more to this spot. Or make it twenty. He asks me if the buzzer has sounded and I tell him No. He really had to know, for Estelle might have punched it before he got to her."

"Hearing the answer he wanted, he bustles around a bit like this—" I monkeyed with some glassware and picked up a bar spoon and pointed with it to the stage. "Note that the Mirror is lighted and empty—I've got the bypass on. Imagine it dark, with Estelle on the altar, a knife in her heart." I dropped the spoon down and, while their eyes were still on the Mirror, I brought metal spoon across the two binding posts which carried the two leads to the push button on the stage. The buzzer gave out with a loud *beep!* I broke the connection by lifting the spoon for a split second, and brought it down again for a second *beep!* "And that is how a man can—*Catch him, Spade!*"

Spade was at him before I yelled. The three cops had him helpless in no time. He was not armed; it had been sheer reflex—a break for freedom. But he was not giving up, even now. "You've got nothing on me. No evidence. Anybody could have jimmied those wires anywhere along the line."

"No, Jack," I contradicted. "I checked for that. Those wires run through the same steel conduit as the power wires, all the way from the control box to the stage. It was here or there, Jack. It couldn't be there; it had to be here."

He shut up. "I want to see my lawyer," was his only answer.

"You'll see your lawyer," Spade assured him jovially. "Tomorrow, or the next day. Right now you're going to go downtown and sit under some nice hot lights for a few hours."

"No, Lieutenant!" It was Hazel.

"Eh? And why not, Miss Dorn?"

"Don't put him under lights. Shut him in a dark closet!"

"Eh? Well, I'll be—That's what I call a bright girl!"

190

It was the mop closet they used. He lasted thirteen minutes, then he started to whimper and then to scream. They let him out and took his confession.

I was almost sorry for him when they led him away. I should not have been—second degree was the most he could get as premeditation was impossible to prove and quite unlikely anyhow. "Not guilty by reason of insanity" was a fair bet. Whatever his guilt, that woman had certainly driven him to it. And imagine the nerve of the man, the pure colossal nerve, that enabled him to go through with lighting up that stage just after he looked up and saw two cops standing inside the door!

I took Hazel home the second time. The bed was still pulled down and she went straight for it, kicking off her shoes as she went. She unzipped the side of her dress and started to pull it over her head, when she stopped. "Eddie!"

"Yes, Beautiful?"

"If I take off my clothes again, are you going to accuse me of another murder?"

I considered this. "That depends," I informed her, "on whether you are really interested in me, or in that agent I was telling you about."

She grinned at me, then scooped up a shoe and threw it. "In you, you lug!" Then she went on shucking off her clothes. After a bit I unlaced my shoes.

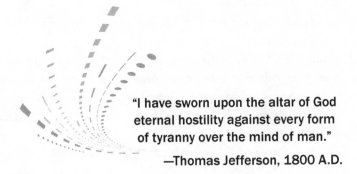

"I have sworn upon the altar of God eternal hostility against every form of tyranny over the mind of man."

—Thomas Jefferson, 1800 A.D.

FOREWORD

My next attempt to branch out was my first book: Rocket Ship Galileo. *I attempted book publication earlier than I had intended to because a boys' book was solicited from me by a major publisher. I was unsure of myself— but two highly respected friends, Cleve Cartmill and Fritz Lang, urged me to try it. So I did ... and the publisher who had asked for it rejected it. A trip to the Moon?* Preposterous! *He suggested that I submit another book-length MS without that silly space-travel angle.*

Instead I sold it to Scribner's and thereby started a sequence: one boys' book each year timed for the Christmas trade. This lasted twelve years and was a very strange relationship, as my editor disliked science fiction, disliked me (a sentiment I learned to reciprocate), and kept me on for the sole reason that my books sold so well that they kept her department out of the red—her words. Eventually she bounced one with the suggestion that I shelve it for a year and then rewrite it.

But by bouncing it she broke the chain of options. Instead of shelving it, I took it across the street ... and won a Hugo with it.

Rocket Ship Galileo *was a fumbling first attempt; I have never been satisfied with it. But it has never been out of print, has appeared in fourteen languages, and has earned a preposterous amount in book royalties alone; I should not kick. Nevertheless I cringe whenever I consider its shortcomings.*

My next fiction (here following) was "Free Men." Offhand it appears to be a routine post-Holocaust story, and the details—idioms, place names, etc.—justify that assumption. In fact it is any *conquered nation in* any *century—*

"That makes three provisional presidents so far," the Leader said. "I wonder how many more there are?" He handed the flimsy sheet back to the runner, who placed it in his mouth and chewed it up like gum.

The third man shrugged. "No telling. What worries me—" A mockingbird interrupted. "Doity, doity, doity," he sang. "Terloo, terloo, terloo, purty-purty-purty-purty."

The clearing was suddenly empty.

"As I was saying," came the voice of the third man in a whisper in the Leader's ear, "it ain't how many worries me, but how you tell a de Gaulle from a Laval. See anything?"

"Convoy. Stopped below us." The Leader peered through bushes and down the side of a bluff. The high ground pushed out toward the river here, squeezing the river road between it and the water. The road stretched away to the left, where the valley widened out into farmland, and ran into the outskirts of Barclay ten miles away.

The convoy was directly below them, eight trucks preceded and followed by halftracks. The following halftrack was backing, vortex gun cast loose and ready for trouble. Its commander apparently wanted elbow room against a possible trap.

At the second truck helmeted figures gathered around its rear end, which was jacked up. As the Leader watched he saw one wheel removed.

"Trouble?"

"I think not. Just a breakdown. They'll be gone soon." He wondered what was in the trucks. Food, probably. His mouth watered. A few weeks ago an opportunity like this would have meant generous rations for all, but the conquerors had smartened up.

He put useless thoughts away. "It's not that that worries me, Dad," he added, returning to the subject. "We'll be able to tell quislings from loyal Americans. But how do you tell men from boys?"

"Thinking of Joe Benz?"

"Maybe. I'd give a lot to know how far we can trust Joe. But I could have been thinking of young Morrie."

"You can trust him."

"Certainly. At thirteen he doesn't drink—and he wouldn't crack if they burned his feet off. Same with Cathleen. It's not age or sex—but how can you tell? And you've *got* to be able to tell."

There was a flurry below. Guards had slipped down from the trucks and withdrawn from the road when the convoy had stopped, in accordance with an orderly plan for such emergencies. Now two of them returned to the convoy, hustling between them a figure not in uniform.

The mockingbird set up a frenetic whistling.

"It's the messenger," said the Leader. "The dumb fool! Why didn't he lie quiet? Tell Ted we've seen it."

Dad pursed his lips and whistled: "Keewah, keewah, keewah, terloo."

The other "mockingbird" answered, "Terloo," and shut up.

"We'll need a new post office now," said the Leader. "Take care of it, Dad."

"Okay."

"There's no real answer to the problem," the Leader said. "You can limit size of units, so that one person can't give away too many—but take a colony like ours. It needs to be a dozen or more to work. That means they all have to be dependable, or they all go down together. So each one has a loaded gun at the head of each other one."

Dad grinned, wryly. "Sounds like the United Nations before the Blow Off. Cheer up, Ed. Don't burn your bridges before you cross them."

"I won't. The convoy is ready to roll."

194

When the convoy had disappeared in the distance, Ed Morgan, the Leader, and his deputy Dad Carter stood up and stretched. The "mockingbird" had announced safety loudly and cheerfully. "Tell Ted to cover us into camp," Morgan ordered.

Dad wheepled and chirruped and received acknowledgment. They started back into the hills. Their route was roundabout and included check points from which they could study their back track and receive reports from Ted. Morgan was not worried about Ted being followed—he was confident that Ted could steal baby 'possums from mama's pouch. But the convoy breakdown might have been a trap— there was no way to tell that all of the soldiers had got back into the trucks. The messenger might have been followed; certainly he had been trapped too easily.

Morgan wondered how much the messenger would spill. He could not spill much about Morgan's own people, for the "post office" rendezvous was all that he knew about them.

The base of Morgan's group was neither better nor worse than average of the several thousand other camps of recalcitrant guerrillas throughout the area that once called itself the United States. The Twenty Minute War had not surprised everyone. The mushrooms which had blossomed over Washington, Detroit, and a score of other places had been shocking but expected—by some.

Morgan had made no grand preparations. He had simply conceived it as a good period in which to stay footloose and not too close to a target area. He had taken squatter's rights in an abandoned mine and had stocked it with tools, food, and other useful items. He had had the simple intention to survive; it was during the weeks after Final Sunday that he discovered that there was no way for a man with foresight to avoid becoming a leader.

Morgan and Dad Carter entered the mine by a new shaft and tunnel which appeared on no map, by a dry rock route which was intended to puzzle even a bloodhound. They crawled through the tunnel, were able to raise their heads when they reached the armory, and stepped out into the common room of the colony, the largest chamber, ten by thirty feet and as high as it was wide.

Their advent surprised no one, else they might not have lived to enter. A microphone concealed in the tunnel had conveyed their shibboleths before them. The room was unoccupied save for a young woman stirring something over a tiny, hooded fire and a girl who sat at a typewriter table mounted in front of a radio. She was wearing earphones and shoved one back and turned to face them as they came in.

"Howdy, Boss!"

"Hi, Margie. What's the good word?" Then to the other, "What's for lunch?"

"Bark soup and a notch in your belt."

"Cathleen, you depress me."

"Well ... mushrooms fried in rabbit fat, but darn few of them."

"That's better."

"You better tell your boys to be more careful what they bring in. One more rabbit with tularemia and we won't have to worry about what to eat."

"Hard to avoid, Cathy. You must be sure you handle them the way Doc taught you." He turned to the girl. "Jerry in the upper tunnel?"

"Yes."

"Get him down here, will you?"

"Yes, sir." She pulled a sheet out of her typewriter and handed it to him, along with others, then left the room.

Morgan glanced over them. The enemy had abolished soap opera and singing commercials but he could not say that radio had been improved. There was an unnewsy sameness to the propaganda which now came over the air. He checked through while wishing for just one old-fashioned, uncensored newscast.

"Here's an item!" he said suddenly. "Get this, Dad—"

"Read it to me, Ed." Dad's spectacles had been broken on Final Sunday. He could bring down a deer, or a man, at a thousand yards— but he might never read again.

"'New Center, 28 April—It is with deep regret that Continental Coordinating Authority for World Unification, North American District, announces that the former city of St. Joseph, Missouri, has been subjected to sanitary measures. It is ordered that a memorial plaque setting forth the circumstances be erected on the former site of St. Joseph as soon as radioactivity permits. Despite repeated warnings the former inhabitants of this lamented city encouraged and succored marauding bands of outlaws skulking around the outskirts of their community. It is hoped that the sad fate of St. Joseph will encourage the native authorities of all North American communities to take all necessary steps to suppress treasonable intercourse with the few remaining lawless elements in our continental society.'"

Dad cocked a brow at Morgan. "How many does that make since they took over?"

"Let's see ... Salinas ... Colorado Springs ... uh, six, including St. Joe."

"Son, there weren't more than sixty million Americans left after Final Sunday. If they keep up, we'll be kind of thinned out in a few years."

"I know." Morgan looked troubled. "We've got to work out ways to operate without calling attention to the towns. Too many hostages."

A short, dark man dressed in dirty dungarees entered from a side tunnel, followed by Margie. "You wanted me, boss?"

"Yes, Jerry. I want to get word to McCracken to come in for a meeting. Two hours from now, if he can get here."

"Boss, you're using radio too much. You'll get him shot and us, too."

"I thought that business of bouncing it off the cliff face was foolproof?"

"Well ... a dodge I can work up, somebody else can figure out. Besides, I've got the chassis unshipped. I was working on it."

"How long to rig it?"

"Oh, half an hour—twenty minutes."

"Do it. This may be the last time we'll use radio, except as utter last resort."

"Okay, boss."

The meeting was in the common room. Morgan called it to order once all were present or accounted for. McCracken arrived just as he had decided to proceed without him. McCracken had a pass for the countryside, being a veterinarian, and held proxy for the colony's underground associates in Barclay.

"The Barclay Free Company, a provisional unit of the United States of America, is now in session," Morgan announced formally. "Does any member have any item to lay before the Company?"

He looked around; there was no response. "How about you?" he challenged Joe Benz. "I heard that you had some things you thought the Company ought to hear."

Benz started to speak, shook his head. "I'll wait."

"Don't wait too long," Morgan said mildly. "Well, I have two points to bring up for discussion—"

"Three," corrected Dr. McCracken. "I'm glad you sent for me." He stepped up to Morgan and handed him a large, much folded piece of paper. Morgan looked it over, refolded it, and put it in his pocket.

"It fits in," he said to McCracken. "What do the folks in town say?"

"They are waiting to hear from you. They'll back you up—so far, anyway."

"All right." Morgan turned back to the group. "First item—we got a message today, passed by hand and about three weeks old, setting up another provisional government. The courier was grabbed right under our noses. Maybe he was a stooge; maybe he was careless—that's neither here nor there at the moment. The message was that the Honorable Albert M. Brockman proclaimed himself provisional President of these United States, under derived authority, and appointed Brigadier General Dewey Fenton commander of armed forces including irregular militia—meaning us—and called on all citizens to unite to throw the Invader out. All formal and proper. So what do we do about it?"

"And who the devil is the Honorable Albert M. Brockman?" asked someone in the rear.

"I've been trying to remember. The message listed government jobs he's held, including some assistant secretary job—I suppose that's the 'derived authority' angle. But I can't place him."

"I recall him," Dr. McCracken said suddenly. "I met him when I was in the Bureau of Animal Husbandry. A career civil servant ... and a stuffed shirt."

There was a gloomy silence. Ted spoke up. "Then why bother with him?"

The Leader shook his head. "It's not that simple, Ted. We can't assume that he's no good. Napoleon might have been a minor clerk under different circumstances. And the Honorable Mr. Brockman may be a revolutionary genius disguised as a bureaucrat. But that's not the point. We need nationwide unification more than anything. It doesn't matter right now who the titular leader is. The theory of derived authority may be shaky but it may be the only way to get everybody to accept one leadership. Little bands like ours can never win back the country. We've got to have unity—and that's why we can't ignore Brockman."

"The thing that burns me," McCracken said savagely, "is that it need never have happened at all! It could have been prevented."

"No use getting in a sweat about it," Morgan told him. "It's easy to see the government's mistakes now, but just the same I think there was an honest effort to prevent war right up to the last. It takes all nations to keep the peace, but it only takes one to start a war."

"No, no, no—I don't mean that, Captain," McCracken answered. "I don't mean the War could have been prevented. I suppose it could have been—once. But everybody knew that another war could happen, and everybody—*everybody*, I say, knew that if it came, it would start with the blasting of American cities. Every congressman, every senator knew that a war would destroy Washington and leave the country with no government, flopping around like a chicken with its head off. They *knew*—why didn't they do something!"

"What could they do? Washington couldn't be protected."

"Do? Why, they could have made plans for their own deaths! They could have slapped through a constitutional amendment calling for an alternate president and alternate congressmen and made it illegal for the alternates to be in target areas—or any scheme to provide for orderly succession in case of disaster. They could have set up secret and protected centers of government to use for storm cellars. They could have planned the same way a father takes out life insurance for his kids. Instead they went stumbling along, fat, dumb, and happy, and let themselves get killed, with no provision to carry out their sworn duties after they were dead. Theory of 'derived authority,' pfui! It's not just disastrous; it's ridiculous! We used to be the greatest country in the world—now look at us!"

"Take it easy, Doc," Morgan suggested. "Hindsight is easier than foresight."

"Hummm! *I* saw it coming. I quit my Washington job and took a country practice, five years ahead of time. Why couldn't a congressman be as bright as I am?"

"Hmmm ... well—you're right. But we might just as well worry over the Dred Scott Decision. Let's get on with the problem. How about Brockman? Ideas?"

"What do you propose, boss?"

"I'd rather have it come from the floor."

"Oh, quit scraping your foot, boss," urged Ted. "We elected you to lead."

"Okay. I propose to send somebody to backtrack on the message and locate Brockman—smell him out and see what he's got. I'll consult with as many groups as we can reach in this state and across the river; and we'll try to manage unanimous action. I was thinking of sending Dad and Morrie."

Cathleen shook her head. "Even with faked registration cards and travel permits they'd be grabbed for the Reconstruction Battalions. I'll go."

"In a pig's eye," Morgan answered. "You'd be grabbed for something a danged sight worse. It's got to be a man."

"I am afraid Cathleen is right," McCracken commented. "They shipped twelve-year-old boys and old men who could hardly walk for the Detroit project. They don't care how soon the radiation gets them—it's a plan to thin us out."

"Are the cities still that bad?"

"From what I hear, yes. Detroit is still 'hot' and she was one of the first to get it."

"I'm going to go." The voice was high and thin, and rarely heard in conference.

"Now, Mother—" said Dad Carter.

"You keep out of this, Dad. The men and young women would be grabbed, but they won't bother with *me*. All I need is a paper saying I have a permit to rejoin my grandson, or something."

McCracken nodded. "I can supply that."

Morgan paused, then said suddenly, "Mrs. Carter will contact Brockman. It is so ordered. Next order of business," he went on briskly. "You've all seen the news about St. Joe—this is what they posted in Barclay last night." He hauled out and held up the paper McCracken had given him. It was a printed notice, placing the City of Barclay on probation, subject to the ability of "local authorities" to suppress "bands of roving criminals."

There was a stir, but no comment. Most of them had lived in Barclay; all had ties there.

"I guess you're waiting for me," McCracken began. "We held a meeting as soon as this was posted. We weren't all there—it's getting harder to cover up even the smallest gathering—but there was no disagreement. We're behind you but we want you to go a little easy. We suggest that you cut out pulling raids within, oh, say twenty miles of Barclay, and that you stop all killing unless absolutely necessary to avoid capture. It's the killings they get excited about—it was killing of the district director that touched off St. Joe."

Benz sniffed. "So we don't do anything. We just give up—and stay here in the hills and starve."

"Let me finish, Benz. We don't propose to let them scare us out and keep us enslaved forever. But casual raids don't do them any real harm. They're mostly for food for the Underground and for minor retaliations. We've got to conserve our strength and increase it and organize, until we can hit hard enough to make it stick. We won't let you starve. I can do more organizing among the farmers and some animals can be hidden out, unregistered. We can get you meat—some, anyhow. And we'll split our rations with you. They've got us on 1800 calories now, but we can share it. Something can be done through the black market, too. There are ways."

Benz made a contemptuous sound. Morgan looked at him.

"Speak up, Joe. What's on your mind?"

"I will. It's not a plan; it's a disorderly retreat. A year from now we'll be twice as hungry and no further along—and they'll be better dug in and stronger. Where does it get us?"

Morgan shook his head. "You've got it wrong. Even if we hadn't had it forced on us, we would have been moving into this stage anyhow. The Free Companies have got to quit drawing attention to themselves. Once the food problem is solved we've got to build up our strength and weapons. We've got to have organization and weapons—nationwide organization and guns, knives, and hand grenades. We've got to turn this mine into a factory. There are people down in Barclay who can use the stuff we can make here—but we can't risk letting Barclay be blasted in the meantime. Easy does it."

"Ed Morgan, you're kidding yourself and you know it."

"How?"

"'How?' Look, you sold me the idea of staying on the dodge and joining up—"

"You volunteered."

"Okay, I volunteered. It was all because you were so filled with fire and vinegar about how we would throw the enemy back into the ocean. You talked about France and Poland and how the Filipinos kept on fighting after they were occupied. You sold me a bill of goods. But there was something you didn't tell me—"

"Go on."

"There never was an Underground that freed its own country. All of them had to be pulled out of the soup by an invasion from outside. Nobody is going to pull *us* out."

There was silence after this remark. The statement had too much truth in it, but it was truth that no member of the Company could afford to think about. Young Morrie broke it. "Captain?"

"Yes, Morrie." Being a fighting man, Morrie was therefore a citizen and a voter.

"How can Joe be so sure he knows what he's talking about? History doesn't repeat. Anyhow, maybe we will get some help. England, maybe—or even the Russians."

Benz snorted. "Listen to the punk! Look, kid, England was smashed like we were, only worse—and Russia, too. Grow up; quit daydreaming."

The boy looked at him doggedly. "You don't know that. We only know what they chose to tell us. And there aren't enough of them to hold down the whole world, everybody, everywhere. We never managed to lick the Yaquis, or the Moras. And they can't lick us *unless we let them*. I've read some history too."

Benz shrugged. "Okay, okay. Now we can all sing 'My Country 'Tis of Thee' and recite the Scout oath. That ought to make Morrie happy—"

"Take it easy, Joe!"

"We have free speech here, don't we? What I want to know is: How long does this go on? I'm getting tired of competing with coyotes for the privilege of eating jackrabbits. You know I've fought with the best of them. I've gone on the raids. Well, haven't I? Haven't I? You can't call *me* yellow."

"You've been on some raids," Morgan conceded.

"All right. I'd go along indefinitely if I could see some sensible plan. That's why I ask, 'How long does this go on?' When do we move? Next spring? Next year?"

Morgan gestured impatiently. "How do I know? It may be next spring; it may be ten years. The Poles waited three hundred years."

"That tears it," Benz said slowly. "I was hoping you could offer some reasonable plan. Wait and arm ourselves—that's a pretty picture! Homemade hand grenades against atom bombs! Why don't you quit kidding yourselves? We're *licked!*" He hitched at his belt. "The rest of you can do as you please—I'm through."

Morgan shrugged. "If a man won't fight, I can't make him. You're assigned noncombatant duties. Turn in your gun. Report to Cathleen."

"You don't get me, Ed. I'm *through.*"

"You don't get *me*, Joe. You don't resign from an Underground."

"There's no risk, I'll leave quietly, and let myself be registered as a straggler. It doesn't mean anything to the rest of you. I'll keep my mouth shut—that goes without saying."

Morgan took a long breath, then answered, "Joe, I've learned by bitter experience not to trust statements set off by 'naturally,' 'of course,' or 'that goes without saying.'"

"Oh, so you don't trust me?"

"As Captain of this Company I can't afford to. Unless you can get the Company to recall me from office, my rulings stand. You're under arrest. Hand over your gun."

Benz glanced around, at blank, unfriendly faces. He reached for his waist. "With your left hand, Joe!"

Instead of complying, Benz drew suddenly, backed away. "Keep clear!" he said shrilly. "I don't want to hurt anybody—but keep clear!"

Morgan was unarmed. There might have been a knife or two in the assembly, but most of them had come directly from the dinner table. It was not their custom to be armed inside the mine.

Young Morrie was armed with a rifle, having come from lookout duty. He did not have room to bring it into play, but Morgan could see that he intended to try. So could Benz.

"Stop it, Morrie!" Morgan assumed obedience and turned instantly to the others. "Let him go. Nobody move. Get going, Joe."

"That's better." Benz backed down the main tunnel, toward the main entrance, weed and drift choked for years. Its unused condition was their principal camouflage, but it could be negotiated.

He backed away into the gloom, still covering them. The tunnel curved; shortly he was concealed by the bend.

Dad Carter went scurrying in the other direction as soon as Benz no longer covered them. He reappeared at once, carrying something. "Heads down!" he shouted, as he passed through them and took out after Benz.

"Dad!" shouted Morgan. But Carter was gone.

Seconds later a concussion tore at their ears and noses.

Morgan picked himself up and brushed at his clothes, saying in annoyed tones, "I never did like explosives in cramped quarters. Cleve—Art. Go check on it. Move!"

"Right, boss!" They were gone.

"The rest of you get ready to carry out withdrawal plan—full plan, with provisions and supplies. Jerry, don't disconnect either the receiver or the line-of-sight till I give the word. Margie will help you. Cathleen, get ready to serve anything that can't be carried. We'll have one big meal. 'The condemned ate hearty.'"

"Just a moment, Captain." McCracken touched his sleeve. "I had better get a message into Barclay."

"Soon as the boys report. You better get back into town."

"I wonder. Benz knows me. I think I'm here to stay."

"Hm ... well, you know best. How about your family?"

McCracken shrugged. "They can't be worse off than they would be if I'm picked up. I'd like to have them warned and then arrangements made for them to rejoin me if possible."

"We'll do it. You'll have to give me a new contact."

"Planned for. This message will go through and my number-two man will step into my shoes. The name is Hobart—runs a feed store on Pelham Street."

Morgan nodded. "Should have known you had it worked out. Well, what we don't know—" He was interrupted by Cleve, reporting.

"He got away, Boss."

"Why didn't you go after him?"

"Half the roof came down when Dad chucked the grenade. Tunnel's choked with rock. Found a place where I could see but couldn't crawl through. He's not in the tunnel."

"How about Dad?"

"He's all right. Got clipped on the head with a splinter but not really hurt."

Morgan stopped two of the women hurrying past, intent on preparations for withdrawal. "Here—Jean, and you, Mrs. Bowen. Go take care of Dad Carter and tell Art to get back here fast. Shake a leg!"

When Art reported Morgan said, "You and Cleve go out and find Benz. Assume that he is heading for Barclay. Stop him and bring him in if you can. Otherwise kill him. Art is in charge. Get going." He turned to McCracken. "Now for a message." He fumbled in his pocket for paper, found the poster notice that McCracken had given him, tore off a piece, and started to write. He showed it to McCracken. "How's that?" he asked.

The message warned Hobart of Benz and asked him to try to head him off. It did not tell him that the Barclay Free Company was moving but did designate the "post office" through which next contact would be expected—the men's rest room of the bus station.

"Better cut out the post office," McCracken advised. "Hobart knows it and we may contact him half a dozen other ways. But I'd like to ask him to get my family out of sight. Just tell him that we are sorry to hear that Aunt Dinah is dead."

"Is that enough?"

"Yes."

"Okay." Morgan made the changes, then called, "Margie! Put this in code and tell Jerry to get it out fast. Tell him it's the strike-out edition. He can knock down his sets as soon as it's out."

"Okay, boss." Margie had no knowledge of cryptography. Instead she had command of jive talk, adolescent slang, and high school double-talk which would be meaningless to any but another American bobby-soxer. At the other end a fifteen-year-old interpreted her butchered English by methods which impressed her foster parents as being telepathy—but it worked.

The fifteen-year-old could be trusted. Her entire family, save herself, had been in Los Angeles on Final Sunday.

Art and Cleve had no trouble picking up Benz's trail. His tracks were on the tailings spilling down from the main entrance to the mine. The earth and rock had been undisturbed since the last heavy rain; Benz's flight left clear traces.

But the trail was cold by more than twenty minutes; they had left the mine by the secret entrance a quarter of a mile from where Benz had made his exit.

Art picked it up where Benz had left the tailings and followed it through brush with the woodsmanship of the Eagle Scout he had been. From the careless signs he left behind Benz was evidently in a hurry and heading by the shortest route for the highway. The two followed him as fast as they could cover ground, discarding caution for speed.

They checked just before entering the highway. "See anything?" asked Cleve.

"No."

"Which way would he go?"

"The Old Man said to head him off from Barclay."

"Yeah, but suppose he headed south instead? He used to work in Wickamton. He might head that way."

"The Boss said to cover Barclay. Let's go."

They had to cache their guns; from here on it would be their wits and their knives. An armed American on a highway would be as conspicuous as a nudist at a garden party.

Their object now was speed; they must catch up with him, or get ahead of him and waylay him.

206

Nine miles and two and a half hours later—one hundred and fifty minutes of dog trot, with time lost lying in the roadside brush when convoys thundered past—they were in the outskirts of Barclay. Around a bend, out of sight, was the roadblock of the Invaders' check station. The point was a bottleneck; Benz must come this way if he were heading for Barclay.

"Is he ahead or behind us?" asked Cleve, peering out through bushes.

"Behind, unless he was picked up by a convoy—or sprouted wings. We'll give him an hour."

A horse-drawn hayrack lumbered up the road. Cleve studied it. Americans were permitted no power vehicles except under supervision, but this farmer and his load could go into town with only routine check at the road block. "Maybe we ought to hide in that and look for him in town."

"And get a bayonet in your ribs? Don't be silly."

"Okay. Don't blow your top." Cleve continued to watch the rig. "Hey," he said presently. "Get a load of that!"

"That" was a figure which dropped from the tail of the wagon as it started around the bend, rolled to the ditch on the far side, and slithered out of sight.

"That was Joe!"

"Are you sure?"

"Sure! Here we go."

"How?" Art objected. "Take it easy. Follow me." They faded back two hundred yards, to where they could cross the road on hands and knees through a drainage pipe. Then they worked up the other side to where Benz had disappeared in weeds.

They found the place where he had been; grass and weeds were still straightening up. The route he must have taken was evident—down toward the river bank, then upstream to the city. There were drops of blood. "Dad must have missed stopping him by a gnat's whisker," Cleve commented.

"Bad job he didn't."

"Another thing—he said he was going to give himself up. I don't think he is, or he would have stayed with the wagon and turned himself in at the check station. He's heading for some hideout. Who does he know in Barclay?"

"I don't know. We'd better get going."

"Wait a minute. If he touches off an alarm, they'll shoot him for us. If he gets by the 'eyes,' we've lost him and we'll have to pick him up inside. Either way, we don't gain anything by blundering ahead. We've got to go in by the chute."

Like all cities the Invader had consolidated, Barclay was girdled by electric-eye circuits. The enemy had trimmed the town to fit, dynamiting and burning where necessary to achieve unbroken sequence of automatic sentries. But the "chute"—an abandoned and forgotten aqueduct—passed under the alarms. Art knew how to use it; he had been in town twice since Final Sunday.

They worked back up the highway, crossed over, and took to the hills. Thirty minutes later they were on the streets of Barclay, reasonably safe as long as they were quick to step off the sidewalk for the occasional Invader.

The first "post office," a clothesline near their exit, told them nothing—the line was bare. They went to the bus station. Cleve studied the notices posted for inhabitants while Art went into the men's rest room. On the wall, defaced by scrawlings of every sort, mostly vulgar, he found what he sought: "Killroy was here." The misspelling of Kilroy was the clue—exactly eighteen inches below it and six to the right was an address: "1745 Spruce—ask for Mabel."

He read it as 2856 Pine—one block beyond Spruce. Art passed the address to Cleve, then they set out separately, hurrying to beat the curfew but proceeding with caution—at least one of them must get through. They met in the backyard of the translated address. Art knocked on the kitchen door. It was opened a crack by a middle-aged man who did not seem glad to see them. "Well?"

"We're looking for Mabel."

"Nobody here by that name."

"Sorry," said Art. "We must have made a mistake." He shivered. "Chilly out," he remarked. "The nights are getting longer."

"They'll get shorter by and by," the man answered.

"We've got to think so, anyhow," Art countered.

"Come in," the man said. "The patrol may see you." He opened the door and stepped aside. "My name's Hobart. What's your business?"

"We're looking for a man named Benz. He may have sneaked into town this afternoon and found someplace to—"

"Yes, yes," Hobart said impatiently. "He got in about an hour ago and he's holed up with a character named Moyland." As he spoke he removed a half loaf of bread from a cupboard, cut four slices, and added cold sausage, producing two sandwiches. He did not ask if they were hungry; he simply handed them to Art and Cleve.

"Thanks, pal. So he's holed up. Haven't you done anything about it? He has got to be shut up at once or he'll spill his guts."

"We've got a tap in on the telephone line. We had to wait for dark. You can't expect me to sacrifice good boys just to shut his mouth unless it's absolutely necessary."

"Well, it's dark now, and we'll be the boys you mentioned. You can call yours off."

"Okay." Hobart started pulling on shoes.

"No need for you to stick your neck out," Art told him. "Just tell us where this Moyland lives."

"And get your throat cut, too. I'll take you."

"What sort of a guy is this Moyland? Is he safe?"

"You can't prove it by me. He's a black market broker, but that doesn't prove anything. He's not part of the organization but we haven't anything against him."

Hobart took them over his back fence, across a dark side street, through a playground, where they lay for several minutes under bushes because of a false alarm, then through many more backyards, back alleys, and dark byways. The man seemed to have a nose for the enemy; there were no more alarms. At last he brought them through a cellar door into a private home. They went upstairs and through a room where a woman was nursing a baby. She looked up, but otherwise ignored them. They ended up in a dark attic. "Hi, Jim," Hobart called out softly. "What's new?"

The man addressed lay propped on his elbows, peering out into the night through opera glasses held to slots of a ventilating louvre. He rolled over and lowered the glasses, pushing one of a pair of earphones from his head as he did so. "Hello, Chief. Nothing much. Benz is getting drunk, it looks like."

"I'd like to know where Moyland gets it," Hobart said. "Has he telephoned?"

"Would I be doing nothing if he had? A couple of calls came in, but they didn't amount to anything, so I let him talk."

"How do you know they didn't amount to anything?"

Jim shrugged, turned back to the louvre. "Moyland just pulled down the shade," he announced.

Art turned to Hobart. "We can't wait. We're going in."

Benz arrived at Moyland's house in bad condition. The wound in his shoulder, caused by Carter's grenade, was bleeding. He had pushed a handkerchief up against it as a compress, but his activity started the blood again; he was shaking for fear his condition would attract attention before he could get under cover.

Moyland answered the door. "Is that you, Zack?" Benz demanded, shrinking back as he spoke.

"Yes. Who is it?"

"It's me—Joe Benz. Let me in, Zack—quick!"

Moyland seemed about to close the door, then suddenly opened it. "Get inside." When the door was bolted, he demanded, "Now—what's your trouble? Why come to me?"

"I had to go someplace, Zack. I had to get off the street. They'd pick me up."

Moyland studied him. "You're not registered. Why not?"

Benz did not answer. Moyland waited, then went on, "You know what I can get for harboring a fugitive. You're in the Underground—aren't you?"

"Oh, no, Zack! I wouldn't do that to you. I'm just a—a straggler. I gotta get registered, Zack."

"That's blood on your coat. How?"

"Uh ... just an accident. Maybe you could let me have clean rags and some iodine."

Moyland stared at him, his bland face expressionless, then smiled. "You've got no troubles we can't fix. Sit down." He stepped to a cabinet and took out a bottle of bourbon, poured three fingers in a water glass, and handed it to Benz. "Work on that and I'll fix you up."

He returned with some torn toweling and a bottle. "Sit here with your back to the window, and open your shirt. Have another drink. You'll need it before I'm through."

Benz glanced nervously at the window. "Why don't you draw the shade?"

"It would attract attention. Honest people leave their shades up these days. Hold still. This is going to hurt."

Three drinks later Benz was feeling better. Moyland seemed willing to sit and drink with him and to soothe his nerves. "You did well to come in," Moyland told him. "There's no sense hiding like a scared rabbit. It's just butting your head against a stone wall. Stupid."

Benz nodded. "That's what I told them."

"Told who?"

"Hunh? Oh, nobody. Just some guys I was talking to. Tramps."

Moyland poured him another drink. "As a matter of fact you *were* in the Underground."

"Me? Don't be silly, Zack."

"Look, Joe, you don't have to kid me. I'm your friend. Even if you did tell me it wouldn't matter. In the first place, I wouldn't have any proof. In the second place, I'm sympathetic to the Underground—any American is. I just think they're wrong-headed and foolish. Otherwise I'd join 'em myself."

"They're foolish all right! You can say that again."

"So you *were* in it?"

"Huh? You're trying to trap me. I gave my word of honor—"

"Oh, relax!" Moyland said hastily. "Forget it. I didn't hear anything; I can't tell anything. Hear no evil, see no evil—that's me." He changed the subject.

The level of the bottle dropped while Moyland explained current events as he saw them. "It's a shame we had to take such a shellacking to learn our lesson but the fact of the matter is, we were standing in the way of the natural logic of progress. There was a time back in '45 when we could have pulled the same stunt ourselves, only we weren't bright enough to do it. World organization, world government. We stood in the way, so we got smeared. It had to come. A smart man can see that."

Benz was bleary but he did not find this comment easy to take. "Look, Zack—you don't mean you *like* what happened to us?"

"Like it? Of course not. But it was necessary. You don't have to like having a tooth pulled—but it has to be done. Anyhow," he went on, "it's not all bad. The big cities were economically unsound anyway. We should have blown them up ourselves. Slum clearance, you might call it."

Benz banged his empty glass down. "Maybe so—but they made slaves out of us!"

"Take it easy, Joe," Moyland said, filling his glass, "you're talking abstractions. The cop on the corner could push you around whenever he wanted to. Is that freedom? Does it matter whether the cop talks with an Irish accent or some other accent? No, chum, there's a lot of guff talked about freedom. No man is free. There is no such thing as freedom. There are only various privileges. Free speech—we're talking freely now, aren't we? After all, you don't want to get up on a platform and shoot off your face. Free press? When did *you* ever own a news-paper? Don't be a chump. Now that you've shown sense and come in, you are going to find that things aren't so very different. A little more orderly and no more fear of war, that's all. Girls make love just like they used to, the smart guys get along, and the suckers still get the short end of the deal."

Benz nodded. "You're right, Zack. I've been a fool."

"I'm glad you see it. Now take those wild men you were with. What freedom have they got? Freedom to starve, freedom to sleep on the cold ground, freedom to be hunted."

"That was it," Benz agreed. "Did you ever sleep in a mine, Zack? Cold. That ain't half of it. Damp, too."

"I can imagine," Moyland agreed. "The Capehart Lode always was wet."

"It wasn't the Capehart; it was the Harkn—" He caught himself and looked puzzled.

"The Harkness, eh? That's the headquarters?"

"I didn't say that! You're putting words in my mouth! You—"

"Calm yourself, Joe. Forget it." Moyland got up and drew down the shade. "You didn't say anything."

"Of course I didn't." Benz stared at his glass. "Say, Zack, where do I sleep? I don't feel good."

"You'll have a nice place to sleep any minute now."

"Huh? Well, show me. I gotta fold up."

"Any minute. You've got to check in first."

"Huh? Oh, I can't do that tonight, Zack. I'm in no shape."

"I'm afraid you'll have to. See me pull that shade down? They'll be along any moment."

Benz stood up, swaying a little. "You framed me!" he yelled, and lunged at his host.

Moyland sidestepped, put a hand on his shoulder and pushed him down into the chair. "Sit down, sucker," he said pleasantly. "You don't expect me to get A-bombed just for you and your pals, do you?" Benz shook his head, then began to sob.

Hobart escorted them out of the house, saying to Art as they left, "If you get back, tell McCracken that Aunt Dinah is resting peacefully."

"Okay."

"Give us two minutes, then go in. Good luck."

Cleve took the outside; Art went in. The back door was locked, but the upper panel was glass. He broke it with the hilt of his knife, reached in and unbolted the door. He was inside when Moyland showed up to investigate the noise.

Art kicked him in the belly, then let him have the point in the neck as he went down. Art stopped just long enough to insure that Moyland would stay dead, then went looking for the room where Benz had been when the shade was drawn.

He found Benz in it. The man blinked his eyes and tried to focus them, as if he found it impossible to believe what he saw. "Art!" he got out at last. "Jeez, boy! Am I glad to see you! Let's get out of here— this place is 'hot.'"

Art advanced, knife out.

Benz looked amazed. "Hey, Art! Art! You're making a mistake. Art. You can't do this—" Art let him have the first one in the soft tissues under the breast bone, then cut his throat to be sure. After that he got out quickly.

Thirty-five minutes later he was emerging from the country end of the chute. His throat was burning from exertion and his left arm was useless—he could not tell whether it was broken or simply wounded.

Cleve lay dead in the alley behind Moyland's house, having done a good job of covering Art's rear.

It took Art all night and part of the next morning to get back near the mine. He had to go through the hills the entire way; the highway was, he judged, too warm at the moment.

He did not expect that the Company would still be there. He was reasonably sure that Morgan would have carried out the evacuation pending certain evidence that Benz's mouth had been shut. He hurried.

But he did not expect what he did find—a helicopter hovering over the neighborhood of the mine.

He stopped to consider the matter. If Morgan had got them out safely, he knew where to rejoin. If they were still inside, he had to figure out some way to help them. The futility of his position depressed him—one man, with a knife and a bad arm, against a helicopter.

Somewhere a bluejay screamed and cursed. Without much hope he chirped his own identification. The bluejay shut up and a mockingbird answered him—Ted.

Art signaled that he would wait where he was. He considered himself well hidden; he expected to have to signal again when Ted got closer, but he underestimated Ted's ability. A hand was laid on his shoulder.

He rolled over, knife out, and hurt his shoulder as he did so. "Ted! Man, do you look good to me!"

"Same here. Did you get him?"

"Benz? Yes, but maybe not in time. Where's the gang?"

"A quarter mile north of back door. We're pinned down. Where's Cleve?"

"Cleve's not coming back. What do you mean 'pinned down'?"

"That damned 'copter can see right down the draw we're in. Dad's got 'em under an overhang and they're safe enough for the moment, but we can't move."

"What do you mean 'Dad's, got 'em'?" demanded Art. "Where's the Boss?"

"He ain't in such good shape, Art. Got a machine gun slug in the ribs. We had a dust-up. Cathleen's dead."

"The hell you say!"

"That's right. Margie and Maw Carter have got her baby. But that's one reason why we're pinned down—the Boss and the kid, I mean."

A mockingbird's call sounded far away. "There's Dad," Ted announced. "We got to get back."

"Can we?"

"Sure. Just keep behind me. I'll watch out that I don't get too far ahead."

Art followed Ted in, by a circuitous and, at one point, almost perpendicular route. He found the Company huddled under a shelf of rock which had been undercut by a stream, now dry. Against the wall Morgan was on his back, with Dad Carter and Dr. McCracken squatting beside him. Art went up and made his report.

Morgan nodded, his face gray with pain. His shirt had been cut away; bandaging was wrapped around his ribs, covering a thick pad. "You did well, Art. Too bad about Cleve. Ted, we're getting out of here and you're going first, because you're taking the kid."

"The baby? How—"

"Doc'll dope it so that it won't let out a peep. Then you strap it to your back, papoose fashion."

Ted thought about it. "No, to my front. There's some knee-and-shoulder work on the best way out."

"Okay. It's your job."

"How do *you* get out, boss?"

"Don't be silly."

"Look here, boss, if you think we're going to walk off and leave you, you've got another—"

"Shut up and scram!" The exertion hurt Morgan; he coughed and wiped his mouth.

"Yes, sir." Ted and Art backed away.

"Now, Ed—" said Carter.

"You shut up, too. You still sure you don't want to be Captain?"

"You know better than that, Ed. They took things from me while I was your deppity, but they wouldn't have me for Captain."

"That puts it up to you, Doc."

McCracken looked troubled. "They don't know me that well, Captain."

"They'll take you. People have an instinct for such things."

"Anyhow, if I am Captain, I won't agree to your plan of staying here by yourself. We'll stay till dark and carry you out."

"And get picked up by an infrared spotter, like sitting ducks? That's supposing they let you alone until sundown—that other 'copter will be back with more troops before long."

"I don't think they'd let me walk off on you."

"It's up to you to *make* them. Oh, I appreciate your kindly thoughts, Doc, but you'll think differently as soon as you're Captain. You'll know you have to cut your losses."

McCracken did not answer. Morgan turned his head to Carter. "Gather them around, Dad."

They crowded in, shoulder to shoulder. Morgan looked from one troubled face to another and smiled. "The Barclay Free Company, a provisional unit of the United States of America, is now in session," he announced, his voice suddenly firm. "I'm resigning the captaincy for reasons of physical disability. Any nominations?"

The silence was disturbed only by calls of birds, the sounds of insects.

Morgan caught Carter's eyes. Dad cleared his throat. "I nominate Doc McCracken."

"Any other nominations?" He waited, then continued, "All right, all in favor of Doc make it known by raising your right hand. Okay— opposed the same sign. Dr. McCracken is unanimously elected. It's all yours, Captain. Good luck to you."

McCracken stood up, stooping to avoid the rock overhead. "We're evacuating at once. Mrs. Carter, give the baby about another table-spoon of the syrup, then help Ted. He knows what to do. You'll follow Ted. Then Jerry. Margie, you are next. I'll assign the others presently.

Once out of the canyon, spread out and go it alone. Rendezvous at dusk, same place as under Captain Morgan's withdrawal plan—the cave." He paused. Morgan caught his eye and motioned him over, "That's all until Ted and the baby are ready to leave. Now back away and give Captain Morgan a little air."

When they had withdrawn McCracken leaned over Morgan the better to hear his weak words. "Don't be too sure you've seen the last of me, Captain. I might join up in a few days."

"You might at that. I'm going to leave you bundled up warm and plenty of water within reach. I'll leave you some pills, too—that'll give you some comfort and ease. Only half a pill for you—they're intended for cows." He grinned at his patient.

"Half a pill it is. Why not let Dad handle the evacuation? He'll make you a good deputy—and I'd like to talk with you until you leave."

"Right." He called Carter over, instructed him, and turned back to Morgan.

"After you join up with Powell's outfit," whispered Morgan, "your first job is to get into touch with Brockman. Better get Mrs. Carter started right away, once you've talked it over with Powell."

"I will."

"That's the most important thing we've got to worry about, Doc. We've got to have unity, and one plan, from coast to coast. I look forward to a day when there will be an American assigned, by name, to each and every one of them. Then at a set time—zzzt!" He drew a thumb across his throat.

McCracken nodded. "Could be. It *will* be. How long do you think it will take us?"

"I don't know. I don't think about 'how long.' Two years, five years, ten years—maybe a century. That's not the point. The only question is whether or not there are any guts left in America." He glanced out where the fifth person to leave was awaiting a signal from Carter, who in turn was awaiting a signal from Art, hidden out where he could watch for the helicopter. "Those people will stick."

"I'm sure of that."

Presently Morgan added, "There's one thing this has taught me: You can't enslave a free man. Only person can do that to a man is himself. No, sir—you can't enslave a free man. The most you can do is kill him."

"That's a fact, Ed."

"It is. Got a cigarette, Doc?"

"It won't do you any good, Ed."

"It won't do me any harm, either—now, will it?"

"Well, not much." McCracken unregretfully gave him his last and watched him smoke it.

Later, Morgan said, "Dad's ready for you, Captain. So long."

"So long. Don't forget. Half a pill at a time. Drink all the water you want, but don't take your blankets off, no matter how hot you get."

"Half a pill it is. Good luck."

"I'll have Ted check on you tomorrow."

Morgan shook his head. "That's too soon. Not for a couple of days at least."

McCracken smiled. "I'll decide that, Ed. You just keep yourself wrapped up. Good luck." He withdrew to where Carter waited for him. "You go ahead, Dad. I'll bring up the rear. Signal Art to start."

Carter hesitated. "Tell me straight, Doc. What kind of shape is he in?"

McCracken studied Carter's face, then said in a low voice, "I give him about two hours."

"I'll stay behind with him."

"No, Dad, you'll carry out your orders." Seeing the distress in the old man's eyes, he added, "Don't you worry about Morgan. A free man can take care of himself. Now get moving."

"Yes, sir."

FOREWORD

This story was tailored in length (1500 words) for Collier's *as a short-short. I then tried it on the American Legion magazine—and was scolded for suggesting that the treatment given our veterans was ever less than perfect. I then offered it to several SF editors—and was told that it was not a science fiction story. (Gee whiz and Gosh wollickers!—space warps and FTL are science but therapy and psychology are not. I must be in the wrong church.)*

But this story does have a major shortcoming, one that usually is fatal. Try to spot it. I will put the answer just after the end.

—— NO BANDS PLAYING, NO FLAGS FLYING— _____

"The bravest man I ever saw in my life!" Jones said, being rather shrill about it.

We—Jones and Arkwright and I—were walking toward the parking lot at the close of visiting hours out at the veterans hospital. Wars come and wars go, but the wounded we have always with us—and damned little attention they get between wars. If you bother to look (few do), you can find some broken human remnants dating clear back to World War One in some of our wards.

So our post always sends out a visiting committee every Sunday, every holiday. I'm usually on it, have been for thirty years—if you can't pay a debt, you can at least try to meet the interest. And you do get so that you can stand it.

But Jones was a young fellow making his first visit. Quite upset, he was. Well, surely, I would have despised him if he hadn't been— this crop was fresh in from Southeast Asia. Jones had held it in, then burst out with that remark once we were outside.

"What do you mean by 'bravery'?" I asked him. (Not but what Jones had plenty to back up his opinion—this lad he was talking about was shy both legs and his eyesight, yet he was chin-up and merry.)

"Well, what do *you* mean by 'bravery'?" Jones demanded, then added, "sir." Respect for my white hair rather than my opinions, I think; there was an edge in his voice.

"Keep your shirt on, son," I answered. "What that lad back there has I'd call 'fortitude,' the ability to endure adversity without losing your morale. I'm not disparaging it; it may be a higher virtue than bravery—but I define 'bravery' as the capacity to *choose* to face danger when you are frightened by it."

"Why do you say 'choose'?"

"Because nine men out of ten meet the test when it's forced on them. But it takes something extra to face up to danger when it scares the crap out of you and there's an easy way to bug out." I glanced at my watch. "Give me three minutes and I'll tell you about the bravest man I've ever met."

I was a young fellow myself back between War One and War Two and had been in a hospital much like this one Arkwright and Jones and I had visited—picked up a spot on my lung in the Canal Zone and had been sent there for the cure. Mind you, this was years ago when lung therapy was primitive. No antibiotics, no specific drugs. The first thing they would try was a phrenectomy—cut the nerve that controls the diaphragm to immobilize the lung and let it get well. If that didn't work, they used artificial pneumothorax. If that failed, they did a "backdoor job"—chop out some ribs and fit you with a corset.

All these were just expedients to hold a lung still so it could get well. In artificial pneumothorax they shove a hollow needle between your ribs so that the end is between rib wall and lung wall, then pump the space in between full of air; this compresses the lung like a squeezed sponge.

But the air would be absorbed after a while and you had to get pumped up again. Every Friday morning those of us on pneumo would gather in the ward surgeon's office for the needle. It wasn't grim—lungers are funny people; they are almost always cheerful. This was an officers' ward and we treated it like a club. Instead of queuing up outside the surgeon's office we would swarm in, loll in his chair, sit on his desk, smoke his cigarettes, and swap lies while he took care of us. Four of us that morning and I was the first.

Taking the air needle isn't bad—just a slight prick as it goes in and you can even avoid that if you want to bother with skin anesthesia. It's over in a few minutes; you put your bathrobe back on and go back to bed. I hung around after I was through because the second patient, chap named Saunders, was telling a dirty story that was new to me.

He broke off in the middle of it to climb up on the table when I got off. Our number-one ward surgeon was on leave and his assistant was taking care of us—a young chap not long out of school. We all liked him and felt he had the makings of a great surgeon.

Getting pumped up is not dangerous in any reasonable sense of the word. You can break your neck falling off a step ladder, choke to death on a chicken bone. You can slip on a rainy day, knock yourself out, and drown in three inches of rain water. And there is just as unlikely a way to hit the jackpot in taking artificial pneumothorax. If the needle goes a little too far, penetrates the lung, and if an air bubble then happens to be forced into a blood vessel and manages to travel all the way back to the heart without being absorbed, it is possible though extremely unlikely to get a sort of vapor lock in the valves of your heart—air embolism, the doctors call it. Given all these improbable events, you can die.

We never heard the end of Saunders' dirty joke. He konked out on the table.

The young doc did everything possible for him and sent for help while he was doing it. They tried this and that, used all the tricks, but the upshot was that they brought in the meat basket and carted him off to the morgue.

Three of us were still standing there, not saying a word—me, re-swallowing my breakfast and thanking my stars that I was through with it, an ex-field-clerk named Josephs who was next up, and Colonel Hostetter who was last in line. The surgeon turned and looked at us. He was sweating and looked bad—may have been the first patient he had ever lost; he was still a kid. Then he turned to Dr. Armand who had come in from the next ward. I don't know whether he was going to ask the older man to finish it for him or whether he was going to put it off for a day, but it was clear from his face that he did not intend to go ahead right then.

Whatever it was, he didn't get a chance to say it. Josephs stood up, threw off his bathrobe and climbed up on the table. He had just lighted a cigarette; he passed it to a hospital orderly and said, "Hold this for me, Jack, while Doctor"—he named our own surgeon—"pumps me up." With that he peels up his pajama coat.

You know the old business about sending a student pilot right back up after his first crack-up. That was the shape our young doctor was in—he had to get right back to it and prove to himself that it was just bad luck and not because he was a butcher. But he couldn't send himself back in; Josephs had to do it for him. Josephs could have ruined him professionally that moment, by backing out and giving him time to work up a real case of nerves—but instead Josephs forced his hand, made him do it.

Josephs died on the table.

The needle went in and everything seemed all right, then Josephs gave a little sigh and died. Dr. Armand was on hand this time and took charge, but it did no good. It was like seeing the same horror movie twice. The same four men arrived to move the body over to the morgue—probably the same basket.

Our doctor now looked like a corpse himself. Dr. Armand took over. "You two get back to bed," he said to Colonel Hostetter and me. "Colonel, come over to my ward this afternoon; I'll take care of your treatment."

But Hostetter shook his head. "No, thank you," he said crisply, "My ward surgeon takes care of my needs." He took off his robe. The young fellow didn't move. The Colonel went up to him and shook his arm. "Come, now Doctor—you'll make us both late for lunch." With that he climbed up on the table and exposed his ribs.

A few moments later he climbed off again, the job done, and our ward surgeon was looking human again, although still covered with sweat.

I stopped to catch my breath. Jones nodded soberly and said, "I see what you mean. To do what Colonel Hostetter did takes a kind of cold courage way beyond the courage needed to fight."

"He doesn't mean anything of the sort," Arkwright objected. "He wasn't talking about Hostetter; he meant the intern. The doctor had to steady down and do a job—not once but twice. Hostetter just had to hold still and let him do it."

I felt tired and old. "Just a moment," I said. "You're both wrong. Remember I defined 'bravery' as requiring that a man had to have a choice … and chooses to be brave in spite of his own fear. The ward surgeon had the decisions forced on him, so he is not in the running. Colonel Hostetter was an old man and blooded in battle—and he had Josephs' example to live up to. So he doesn't get first prize."

"But that's silly," Jones protested. "Josephs was brave, sure—but, if it was hard for Josephs to offer himself, it was four times as hard for Hostetter. It would begin to look like a jinx—like a man didn't stand a chance of coming off that table alive."

"Yes, yes!" I agreed. "I know, that's the way *I* felt at the time. But you didn't let me finish. I know for *certain* that it took more bravery to do what Josephs did.

"The autopsy didn't show an air embolism in Josephs, or anything else. Josephs died of fright."

THE END

The Answer: I'll bury this in other words to keep your eye from picking it up at once; the shortcoming is that this is a true story. I was there. I have changed names, places, and dates but not the essential facts.

FOREWORD

You may not be old enough to remember the acute housing shortage follow-ing World War II (the subject of this story) but if you are over six but not yet old enough for the undertaker, you are aware of the current problem of getting in out of the rain ... a problem especially acute for the young couple with one baby and for the retired old couple trying to get by on Social "Security" plus savings if any. (I am not suggesting that it is easy for those between youth and old age; the present price of mortgage money constitutes rape with violence; the price tag on an honestly-constructed—if you can find one—two-bedroom house makes me feel faint.)

In 1960 in Moscow Mrs. Heinlein and I had as Intourist courier a sweet child named Ludmilla—23, unmarried, living with her father, mother, brother and sisters. She told us that her ambition in life was for her family not to have to share a bathroom with another family.

The next aesthete who sneers at our American "plumbing culture" in my presence I intend to cut into small pieces and flush him down that W.C. he despises.

Any old pol will recognize the politics in this story as the Real McCoy. Should be. Autobiographical in many details. Which details? Show me a warrant and I'll take the Fifth.

Ever step on a top step that wasn't there?

That's the way I felt when I saw my honorable opponent for the office of city councilman, third district.

Tom Griffith had telephoned at the close of filing, to let me know my opponents. "Alfred McNye," he said, "and Francis X. Nelson."

"McNye we can forget," I mused. "He files just for the advertising. It's a three-way race—me, this Nelson party, and the present encumbrance, Judge Jorgens. Maybe we'll settle it in the primaries." Our fair city has the system laughingly called "non-partisan"; a man can be elected in the primary by getting a clear majority.

"Jorgens didn't file, Jack. The old thief isn't running for re-election."

I let this sink in. "Tom, we might as well tear up those photostats. Do you suppose Tully's boys are conceding our district?"

"The machine *can't* concede the third district, not this year. It must be Nelson."

"I suppose so ... it can't be McNye. What d'you know about him?"

"Nothing."

"Nor I. Well, we'll look him over tonight." The Civic League had called a "meet-the-candidates" meeting that night. I drove out to the trailer camp where I hang my hat—then a shower, a shave, put on my hurtin' shoes, and back to town. It gave me time to think.

It's not unusual for a machine to replace—temporarily—a man whose record smells too ripe with a citizen of no background to be sniped at. I could visualize Nelson—young, manly looking, probably a lawyer and certainly a veteran. He would be so politically naive that he would stand without hitching, or so ambitious that it would blind him to what he must do to keep the support of the machine. Either way the machine could use him.

I got there just in time to be introduced and take a seat on the platform. I couldn't spot Nelson but I did see Cliff Meyers, standing with some girl. Meyers is a handyman for Boss Tully—Nelson would be around close.

McNye accepted the call of the peepul in a few hundred well-worn words, then the chairman introduced Nelson. "—a veteran of this war and candidate for the same office."

The girl standing with Meyers walked up and took the stage.

They clapped and somebody in the balcony gave a wolf whistle. Instead of getting flustered, she smiled up and said, "Thank you!"

They clapped again, and whistled and stomped. She started talking. I'm not bright—I had trouble learning to wave bye-bye and never did master patty-cake. I expected her to apologize for Nelson's absence and identify herself as his wife or sister or something. She was into her fourth paragraph before I realized that *she* was Nelson.

Francis X. Nelson—*Frances* X. Nelson. I wondered what I had done to deserve this. Female candidates are poison to run against at best; you don't dare use the ordinary rough-and-tumble, while she is free to use anything from a blacksnake whip to mickeys in your coffee.

Add to that ladylike good looks, obvious intelligence, platform poise—and a veteran. I couldn't have lived that wrong. I tried to catch Tom Griffith's eye to share my misery, but he was looking at *her* and the lunk was lapping it up.

Nelson—*Miss* Nelson—was going to town on housing. "You promised him that when he got out of that foxhole nothing would be too good for him. And what did he get? A shack in shanty-town, the sofa in his in-laws' parlor, a garage with no plumbing. If I am elected I shall make it my first concern—"

You couldn't argue against it. Like good roads, good weather, and the American Home, everybody is for veterans' housing.

When the meeting broke up, I snagged Tom and we rounded up the leaders of the Third District Association and adjourned to the home of one of the members. "Look, folks," I told them, "when we caucused and I agreed to run, our purpose was to take a bite out of the machine by kicking out Jorgens. Well, the situation has changed. It's not too late for me to forfeit the filing fee. How about it?"

Mrs. Holmes—Mrs. Bixby Holmes, as fine an old warhorse as ever swung a gavel—looked amazed. "What's gotten into you, Jack? Getting rid of Jorgens is only half of it. We have to put in men we can depend on. For this district, you're it."

I shook my head. "I didn't want to be the candidate; I wanted to manage. We should have had a veteran—"

"There's nothing wrong with your war record," put in Dick Blair.

"Maybe not, but it's useless politically. We needed a veteran." I had shuffled papers in the legal section of the Manhattan project—in civilian clothes. Dick Blair, a paratrooper and Purple Heart, had been my choice. But Dick had begged off, and who is to tell a combat veteran that he has got to make further sacrifice for the dear peepul?

"I abided by the will of the group, because Jorgens was not a veteran either. Now look at the damn thing—What makes you think I can beat her? She's got political sex-appeal."

"She's got more than political sex-appeal"—this from Tom.

When Dr. Potter spoke we listened; he's the old head in our group. "That's the wrong tack, Jack. It does not matter whether you win."

"I don't believe in lost causes, Doctor."

"I do. And so will you, someday. If Miss Nelson is Tully's choice to succeed Jorgens, then we must oppose her."

"She is with the machine, isn't she?" asked Mrs. Holmes.

"Sure she is," Tom told her. "Didn't you see that Cliff Meyers had her in tow? She's a stooge—the Stooge with the Light Brown Hair."

I insisted on a vote; they were all against me. "Okay," I agreed, "if you can take it, I can. This means a tougher campaign. We thought the dirt we had on Jorgens was enough; now we've got to dig."

"Don't fret, Jack," Mrs. Holmes soothed me. "We'll dig. I'll take charge of the precinct work."

"I thought your daughter in Denver was having a baby?"

"So she is. I'll stick."

I ducked out soon after, feeling much better, not because I thought I could win, but because of Mrs. Holmes and Dr. Potter and more like them. The team spirit you get in a campaign is pretty swell; I was feeling it again and recovering my pre-War zip.

Before the War our community was in good shape. We had kicked out the local machine, tightened up civil service, sent a police lieutenant to jail, and had put the bidding for contracts on an honest-to-goodness competitive basis—not by praying on Sunday, either, but by volunteer efforts of private citizens willing to get out and punch doorbells.

Then the War came along and everything came unstuck.

Naturally, the people who can be depended on for the in-and-out-of-season grind of volunteer politics are also the ones who took the War the most seriously. From Pearl Harbor to Hiroshima they had no time for politics. It's a wonder the city hall wasn't stolen during the War—bolted to its foundations, I guess.

On my way home I stopped at a drive-in for a hamburger and some thought. Another car squeezed in close beside me. I glanced up, then blinked my eyes. "Well, I'll be—Miss Nelson! Who let you out alone?"

She jerked her head around, ready to bristle, then turned on the vote-getter. "You startled me. You're Mr. Ross, aren't you?"

"Your future councilman," I agreed. "You startled *me*. How's the politicking? Where's Cliff Meyers? Dump him down a sewer?"

She giggled. "Poor Mr. Meyers! I said goodnight to him at my door, then came over here. I was hungry."

"That's no way to win elections. Why didn't you invite him in and scramble some eggs?"

"Well, I just didn't want—I mean I wanted a chance to think. You won't tell on me?" She gave me the you-great-big-strong-man look.

"I'm the enemy—remember? But I won't. Shall I go away, too?"

"No, don't. Since you are going to be my councilman, I ought to get acquainted. Why are you so sure you will beat me, Mr. Ross?"

"Jack Ross—your friend and mine. Have a cigar. I'm not at all sure I can beat you. With your natural advantages and Tully's gang behind you I should 'a stood in bed."

Her eyes went narrow; the vote-getter smile was gone. "What do you mean?" she said slowly. "I'm an independent candidate."

It was my cue to crawl, but I passed. "You expect me to swallow that? With Cliff Meyers at your elbow—" The car hop interrupted us; we placed our orders and I resumed. She cut in.

"I *do* want to be alone," she snapped and started to close her window.

I reached out and placed a hand on the glass. "Just a moment. This is politics; you are judged by the company you keep. You show up at your first meeting and Cliff Meyers has you under his wing."

"What's wrong with that? Mr. Meyers is a perfect gentleman."

"And he's good to his mother. He's a man with no visible means of support, who does chores for Boss Tully. I thought what everybody thought, that the boss had sent him to chaperone a green candidate."

"It's not true!"

"No? You're caught in the jam cupboard. What's your story?"

She bit her lip. "I don't have to explain anything to you."

"No. But if you won't, the circumstances speak for themselves." She didn't answer. We sat there, ignoring each other, while we ate. When she switched on the ignition, I said, "I'm going to tail you home."

"It's not necessary, thank you."

"This town is a rough place since the War. A young woman should not be out alone at night. Even Cliff Meyers is better than nobody."

"That's why I let them—Do as you see fit!" I had to skim red lights, but I kept close behind her. I expected her to rush inside and slam the door, but she was waiting by the curb. Thank you for seeing me home, Mr. Ross."

"Quite all right." I went up on her front porch with her and said goodnight.

"Mr. Ross—I shouldn't care what you think, but I'm not with Boss Tully. I'm independent." I waited. Presently she said, "You don't believe me." The big, beautiful eyes were shiny with tears.

"I didn't say so—but I'm waiting for you to explain."

"But what is there to explain?"

"Plenty." I sat down on the porch swing. "Come here, and tell papa. Why did you decide to run for office?"

"Well ..." She sat down beside me; I caught a disturbing whiff of perfume. "It started because I couldn't find an apartment. No, it didn't—it was farther back, out in the South Pacific. I could stand the insects and the heat. Even the idiotic way the Army does things didn't fret me much. But we had to queue up to use the wash basins. There was even a time when baths were rationed. I hated it. I used to lie on my cot at night, awake in the heat, and dream about a bathroom of my own. A bathroom of my own! A deep tub of water and time to soak. Shampoos and manicures and big, fluffy towels! I wanted to lock myself in and live there. Then I got out of the Army—"

"Yes?"

She shrugged. "The only apartment I could find carried a bonus bigger than my discharge pay, and I couldn't afford it anyhow."

"What's wrong with your own home?"

"This? This is my aunt's home. Seven in the family and I make eight—one bathroom. I'm lucky to brush my teeth. And I share a three-quarters bed with my eight-year-old cousin."

"I see. But that doesn't tell why you are running for office."

"Yes, it does. Uncle Sam was here one night and I was boiling over about the housing shortage and what I would like to do to Congress. He said I ought to be in politics; I said I'd welcome the chance. He phoned the next day and asked how would I like to run for his seat? I said—"

"Uncle Sam—Sam Jorgens!"

"Yes. He's not my uncle, but I've known him since I was little. I was scared, but he said not to worry, he would help me out and advise me. So I did and that's all there is to it. You see now?"

I saw all right. The political acumen of an Easter bunny—except that the bunny rabbit was likely to lick the socks off me. "Okay," I told her, "but housing isn't the only issue. How about the gas company franchise, for example and the sewage disposal plant? And the tax rate? What airport deal do you favor? Do you think we ought to ease up on zoning and how about the freeways?"

"I'm going after housing. Those issues can wait."

I snorted. "They won't let you wait. While you're riding your hobbyhorse, the boys will steal the public blind—again."

"Hobbyhorse! Mister Smarty-Britches, getting a house is the most important thing in the world to the man who hasn't one. You wouldn't be so smug if you were in that fix."

"Keep your shirt on. Me, I'm sleeping in a leaky trailer. I'm strong for plenty of housing—but how do you propose to get it?"

"How? Don't be silly. I'll back the measures that push it."

"Such as? Do you think the city ought to get into the building business? Or should it be strictly private enterprise? Should we sell bonds and finance new homes? Limit it to veterans, or will you help me, too? Heads of families only, or are you going to cut yourself in on it? How about pre-fabrication? Can we do everything you want to do under a building code that was written in 1911?" I paused for breath. "Well?"

"You're being nasty, Jack."

"I sure am. But that's not half of it. I'll challenge you to debate on everything from dog licenses to patent paving materials. A nice, clean campaign and may the best man win—providing his name is Ross."

"I won't accept."

"You'll wish you had, before we're through. My boys and girls will be at all your meetings, asking embarrassing questions."

She looked at me. "Of all the dirty politics!"

"You're a candidate, kid; you're supposed to know the answers."

She looked upset. "I *told* Uncle Sam," she said, half to herself, "that I didn't know enough about such things, but he said—"

"Go on, Frances. What did he say?"

She shook her head. "I've told you too much already."

"I'll tell you. You were not to worry your pretty head, because he would be there to tell you how to vote. That was it, wasn't it?"

"Well, not in so many words. He said—"

"But it amounted to that. And he brought Meyers around and said Meyers would show you the ropes. You didn't want to cause trouble, so you did what Meyers told you to do. Right?"

"You've got the nastiest way of putting things."

"That's not all. You honestly think you are independent. But you do what Sam Jorgens tells you and Sam Jorgens—your sweet old Uncle Sam—won't change his socks without Boss Tully's permission."

"I don't believe it!"

"Check it. Ask some of the newspaper boys. Sniff around."

"I shall."

"Good. You'll learn about the birds and the bees." I stood up. "I've worn out my welcome. See you at the barricades, comrade."

I was halfway to the street when she called me back. "Jack!"

"Yes, Frances?" I went back up on the porch.

"I'm going to find out what connection, if any, Tully has with Uncle Sam, but, nevertheless and notwithstanding, I'm an independent. If I've been led around by the nose, I won't be for long."

"Good girl!"

"That's not all. I'm going to give you the fight of your life, whip the pants off you, and wipe that know-it-all look off your face!"

"Bravo! That's the spirit, kid. We'll have fun."

"Thanks. Well, goodnight."

"Just a second." I put an arm around her shoulders. She leaned away from me warily. "Tell me, darling: who writes your speeches?"

I got kicked in the shins, then the screen door was between us. "Goodnight, Mr. Ross!"

"One more thing—your middle name, it can't be 'Xavier.' What *does* the X stand for?"

"Xanthippe—want to make something of it?" The door slammed.

I was too busy the following month to worry about Frances Nelson. Ever been a candidate? It is like getting married and having your appendix out, while going over Niagara Falls in a barrel. One or more meetings every evening, breakfast clubs on Saturdays and Sundays, a Kiwanis, Rotary, or Lions, or Chamber of Commerce lunch to hit at noon, an occasional appearance in court, endless correspondence, phone calls, conferences, and, to top it off, as many hours of doorbell pushing as I could force into each day.

It was a grass-roots campaign, the best sort, but strenuous. Mrs. Holmes, by scraping the barrel, rounded up volunteers to cover three-quarters of the precincts; the rest were my problem. I couldn't cover them all, but I could durn well try.

And every day there was the problem of money. Even with a volunteer, unpaid organization, politics costs money—printing, postage, hall rental, telephone bills, and there is gasoline and lunch money for people who can't carry their own expenses. A dollar here and a dollar there and soon you are three thousand bucks in the red.

It is hard to tell how a campaign is going; you tend to kid each other. We made a mid-stream spot check—phone calls, a reply post-card poll, and a doorbell sampling. And Tom and I and Mrs. Holmes got out and sniffed the air. All one day I bought gasoline here, a cola there, and a pack of cigarettes somewhere else, talking politics as I did so, and never offering my name. By the time I met Tom and Mrs. Holmes at her home I felt that I knew my chances.

We got our estimates together and looked them over. Mine read: "Ross 45%; Nelson 55%; McNye a trace." Tom's was: "fifty-fifty, against us." Mrs. Holmes had written, "A dull campaign, a light vote, and a trend against us." The computed results of the formal polls read; Ross 43%, Nelson 52%, McNye 5%—probable error plus-or-minus 9%.

I looked around. "Shall we cut our losses, or go on gallantly to defeat?"

"We aren't licked yet," Tom pointed out.

"No, but we're going to be. All we offer is the assumption that I'm better qualified than the little girl with the big eyes—a notion in which Joe Public is colossally uninterested. How about it, Mrs. Holmes? Can you make it up in the precincts?"

She faced me. "Jack, to be frank, it's all uphill. I'm working the old faithfuls too hard and I can't seem to stir out any new blood."

"We need excitement," Tom complained. "Let's throw some mud."

"At what?" I asked. "Want to accuse her of passing notes in school, or shall we say she sneaked out after taps when she was a WAC? She's got no record."

"Well, tackle her on housing. You've let her hog the best issue."

I shook my head. "If I knew the answers, I wouldn't be living in a trailer. I won't make phony promises. I've drawn up three bills, one to support the Federal Act, one to revise the building code, and one for a bond election for housing projects—that last one is a hot potato. None of them are much good. This housing shortage will be with us for years."

Tom said, "Jack, you shouldn't run for office. You don't have the fine, free optimism that makes a good public figure."

I grunted. "That's what I told you birds. I'm the manager type. A candidate who manages himself gets a split personality."

Mrs. Holmes knit her brows. "Jack—you know more about housing than she does. Let's hold a rally and debate it."

"Okay with me—I just work here. I once threatened to make her debate everything from streetcars to taxes. How about it, Tom?"

"Anything to make some noise."

I phoned at once. "Is this the Stooge with the Light Brown Hair?"

"That must be Jack Ross. Hello, Nasty. How's the baby-kissing?"

"Sticky. Remember I promised to debate the issues with you? How about 8 p.m. Wednesday the 15th?"

She said, "Hold the line—" I could hear a muffled rumble, then she said, "Jack? You tend to your campaign; I'll tend to mine."

"Better accept, kid. We'll challenge you publicly. Is Miss Nelson afraid to face the issues, quote and unquote."

"Goodbye, Jack."

"Uncle Sam won't let you, will he?" The phone clicked in my ear.

We went ahead anyway. I sold some war bonds and ordered a special edition of the Civic League News, with a Ross-for-Councilman front page, as a throw-away to announce the rally—prizes, entertainment, movies, and a super-colossal, gigantic debate between Ross in this corner and Nelson in that. We piled the bundles of papers in Mrs. Holmes' garage late Sunday night. Mrs. Holmes phoned about seven-thirty the next morning—"Jack," she yipped, "come over right away!"

"On my way. What's wrong?"

"Everything. Wait till you get here." When I did, she led me out to her garage; someone had broken in and had slit open our precious bundles—then had poured dirty motor oil on them.

Tom showed up while we were looking at the mess. "Pixies everywhere," he observed. "I'll call the Commercial Press."

"Don't bother," I said bitterly. "We can't pay for another run." But he went in anyhow. The kids who were to do the distributing started to show up; we paid them and sent them home. Tom came out. "Too late," he announced. "We would have to start from scratch—no time and too expensive."

I nodded and went in the house. I had a call to make myself. "Hello," I snapped, "is this Miss Nelson, the Independent Candidate?"

"This is Frances Nelson. Is this Jack Ross?"

"Yes. You were expecting me to call, I see."

"No, I knew your sweet voice. To what do I owe the honor?"

"I'd like to show you how well your boys have been campaigning."

"Just a moment—I've an appointment at ten; I can spare the time until then. What do you mean; how my boys have been campaigning?"

"You'll find out." I hung up.

I refused to talk until she had seen the sabotage. She stared. "It's a filthy, nasty trick, Jack—but why show it to me?"

"Who else?"

"But—Look, Jack, I don't know who did this, but it has nothing to do with me." She looked around at us. "You've got to believe me!" Suddenly she looked relieved. "I know! It wasn't me, so it must have been McNye."

Tom grunted. I said gently, "Look, darling, McNye is nobody. He's a seventeenth-rater who files to get his name in print. He wouldn't use sabotage because he's not out to win. It *has* to be you—wait!—not you personally, but the machine. This is what you get into when you accept the backing of wrong 'uns."

"But you're wrong! You're wrong! I'm not backed by the machine."

"So? Who runs your campaign? Who pays your bills?"

She shook her head. "A committee takes care of those things. My job is to show up at meetings and speak."

"Where did the committee come from? Did the stork bring it?"

"Don't be ridiculous. It's the Third District Home-Owners' League. They endorsed me and set up a campaign committee for me."

I'm no judge of character, but she was telling the truth, as she saw it. "Ever hear of a dummy organization, kid? Your only connection with this Home-Owners' League is Sam Jorgens ... isn't it?"

"Why, no—that is—Yes, I suppose so."

"And I told you Jorgens was a tame dog for Boss Tully."

"Yes, but I checked on that, Jack. Uncle Sam explained the whole thing. Tully used to support him, but they broke because Uncle Sam wouldn't take the machine's orders. It's not his fault that the machine used to back him."

"And you believed him."

"No, I made him prove it. You said to check with the newspapers— Uncle Sam had me talk with the editor of the *Herald*." Tom snorted.

"He means," I told her, "that the *Herald* is part of the machine. I meant talk to reporters. Most of them are honest and all of them know the score. But I can't see how you could be so green. I know you've been away, but didn't you read the papers before the War?"

It developed that, what with school and the War, she hadn't been around town much since she was fifteen. Mrs. Holmes broke in, "Why, she's not eligible, Jack! She doesn't have the residence requirements."

I shook my head. "As a lawyer, I assure you she does. Those things don't break residence—particularly as she enlisted here. How about making us all some coffee, Mrs. Holmes?"

Mrs. Holmes bristled; I could see that she did not want to fraternize with the enemy, but I took her arm and led her into the house, whispering as I went. "Don't be hard on the kid, Molly. You and I made mistakes while we were learning the ropes. Remember Smythe?"

Smythe was as fine a stuffed shirt as ever took a bribe—we had given him our hearts' blood. Mrs. Holmes looked sheepish and relaxed. We chatted about the heat and presidential possibilities, then Frances said, "I'm conceding nothing, Jack—but I'm going to pay for those papers."

"Skip it," I said. "I'd rather bang Tully's heads together. But see here—you've got an hour yet; I want to show you something."

"Want me along, Jack?" Tom suggested, looking at Frances.

"If you like. Thanks for the coffee, Mrs. Holmes—I'll be back to clean up the mess." We drove to Dr. Potter's office and got the photostats we had on Jorgens out of his safe. We didn't say anything; I just arranged the exhibits in logical order. Frances didn't talk either, but her face got whiter and whiter. At last she said, "Will you take me home now, Mr. Ross?"

We bumped along for the next three weeks, chasing votes all day, licking stamps and stenciling auto-bumper signs late at night and never getting enough sleep. Presently we noticed a curious fact—McNye was coming up. First it was billboards and throw-aways, next was publicity—and then we began to get reports from the field of precinct work for McNye.

We couldn't have been more puzzled if the Republican Party had nominated Norman Thomas. We made another spot check. Mrs. Holmes and Dr. Potter and I went over the results. Ross and Nelson, neck and neck—a loss for Nelson; McNye a strong third and coming up fast. "What do you think, Mrs. Holmes?"

"The same you do. Tully has dumped Nelson and bought up McNye."

Potter agreed. "It'll be you and McNye in the runoff. Nelson is coasting on early support from the machine. She'll fizzle."

Tom had come in while we were talking. "I'm not sure," he said. "Tully needs a win in the primary, or, if that fails, a run-off between the girl and McNye. We've got an organization, she hasn't."

"Tully can't count on me running third. In fact, I'll beat out Frances for second place at the very worst."

Tom looked quizzical. "Seen tonight's *Herald*, Jack?"

"No. Have they discovered I'm a secret drinker?"

"Worse than that." He chucked us the paper. "CLAIM ROSS INELIGIBLE COUNCILMANIC RACE" it read; there was a 3-col cut of my trailer, with me in the door. The story pointed put that a city father must have lived two years in the city and six months in his district. The trailer camp was outside the city limits.

Dr. Potter looked worried. "Can they disqualify you, Jack?"

"They won't take it to court," I told him. "I'm legal as baseball. Residence isn't geographical location; it's a matter of intent—your home is where you intend to return when you're away. I'm registered at the flat I had before the War, but I turned it over to my partner when I went to Washington. My junk is still in it, but he's got a wife and twins. Hence the trailer, a temporary exigency of no legal effect."

"Hmmm … how about the political effect?"

"That's another matter."

"You betcha it is," agreed Tom. "How about it, Mrs. Holmes?"

She looked worried. "Tom is right. It's tailor-made for a word-of-mouth campaign combined with unfavorable publicity. Why vote for a man who doesn't even live in your district?—that sort of thing."

I nodded. "Well, it's too late to back out, but, let's face it, folks— We've wasted our nickel."

For once they did not argue. Instead Potter said, "What sort of person is Miss Nelson? Could we possibly back her in the finals?"

"She's a good kid," I assured him. "She got taken in and hated to admit it, but she's better than McNye."

"I'll say she is," agreed Tom.

"She's a lady," stated Mrs. Holmes.

"But," I objected, "we can't elect her in the finals. We can't pin anything on McNye and she's too green to stand up to what the machine can do to her in a long campaign. Tully knows what he's doing."

"I'm afraid you're right," Potter agreed.

"Jack," said Tom, "I take it you think we're licked now."

"Ask Mrs. Holmes."

Mrs. Holmes said, "I hate to say so, and I'm not quitting, but it would take a miracle to put Jack on the final ballot."

"Okay," said Tom, "let's quit being boy scouts and have some fun the rest of the campaign. I don't like the way Boss Tully campaigns. We've played fair; what we've gotten in return is shenanigans."

"What do you want to do?"

He explained. Presently I nodded and said, "I'm all for it—and a wrinkle of my own. It'll be fun, and it just might work."

"Well, call her up then!"

I got Frances Nelson on the phone. "Jack Ross, Frances. Haven't seen you around much, sweetheart. How's the campaign?"

She sounded tired. "Oh, that—What campaign, Jack?"

"Did you withdraw? I haven't seen any announcement."

"It wasn't necessary. I had a show-down with Jorgens and after that my campaign just disappeared. The committee vanished away. Look, Jack, I'd like to see you—to apologize."

"Forget it, I want to see you, too. I'll pick you up."

We laid it on the line. "I'm dropping out of the race, Frances. We want to throw our organizational support to you—provided."

She stared. "But you can't, Jack. I'm going to vote for you."

"Huh? Never mind, you won't get a chance to." I showed her the *Herald* story. "It's a phony, but it licks me anyhow. I should have played up my homeless condition but, like a dope, I let them do it. It's too late now—when a candidate has to explain things he's back on his heels and ready for the knockout. I was a fifty-fifty squeeze at best; this tips the balance."

She was staring at the picture, bug-eyed, knuckles pressed to her mouth. "Jack—Oh, dear! I've gone and done it again."

"Done what?"

"Got you into this mess. I told Sam Jorgens all about our first talk, including how you had to camp out in a trailer. I—"

I brushed it aside. "No matter. They would have stumbled on it anyhow. See here—we're going to take you on. We might even elect you."

"But I don't want the job, Jack. I want you to have it."

"Too late, Frances. But we want to beat that spare tire, McNye. The machine is still using you, to beat me in the primary by splitting the non-machine vote; then they'll settle your hash. I've got a gimmick for that. But first—you call yourself an independent. Well, you aren't now."

"What do you mean? I won't be anything else."

"They gave women the vote! Look, darling, a candidate can be unbossed, but not independent. Independence is an adolescent notion. To merit support you have to commit yourself—and there goes your independence."

"But I—Oh, politics is a rotten business!"

"You make me tired! Politics is just as clean—or as dirty—as the people who practice it. The people who say it's dirty are too lazy to do their part in it." She dropped her face into her hands. I took her by the shoulders, and shook her. "Now you listen to me. I'm going over our program, point by point. If you agree with it and commit yourself, you're our candidate. Right?"

"Yes, Jack." It was just a whisper.

We ran through it. There was no trouble, it was sane and sensible, likely to appeal to anyone with no ax to grind. The points she did not understand we let lay over. She liked especially my housing bills and began to perk up and sound like a candidate.

"Okay," I said finally. "Here's the gimmick. I'll get my name off the ballot so that the race will be over in the primary. It's too late to do it myself, but they've played into my hands. It'll be a court order, for ineligibility through non-residence."

Dr. Potter looked up sharply. "Come again, son? I thought you said your legal position was secure."

I grinned. "It is—if I fight. But I won't. Here's the gag—we bring a citizen's suit through a couple of dummies. The court orders me to show cause. I default. Court has no option but to order my name stricken from the ballot. One, two, three."

Tom cheered. I bowed. "Now Dr. Potter is your new campaign chairman. You go on as before, going where you are sent and speaking your piece. Oh, yes—I'm going to give you some homework on other issues than housing. As for Tom and me—we're the special effects department. Just forget us."

Three days later I was off the ballot. Tom handled it so that it looked like McNye and Tully. Mrs. Holmes had the delicate job of convincing our precinct workers that Frances was our new white hope. Dr. Potter and Dick Blair got Frances endorsed by the Civic League—the League would endorse a giant panda against a Tully man. And Dick Blair worked up a veterans' division.

Leaving Tom and me free for fun and games.

First we got a glamor pic of Frances, one that made her look like Liberty Enlightening the World, with great sorrowful eyes and a noble forehead, and had it blown up for billboards—6-sheets; 24-sheets look like too much dough.

We got a "good" picture of McNye, too—good for us. Like this— you send two photographers to a meeting where your man is to speak. One hits him with a flash bulb; the second does also, right away, before the victim can recover from his reflex. Then you throw the first pic away. We got a picture which showed McNye as pop-eyed, open-mouthed, and idiotic—a Kallikak studying to be a Jukes. It was so good we had to tone it down. Then I went up state and got some printing done, very privately.

We waited until the last few days, then got busy. First we put snipe sheets on our own billboards, right across Frances' beautiful puss so that those eyes looked appealingly at you over the paster. "VOTE FOR McNYE" they read. Two nights later it was quarter cards, this time with his lovely picture: VOTE FOR McNYE—A WOMAN'S PLACE IS IN THE HOME. We stuck them up on private property, too.

Tom and I drove around the next day admiring our handiwork, "It's beautiful," Tom said dreamily. "Jack, do you suppose there is any way we could get the Communist Party to endorse McNye?"

"I don't see how," I admitted, "but if it doesn't cost too much I've still got a couple of war bonds."

He shook his head. "It can't work, but it's a lovely thought."

We saved our double whammy for the day before election. It was expensive—but wait. We hired some skid-row characters on Saturday, through connections Tom has, and specified that they must show up with two-day beards on Monday. We fed each one a sandwich loaded with garlic, gave him literature and instructions—ring the doorbell, blow his breath in the victim's face, and hand her a handbill, saying abruptly, "Here's how you vote, lady!" The handbill said, "VOTE FOR McNYE" and had his special picture. It had the rest of Tully's slate too, and some choice quotes of McNye's best double talk. Around the edge it said "100% American—100% American."

We pushed the stumblebums through an average of four precincts apiece, concentrating on the better neighborhoods.

That night there was an old-fashioned torchlight parade—Mrs. Holmes' show, and the wind-up of the proper campaign. It started off with an elephant and donkey (Heaven knows where she borrowed the elephant!) The elephant carried signs: I'M FOR FRANCES; the donkey, SO AM I. There was a kid's band, flambeaux carried by our weary volunteers, and a platoon of WAC and WAVE veterans marching ahead of the car that carried Frances. She looked scared and lovely.

Tom and I watched it, then got to work. No sleep that night—

More pasters. Windshield size this time, 3" x 10", with glue on the printed side. I suppose half the cars in town have no garages, housing being what it is. We covered every block in the district before dawn, Tom driving and me on the right with a pail of water, a sponge, and stickers. He would pull alongside a car; I would slap a sticker on the windshield where it would stare the driver in the face—and have to be scraped off. They read: VOTE FOR McNYE—KEEP AMERICA PURE.

We figured it would help to remind people to vote.

I voted myself when the polls opened, then fell into bed.

I pulled myself together in time to get to the party at the headquarters—an empty building we had borrowed for the last month of the campaign. I hadn't given a thought to poll watchers or an honest count—that was Mrs. Holmes' baby—but I didn't want to miss the returns.

One election party is like another—the same friendly drunks, the same silent huddle around the radio, the same taut feeling. I helped myself to some beer and potato chips and joined the huddle.

"Anything yet?" I asked Mrs. Holmes. "Where's Frances?"

"Not yet. I made her lie down."

"Better get her out here. The candidate has to be seen. When people work for a pat on the back, you've got to give 'em the pat."

But Frances showed up about then, and went through the candidate routine—friendly, gracious, thanking people, etc. I began to think about running her for Congress.

Tom showed up, bleary-eyed, as the first returns came in. All McNye. Frances heard them and her smile slipped. Dr. Potter went over to her and said, "It's not important—the machine's precincts are usually first to report." She plastered her smile back on.

McNye piled up a big lead. Then our efforts began to show—Nelson was pulling up. By 10:30 it was neck and neck. After a while it began to look as if we had elected a councilman.

Around midnight McNye got on the air and conceded.

So I'm a councilman's field secretary now. I sit outside the rail when the council meets; when I scratch my right ear, Councilman Nelson votes "yes"; if I scratch my left ear, she votes "no"—usually.

Marry her? *Me?* Tom married her. They're building a house, one bedroom and *two* bathrooms. When they can get the fixtures, that is.

FOREWORD

When the U.S.S.R. refused our proposals for controlling the A-bomb, I swore off "World-Saving." No more preaching. No more attempts to explain the mortal peril we were in. No, sir!

A year and a half later, late '47, I backslid. If it could not be done by straightforward exposition, perhaps it could be dramatized as fiction.

Again I fell flat on my face.

Fifteen years later there was a tremendous flap over Soviet medium-range missiles in Cuba. Then they were removed—or so we were told—and the flap died out. Why? Why both ways? For years we have had Soviet submarines on both coasts; are they armed with slingshots? Or powder puffs?

This story is more timely today, over thirty years later, than it was when it was written; the danger is enormously greater.

And again this warning will be ignored. But it won't take much of your time; it's a short-short, a mere 2200 words.

"Paddy, shake hands with the guy who built the atom bomb," Professor Warner said to the bartender. "He and Einstein rigged it up in their own kitchen one evening."

"With the help of about four hundred other guys," amended the stranger, raising his voice slightly to cut through the rumble of the subway.

"Don't quibble over details. Paddy, this is Doctor Mansfield. Jerry, meet Paddy—Say, Paddy, what *is* your last name?"

"Francis X. Hughes," answered the barkeep as he wiped his hand and stuck it out. "I'm pleased to meet any friend of Professor Warner."

"I'm pleased to meet you, Mr. Hughes."

"Call me Paddy, they all do. You really are one of the scientists who built the atom bomb?"

"I'm afraid so."

"May the Lord forgive you. Are you at N.Y.U., too?"

"No, I'm out at the new Brookhaven Laboratory."

"Oh, yes."

"You've been there?"

Hughes shook his head. "About the only place I go is home to Brooklyn. But I read the papers."

"Paddy's in a well-padded rut," explained Warner. "Paddy, what are you going to do when they blow up New York? It'll break up your routine."

He set their drinks before them and poured himself a short beer. "If that's all I've got to worry about I guess I'll die of old age and still in my rut, Professor."

Warner's face lost its cheerful expression for a moment; he stared at his drink as if it had suddenly become bitter. "I wish I had your optimism, Paddy, but I haven't. Sooner or later, we're in for it."

"You shouldn't joke about such things, Professor."

"I'm not joking."

"You can't be serious."

"I wish I weren't. Ask him. After all, he built the damned thing."

Hughes raised his brows at Mansfield who replied, "I'm forced to agree with Professor Warner. They will be able to do it—atom-bomb New York I mean. I *know* that; it's not a guess—it's a certainty. Being able to do it, I'm strongly of the opinion that they *will* do it."

"Who do you mean by 'they'?" demanded the bartender. "The Russians?"

"Not necessarily. It might be anybody who first worked up the power to smash us."

"Sure," said Warner. "Everybody wants to kick the fat boy. We're envied and hated. The only reason we haven't been smeared is that no one has had what it takes to do it—up to now, that is!"

"Just a minute, gentlemen—" put in Hughes. "I don't get it. You're talking about somebody—anybody—atom-bombing New York. How can they do it? Didn't we decide to hang on to the secret? Do you think some dirty spy has gotten away with it while we weren't watching?"

Mansfield looked at Warner, then back at Hughes and said gently, "I hate to disturb your peace of mind, Mr. Hughes—Paddy—but there is no secret. Any nation that is willing to go to the trouble and expense can build an atom bomb."

"And that's official," added Warner, "and it's a lead-pipe cinch that, power politics being what it is, a dozen different nations are working on the problem right now."

Hughes had been looking perturbed; his face cleared. "Oh, I see what you mean. In time, they can dig it out for themselves. In that case, gentlemen, let's have a round on the house and drink to their frustration. I can't be worrying about what might happen twenty years from now. We might none of us be spared that long what with taxicabs and the like."

Mansfield's brows shot up. "Why do you say twenty years, Paddy?"

"Eh? Oh, I seem to remember reading it in the papers. That general, wasn't it? The one who was in charge of the atom-bomb business."

Mansfield brushed the general aside. "Poppycock! That estimate is based on entirely unwarranted national conceit. The time will be much shorter."

"How much shorter?" demanded Hughes. Mansfield shrugged.

"What would you do, Paddy," Warner asked curiously, "if you thought some nation—let's say some nation that didn't like us—had already managed to manufacture atom bombs?"

The saloon cat came strolling along the top of the bar. Hughes stopped to feed it a slice of cheese before replying. "I do not have your learning, gentlemen, but Paddy Hughes is no fool. If someone is loose in the world with those devil's contraptions, New York is a doomed city. America is the champion and must be beaten before any new bully boy can hope to win—and New York is one of the spots he would shoot at first. Even Sad Sack—" He jerked a thumb at the cat. "—is bright enough to flee from a burning building."

"Well, what do you think you would do?"

"I don't 'think' what I'd do, I *know* what I'd do; I've done it before. When I was a young man and the Black-and-Tans were breathing down the back o' my neck, I climbed on a ship with never a thought of looking back—and any man who wanted them could have my pigs and welcome to them."

Warner chuckled. "You must have been quite the lad, Paddy. But I don't believe you would do it—not now. You're firmly rooted in your rut and you like it—like me and six million others in this town. That's why decentralization is a fantasy."

Hughes nodded. "It would be hard." That it would be hard he understood. Like leaving home it would be to quit Schreiber's Bar-Grill after all these years—Schreiber couldn't run it without him; he'd chase all the customers away. It would be hard to leave his friends in the parish, hard to leave his home—what with Molly's grave being just around the corner and all. And if the cities were to be blown up a man would have to go back to farming. He'd promised himself when he hit the new country that he'd never, never, never tackle the heart-breaking load of tilling the soil again. Well, perhaps there would be no landlords when the cities were gone. If a man must farm, at least he might be spared that. Still, it would be hard—and Molly's grave off somewhere in the rubble. "But I'd do it."

"You think you would."

"I wouldn't even go back to Brooklyn to pick up my other shirt. I've my week's pay envelope right here." He patted his vest. "I'd grab my hat and start walking." The bartender turned to Mansfield. "Tell me the truth, Doctor—if it's not twenty years, how long will it be?"

Mansfield took out an envelope and started figuring on the back of it. Warner started to speak, but Hughes cut him off. "Quiet while he's working it out!" he said sharply.

"Don't let him kid you, Paddy," Warner said wryly. "He's been lying awake nights working out this problem ever since Hiroshima."

Mansfield looked up. "That's true. But I keep hoping I'll come out with a different answer. I never do."

"Well, what *is* the answer?" Hughes insisted.

Mansfield hesitated. "Paddy, you understand that there are a lot of factors involved, not all of them too clear. Right? In the first place, it took us about four years. But we were lavish with money and lavish with men, more so maybe than any other nation could be, except possibly Russia. Figured on that alone it might take several times four years for another country to make a bomb. But that's not the whole picture; it's not even the important part. There was a report the War Department put out, the Smyth Report—you've heard of it?—which gives anyone who can read everything but the final answers. With that report, with competent people, uranium ore, and a good deal less money than it cost us, a nation ought to be able to develop a bomb in a good deal less time than it took us."

Hughes shook his head. "I don't expect you to explain, Doctor; I just want to know your answer. How long?"

"I was just explaining that the answer had to be indefinite. I make it not less than two and not more than four years."

The bartender whistled softly. "Two years. Two years to get away and start a new life."

249

"No, no, no! Mr. Hughes," Mansfield objected. "Not two years from now—two years from the time the first bomb was dropped."

Hughes' face showed a struggle to comprehend. "But, gentlemen," he protested, "it's been *more* than two years since the first bomb was dropped."

"That's right."

"Don't blow your top, Paddy," Warner cautioned him. "The bomb isn't everything. It might be ten years before anybody develops the sort of robot carrier that can go over the north pole or the ocean and seek out a particular city with an atom bomb. In the meantime we don't have too much to fear from an ordinary airplane attack."

Mansfield looked annoyed. "You started this, Dick. Why try to hand out soothing syrup now? With a country as wide open as this one you don't need anything as fancy as guided missiles to pull a Pearl Harbor on it. The bombs would be assembled secretly and set off by remote control. Why, there might be a tramp steamer lying out there in the East River right now—"

Warner let his shoulders slump. "You're right, of course."

Hughes threw down his bar towel. "You're telling me that New York is as likely to be blown up right now as at any other time."

Mansfield nodded. "That's the size of it," he said soberly.

Hughes looked from one to the other. The cat jumped down and commenced rubbing up against his ankle, purring. He pushed it away with his foot, "It's not true! I know it's not true!"

"Why not?"

"Because! If it was true would you be sitting here, drinking quietly? You've been having a bit of fun with me, pulling my leg. Oh, I can't pick the flaw in your argument, but you don't believe it yourselves."

"I wish I didn't believe it," said Mansfield.

"Oh, we believe it, Paddy," Warner told him. "To tell you the truth, I'm planning to get out. I've got letters out to half a dozen cow colleges; I'm just waiting until my contract expires. As for Doc Mansfield, he can't leave. This is where his lab is located."

Hughes considered this, then shook his head. "No, it won't wash. No man in his right mind will hang on to a job when it means sitting on the hot squat, waiting for the Warden to throw the switch. You're pulling my leg."

Mansfield acted as if Hughes had not spoken. "Anyhow," he said to Warner, "the political factors might delay the blow-off indefinitely."

Warner shook his head angrily. "Now who's handing out soothing syrup? The political factors speed up the event, not delay it. If a country intends to defeat us someday, it's imperative that she do it as quickly as possible, before we catch wind of her plans and strike first. Or before we work out a real counter weapon—if that's possible."

Mansfield looked tired, as if he had been tired for a long time. "Oh, you're right. I was just whistling to keep my courage up. But we won't develop a counter weapon, not a real one. The only possible defense against atomic explosion is not to be there when it goes off." He turned to the barman. "Let's have another round, Paddy."

"Make mine a Manhattan," added Warner.

"Just a minute. Professor Warner. Doctor Mansfield. You were not fooling with me? Every word you had to say is God's own truth?"

"As you're standing there, Paddy."

"And Doctor Mansfield—Professor Warner, do you trust Doctor Mansfield's figuring?"

"There's no man in the United States better qualified to make such an estimate. That's the truth, Paddy."

"Well, then—" Hughes turned toward where his employer sat nodding over the cash register on the restaurant side of the room and whistled loudly between his teeth. "Schreiber! Come take the bar." He started stripping off his apron.

"Hey!" said Warner, "where you going? I ordered a Manhattan."

"Mix it yourself," said Hughes. "I've quit." He reached for his hat with one hand, his coat with the other, and then he was out the door.

Forty seconds later he was on an uptown express; he got off at 34th Street and three minutes thereafter he was buying a ticket, west. It was ten minutes later that he felt the train start to roll under him, headed out of the city.

But it was less than an hour later when his misgivings set in. Had he been too hasty? Professor Warner was a fine man, to be sure, but given to his little jokes, now and again. Had he been taken in by a carefully contrived hoax? Had Warner said to his friend, we'll have some fun and scare the living daylights out of the old Irishman?

Nor had he made any arrangements for someone to feed Sad Sack. The cat had a weak stomach, he was certain, and no one else gave the matter any attention at all. And Molly's grave—Wednesday was his day to do his gardening there. Of course Father Nelson would see that it was watered, just for kindness' sake, but still—

When the train paused at Princeton Junction he slipped off and sought out a telephone. He had in mind what he meant to say if he was able to reach Professor Warner—a good chance, he thought, for considering the hour the gentlemen probably stayed on for a steak. Professor Warner, he would say, you've had your fun and a fine joke it was as I would be the first to say and to buy a drink on it, but tell me—man to man—was there anything *to* what you and your friend was telling me? That would settle it, he thought.

The call went through promptly and he heard Schreiber's irritated voice. "Hello," he said.

The line went dead. He jiggled the hook. The operator answered, "One moment, please—" then, "This is the Princeton operator. Is this the party with the call to New York?"

"Yes. I—"

"There has been a temporary interruption in service. Will you hang up and try again in a few minutes, please?"

"But I was just talking—"

"Will you hang up and try again in a few minutes, puh*lease*?"

He heard the shouting as he left the booth. As he got outdoors he could see the great, gloriously beautiful, gold and purple mushroom still mounting over where had been the City of New York.

END OF VOLUME ONE